TULSA

A NOVEL

CHRISTOPHER HARRIS

**ASPHALT
HOUSE**

Asphalt House paperback edition September 2018

Cover design by Dillon McGaughey

ISBN: 0692170138
ISBN-13: 978-0692170137

ACKNOWLEDGMENTS

Thanks to Chris Walsh, Phil McRae, Dillon McGaughey and Craig Clark for guidance, and to the real world for not yet quite turning into this. (Checks watch.)

"The whole conviction of my life now rests upon the belief that loneliness, far from being a rare and curious phenomenon, is the central and inevitable fact of human existence."

—Thomas Wolfe

"No phone, no pool, no pets, no cigarettes."

—Christopher McCandless via Roger Miller

1

Facts are facts:
I lost my head.
We blocked what was once and may yet again be
Highway 49. Clooney parked the Tacoma crosswise and he
and I waited against a boulder. This was during a time of high
philosophy. People you'd never expect spoke of meaning, and
recognized that it was a luxury the future might not afford.
Clooney talked about once owning a fleet of rental vans. "I'd
like to go back and start 'em all in a big circle with the
exhausts facing in and just smell the smell." He wore a safari
jacket I wanted, but he filled it out as I never could've, he was
handsome. In the middle of the road, Majido pressed back his
cuticles with a matchstick because he'd seen it in a movie. I
was doing something.

A puff of ginger arose to the south, down where the
blacktop lost definition: a truck, coming our way. Overgrown
weeds blocked this peak, and whoever was inside the truck
wouldn't see us until they drew close. Majido crossed the
road as if to hide but then just stood there sneezing.

Clooney waved his arms. His jacket cuffs were rolled up
and his lapels were crooked, this blond foursquare weekender
out of a catalogue. It was a much bigger truck than ours,

ominously polished, and it stopped a hundred feet away. Clooney mimed welcoming laughter. By the time the driver thought to turn around, Majido was standing in his rearview.

The driver was a teenage boy. He was alone. Clooney smiled with half his mouth and waved him forward and it was crazy to think this could work. Surely the boy would throw it into reverse and send Majido scrambling. But such was Clooney's power: all that chrome advanced. The boy had his window down. At first he looked like a Cub Scout, but it turned out he was wearing a Union soldier's blueback uniform.

"What!" he said.

"We don't like doing this," said Clooney. "But there's three of us and one of you, and I know you're only a kid. But things are tough enough, so why don't you come on out of there and hand over the keys. We'll drop you off at the next town."

The boy said, "Fuck you."

Clooney had a laugh people liked. You wanted to amuse him. "For future reference," he said, "imagine if I was a different kind of person. Somebody wanting to fuck…that might actually happen to you. Then where would you be?"

"Move your fucking junker," said the boy, and he honked his horn. Majido jumped into the bed, and the truck rocked and the boy's profile bobbed as would a castaway set adrift. Majido rummaged up there beneath a plastic sheet. The boy yanked his neck around to see behind.

"You can check us," said Clooney. "We're not armed. Give us the keys and I guarantee nobody's getting hurt."

"There's a tank back here," Majido said. "Gas, maybe even diesel."

"What's your name?" Clooney said. He'd come around to the driver-side door. "You want something to eat? We've got a bunch of snacks, glad to share." He asked me: "What do we have?"

I tried to remember. Packaged apple pies and

unrefrigerated eggs and ten different kinds of chips mysteriously left in a distributor's cardboard box on the side of the road. But I realized Clooney didn't want me to answer. He wanted me to check both directions to make sure no other cars were coming. It was a cool evening after a hot boring day and I had the fluffed-out flannel feeling of nothing, nothing happening, nothing would happen…which was ridiculous because things had done nothing *but* happen, but in those days it was still easy to trust a mood the way I'd always done. The boy's door made a newfangled wrenching sound and I stepped alongside Clooney thinking I could help ease the boy's transition into captivity. Clooney said, "Come on down from there. Seriously, your parents must be w—" and I felt a sizzle on one side of my jaw as the boy shot Clooney in the face.

His face exploded. The boy's handgun turned my way. I truly didn't have a weapon. For a moment Clooney tried to keep his balance but he was dead. Chemical misinformation caused his arms to bend and his legs to surf. I saw Majido coming down out of the bed pointing his rifle at the boy and pulling the trigger but nothing happened. I saw a parking permit glued to the inside of the windshield. I reached up into the pickup and grabbed the boy before he could shoot me and I had him by his Union soldier's shirt and pulled him out of the truck and flung him onto the road, and the boy was light and his gun went flying and the boy landed shoulder- and face-first on the asphalt and I stepped on his gun hand and he yelled and I saw Clooney's body fall over twitching a few feet away and I picked up a big rock and smashed the boy's head four, five, six times, and the boy was a wet mess and wasn't moving and would never move again.

I picked up the boy's weapon. It was big and it burned my hand. Majido looked at the bodies and I wanted to throw up. It was actually the first time I'd seen a person killed up close, let alone done it myself.

"What just happened!" said Majido.

I looked at Clooney.

Had he really owned rental vans? I'd also heard him say he was in public relations. His chin was tucked into the safari jacket—stubble and zippers and crimson-soaked poplin—and his remaining cheekbone was nudging the road and his upper lip was dearly turned out. It felt like an accident. I was still trying to assemble the evening the way he'd assumed it would go.

Majido was going to tell me it was bound to happen, that we'd been dancing around the possibility of actual violence. And that was right. But I didn't want to hear it: we were strangers and comrades of convenience, and it hadn't been so bad. Or else he was about to berate me for insufficient backup, or for losing control. Or he was about to shoot me.

He hopped around the hardtop. He said, *"This is all so completely fucked!"*

And I couldn't look at the boy.

The sun set behind boulders. Majido was shaking his head. His rash had returned. I don't know how much time passed.

He said, "Okay, fuck. We've got two trucks now. And there's a lot of good shit back there."

I had the gun, I still held the rock, my hands were smeared with blood.

"Too much stuff combined to fit into either," said Majido.

"..."

"So: we convoy?"

What did I say? Had I said anything? Majido had been a security guard. He was a cartoon character. He was fat and slept in his cowboy boots.

"No," I said. "You go ahead without me."

He didn't try to talk me out of it. He moved the Tacoma off the highway and we staggered carrying one of our filled-up fifty-gallon tanks over to the boy's truck. It banged into the bed, metal on metal almost crushing my fingers. Majido climbed aboard. He said, "We can't expect the world to just keep being the world."

Now all I could do was look at the bodies.

"You're still keeping track of the days," Majido said from up in the cabin. "What day is it?"

"…"

"What day?"

"October 10th."

"Here's what we do. One month. Meet right back here. Find as much as you can, I'll do the same. We're still partners. Maybe find a tanker truck. If we can get a full tanker truck, that'd get us in easy, right?"

"Maybe," I said. "Yes."

"So keep counting the days. This exact spot. We pool whatever gas we've got and see where we are. Maybe it's what the three of us should've been doing, working on our own. Maybe we'll find more this way."

"…"

"If the other guy doesn't show up, it means…." He looked at Clooney. "Tell you what. The 10th of every month, I'll come right back here if I can, and you do the same. We're still partners. Say it."

"We're still partners."

"I'll see you then." Majido drove away south, back toward Shreveport. I wondered if we were still partners.

I tried to dig a hole, but the ground was rocky and even the flat patches were hard, and we didn't have a shovel in the Tacoma. So I dragged Clooney off the road to a spot with a fine view of a valley and stacked rocks on top of him. Halfway through, I thought I should've gone through his pockets or taken his shoes, but that was grisly work for which I wasn't quite yet ready. I made the pile immovably high then wondered if the weight would squeeze the blood out of his body and make an observable puddle. Then I figured it didn't matter.

I also dragged the boy's body off the road but I didn't

cover him. I sat in the Tacoma for a while. It was getting dark and when there were three of us our habit had been to make camp far off the road. Now probably I'd just sleep in the truck. But I wasn't tired and I turned the ignition.

I three-pointed our truck north and the headlights revealed slate and earth…and then a pair of legs. A woman stood in the road blocking my way.

She said, "I know a safe place that needs you."

2

They locked me in a candlelit cinderblock barracks with a moron named Fein.

There were two bunks, a long table, a room-temperature water cooler and a stack of ancient *Entertainment Weeklies*. They brought us food: grits and carrots and fresh skim milk. Fein wouldn't eat, so I doubled up. He paced the dirt floor.

"Been here three days," he said. "Motherfuckers keep asking the same motherfucking questions. What'd they ask you?"

"Nothing yet."

"Shit. Shit! I must be giving the wrong answers. Like, what could I say to get me out of here? What motherfucking lies could I make up?" He had one of the magazines. "I was just minding my business." I could see him smile as he started tearing out pages, tearing them to shreds. "Guy in a super-old truck says do I want a lift. Says do I have a place to sleep. I don't know what I expected. I mean, what'd they tell you? Same guy, red truck?"

"Mine was a woman."

"I'm losing it," said Fein. "Jesus Christ. What, they're gonna eat us?"

I chose a bunk.

"We'll team up," he said. "Everybody underestimates me. I'll file down this spoon, next time someone comes in we stab and run. I'm being serious: people are acting crazy."

"No question," I said.

I slept but couldn't make myself dream of specific gone things. Instead I was on a golf course with someone important who kept cheating. I suspected there were assassins in the trees. When I woke the candles were out and the barracks doorframe was bright and Fein wasn't there.

I washed out my mouth and wet my face and hair. The water that came off me had the boy's blood mixed in.

The deadbolt clicked and the barracks filled with light. It wasn't the woman. It was a tall guy wearing a suede holster on his hip. He let his right hand brush against his weapon and squinted at me. He sat at the table and said, "See if you follow my logic. Man has a truck and some water and some food and a big tank of gas. Why does the man voluntarily give that up? It's suspicious behavior."

I said, "She told me you have a farm."

"Oh, so you're a trusting fellow. Got it. Problem with that is, she watched you beat someone to death."

"…"

"And there was another guy with you, where's he now? What's the plan? You get in good with us first, then what?"

"…"

"I heard there are people in cities still going to work. Get up in the morning, make the commute, settle down at your desk and write ad copy for dog food. A failure of adaptation. That's not an issue with me. I'm ex-Army ranger, this is what the training *is*. Suddenly everything's on fire, what do you do? Suddenly the ground splits open, eats a million people. Suddenly the enemy controls the roads. Tell me what makes you think we won't just keep all your shit and leave you in here to rot."

"You're not a ranger," I said. "And that other guy Fein is

a plant."

"A plant."

"Not real. Fake prisoner."

The cowboy with the gun was cool. His forearm bore a complicated tattoo: interlocking flowers from wrist to elbow. He spoke well, his face was nuanced. Five months had taught me something: he was no soldier. He'd been a musician, or a graphic designer. He said, "They've got him in another building and they're making him tell us what you told him."

"Okay."

"Why'd you hand over your truck? Generosity is suspicious from a murderer. Which means there's a very good chance you never leave this room. That's what this is. If I'm not convinced you can be trusted, I can guarantee you won't like the result."

" . . ."

"Where are you from? What do you do for a living?"

"You first," I said. "What is this? Is there really even a farm?"

He didn't answer. We watched each other for a while. He smiled a frown. I thought that everyone in the world had seen too many movies. He bid courteous adieu and walked out with the cooler's water jug.

What was I? I was several things. I was a reporter, but not the kind who goes undercover or breaks scandals. I worked for a business news site whose editorial mission was to parrot things executives said about their own companies. Before that, I wrote copy for an art book publisher: purple captions beneath reproductions of great works. I painted monstrous houses and walked bourgeois dogs. I liked to think the common thread was the tolerance and handling of feces. I hadn't been begging for some prehistoric configuration of manhood to come collapsing down on me, but I'd recognized—as so many recognized—the uselessness of my days. Yet the moment I killed that boy proved that whatever small longing I'd once felt for "living closer the marrow" was just one more piece of turd-handling self-delusion.

They didn't bring food that day.

I read about Hollywood's Young Couples Built To Last, all of whom had broken up in intervening years, and why a megaflop sequel I remembered would signal the end of studio blockbusters, which it obviously hadn't. I wondered if people in Los Angeles had electricity, and if they were still making movies.

The woman hadn't told me much. She and her friends had food and water and nobody's boot was on their necks, but she'd lobbied to find someone tough, in anticipation of a time when boots would become more plentiful. She was a squat Mexican in a black cowboy hat. She said she'd been a housemaid. I said hop in and we drove about thirty minutes into the heart of nowhere.

I tried to sleep. She hadn't said anything else and I hadn't asked more questions, and I must've gone along because it's what I always did. I was the one who rents the first apartment he sees and stays for ten years. I was the one who goes to movies and bars and coffee shops alone assuming at some point he'll meet someone to love but it never happens. I was the one who eschews politics because he can't be bothered to tell the difference. I didn't resent. I liked doing my taxes.

Someone nudged me. The doorframe was dark again, candles were lit. It was Fein and his face was bleeding.

"I didn't give you up," he said.

It was the first time I'd been this hungry, the first time since whatever happened happened. The first few weeks were easy: I had nonperishable food in the apartment and everyone shared because we assumed it was temporary. Even after we were booted out, every day I'd found something to eat. Folks handing out vegetables from the back of a van. A supermarket guarded by shotgun-wielding private security, distributing its expiring wares to families and stragglers rather than forking them over to looters or a militia. And Clooney, who picked me out in a suburb of Tulsa and whose Tacoma for a time was itself a convenience store.

But right now, I was shaky. My stomach hurt.

I said, "What?"

"They asked me about you. I didn't tell them anything."

"You don't know anything."

Fein had something in his waistband. He presented it to me: a metal pry-bar with a hooked edge. "It'll take two of us to break the lock."

"…"

"I don't understand why you don't like me," he said.

"Where'd you get it?"

"The other place they interrogate people is a toolshed."

"Convenient," I said.

"What the fuck do you care? I'm starving, you're starving. There's a dirt road out there and a highway. You don't want to try and break out?" Fein was an actor. He spoke too closely, too recklessly. I was almost sure.

I said, "You have no idea why they're holding you like this."

"Is my face bad? Jesus, I don't know. They ask me over and over: 'Who are you working with? Who sent you here? Why'd you get in the truck? When was the last time you saw a soldier? When was the last time you saw a gun?' I'm a goddamn insurance adjuster. What do I know about…? But if I tell the truth they just ask again!"

"…"

"We should be in this together. I trust you. I trust you, okay? You don't have to tell me anything about yourself. You're in here like me."

I wondered what Clooney would say. About two days since he'd died; Majido had probably already forgotten about him. Clooney would've charmed them all.

Fein said, "My friends and I always joked about the apocalypse. Who'd be most useless, who'd be the first one to get eaten. We pretended it was funny but really deep down it was sad. Nobody knew how anything worked. Nobody could fix anything. At some point being a man went from killing what you need to having nice shoes, and it made us sad so we fucking laughed about it. Now people are killing, though. We're back to that." He pretended to clean his glasses. "You kill anybody?"

"Sure," I said. "Dozens."

"So who the fuck cares if it's a couple guards out there? Let's fucking bust *out*."

I was still in the cot and I turned over, away from him. I probably wanted them to be legit—the woman, the cowboy, the farm—because I was an ox in search of a yoke.

The next morning I was in rough shape. The door opened and I cowered from the light. Two guys came in and rousted Fein, who whined and spat and left behind his glasses. The tattooed cowboy entered. He put a pitcher of water on the table.

I was so thirsty. I said, "I thought a farm sounded like a smart place to be. Nobody seems to have confidence things are ever coming back." I told him where I was from and what I did for a living.

"Someone's more cooperative today," he said, and he nodded at the water jug. I held it in both hands and swallowed half its contents. "Who was the person Xochitl saw you kill?" I told him. "Why do you think the guy staying in here with you is a plant?"

I said, "You wouldn't willingly keep anybody around who's really that stupid and annoying."

"We can't afford to let many people stay," he said. "You have to prove you can take direction."

"I can. Believe me."

"I *am* a goddamn ranger," he said, and left me alone again. I drank the rest of the water and fell back asleep. Was there really even a farm at all?

Fein didn't return that night. The candles remained out. I felt around the room until I stumbled over his cot and found the pry-bar. But what was the winning move? Stay captive and prove my docility? Break out and prove my mettle? When it was light I hid the pry-bar against the barracks wall beneath my cot.

The cowboy came in again. This time I tried to look behind him, to see outside, and meanwhile he might've riffled through Fein's blanket. He'd brought more water.

He said, "I've thought about what they must be doing with all the prisons. At some point they'll have to let everyone out, right? Violent offenders roaming the countryside."

"…"

"That's fine. Drink up. All right, you say you're from Tulsa. Is there electricity there?"

"No."

"And what do people there think?"

"I need to eat something."

"…"

I said, "They don't know. It just went out."

"No theories."

"Nothing but theories."

"You didn't work with someone who had inside information?"

"I worked from home. The second I had no Internet I was unemployed."

The cowboy said, "So what do you think they did with the prisons? They couldn't have fed the inmates for long. Did they let them go, or did they leave them locked up and just walk away?"

"…"

"I don't believe you," he said. "I don't believe that boy was the first person you've killed. In fact, I think you've killed dozens."

"One," I said. "Just one. Please. I'm starving."

"People don't just turn into animals. You've had practice."

"*Please.*"

He said, "Maybe tomorrow. You're not there yet."

"Please don't go."

But he left and I crawled beneath my cot and the pry-bar was real.

Things were bad. My stomach pulled at the rest of me and my eyes hurt and my head was mashed at the temples and my brain misfired. Gravity tripled. I wasn't haunted by Clooney's ghost. I was crushed by aloneness in ways the world had only just gotten around to re-inventing.

I was not—had never been—tough. I slung one arm and one leg over the cot's side and drooled. I was starving and could no longer sleep and I may have pissed myself.

The pry-bar beneath me pulsed.

Fein came in, or I thought he did. He stood over me breathing through his mouth. I couldn't look up: not physically incapable, just scared. He said, "I made a deal. I gave you up. They're gonna shish-kebab your asshole 'til it comes out your mouth and roast you over an open fire. They're just taking off your excess fat. Muscle tastes better."

I was sweating hot water. I could hear the night. Deprived of the enzymes to which it was accustomed, my brain was transforming anything it could find into nonsense. For a while I thought the loathsome president was giving a speech in the barracks corner. I tried to listen.

The cowboy came back in. It was still night, though I couldn't know which one. He noticed the torn-up pieces of magazine on the floor and bent to pick them up, and I was standing behind him holding the pry-bar. I noticed myself mid-swing: I got him on the shoulder and coiled myself for another strike and I had a sense he was letting me, he'd taken the blow too easily, he was standing and the door was still open and nobody was charging in to disarm me, I knew despite his weird acquiescence I could kill him and get away and yet my weakness was everywhere. My knees were bone-on-bone.

Or I could've stopped. I could've dropped the pry-bar

and run. Why did I want his blood, too?

I took another hack.

But the cowboy saw it coming and he dropped away and kicked my legs and I crumpled. He pinned me to the floor and said, "How many people have you killed?"

"…"

"How many people?"

I understood.

"Dozens," I said.

The pressure on my chest lessened. "I can use you," he said. "Just remember who's boss."

He raised me up and walked me outside and I saw two women pass by, holding candles, with veils covering their faces. He said, "We had a landline that worked for a week."

"…"

"Powered through the copper wires in the ground, lasted as long as the phone company's backup generators. But nobody called, and almost nobody answered. At some point we just started dialing random numbers in random area codes. Any time we got someone, they said the same thing: everything was out."

It was so black. I could hear a cold wind moving through trees and grass, and it made me nostalgic and horrified and comforted and confused, I was hot and it cooled me but then I was freezing. I was haywire from hunger. We were walking in the dark toward a distant buzz.

"Don't be fooled," said the cowboy. "Everyone here knows what you are. Step out of line, you answer to me."

We were indoors again. I was collapsing. Several sets of arms had me and my legs were still going like a unicyclist's. There was a huge fireplace in the center of this room; its heat felt like vacations I'd never had companionship enough to take.

They gave me soup and I kept half of it down.

3

In sunlight, I woke when someone stepped on my foot.
She had a finger to her lips. It was the Mexican woman I'd
driven here: Xochitl. A few other people were sleeping
around the fire. She brandished a twitching silver splinter that
turned out to be the key to the Tacoma. The person closest
to us was a dozing woman whose veil dented and undented in
time with her chest. Xochitl threw the key at me and I missed
and it hit me in the face.

On the way outside we passed a cupboard, on top of
which was a basket of long-dead cell phones.

We stepped out of a sprawling single-floor farmhouse
and looked down into a beige valley. Faraway crops leaned.
Small people and animals tugged at farm equipment.
Corrugated earth sprouted green tussocks. Birds flew south in
a flectional formation. Of course there were places like this,
of course they hadn't all immediately been ravaged. I
followed Xochitl and she said, "Nothing but bread and water
for you today." I said nothing. My stomach was a bramble of
pain and I hated everyone.

The Tacoma was one of a few cars in a circular driveway.
This wasn't where I'd parked it, and I couldn't see the

cinderblock barracks. The farmhouse was white but the small enclosure at its furthest edge was painted pink, and the driveway surrounded it. The Tacoma's bed was brimming with new clutter. Xochitl had left warm bread slices on the driver seat.

"So that's it," I said. "We're friends."

She shrugged and got in the passenger side.

In the new world maybe you lost and acquired companions like changing clothes. I got in, too.

"You knew what they were going to do to me," I told her.

"I didn't know you'd be stubborn," she said.

"Explain it to me. You wanted me to say I'm a mass murderer, which is a lie. If that's the litmus that lets people stay here, what kind of messed-up place is this?"

"What kind of messed-up place is everyplace?" Xochitl tore off a piece of crust. She had black eyes and a middle part and enormous cheekbones and acne scars and a Mayan nose, she was early-thirties with teeth that looked older. "I'm sorry."

"..."

"..."

"Screw them," I said. "Screw you." I ate the bread. "Wouldn't you be better off with an actual mass murderer?"

She hugged herself and didn't answer.

I turned the key and drove a dirt road that split wheat fields. Surely we were both thinking I'd toss her out when we got far enough away. We reached the paved highway and I stopped.

"Your tank is still in back," she said. "Hidden underneath the trash. We didn't take any gas. I'll get out now if you want."

"Did you really think I wouldn't be mad?"

"But you're a big boy. You've been living out there five months. You've seen worse and you've done worse."

"I want to find that cowboy with the holster."

"His name is Charles, and I don't think you do."

"..."

"It's really so much better? 'Actually, I only killed one person.' That makes you innocent?"

"More innocent," I said. But the last penny dropped. I did, I smashed in a teenage boy's skull. I would never get away from it. I was a stranger to myself, I was the cardboard cutout of a man being operated by something unseen and looking for an excuse.

"You're not mad he starved you," said Xochitl. "You're mad he scared you."

Roaming the suburbs and then the countryside looking for gas, Clooney and Majido and I…we'd positioned ourselves as mere scoundrels, we'd made it a grim lark. But again my hand felt the final pressure as I'd slammed down the rock one last unnecessary time and bone had given way. I said, "What did you really bring me here for?"

"We have too many pacifists," she said.

"But not Charles."

"He knows we need you."

The highway around us was vacant. "If I hadn't been…. If you hadn't seen me doing it, you would've just passed me by?"

She said, "Do you know anything real about the electricity? Everyone says they know. They say, 'I'm friends with someone in Washington or New York.' Someone says there's TV in New York, everything there is pretty normal. Someone else says New York has been bombed and destroyed."

"..."

Xochitl put on sunglasses. "Do you think it's the whole United States? Do you think it's the whole world?"

"Until just now I'd have told you *I'm* a pacifist," I said. The engine was still running as we sat in park. My previous accomplices hadn't allowed such wastefulness. "You're really a maid?"

She looked through the windshield and said, "Not anymore."

What was I doing when the electricity stopped? I was masturbating. It was a Wednesday afternoon, my pants were around my ankles and I had my laptop in bed. I was supposed to be writing. Hairless bodies writhed. The lights went out and I cursed because the video began to buffer. But an outage was no disaster work-wise: I had a full computer charge and a personal hotspot on my phone. I closed my eyes and finished and fell asleep thinking about what was on TV that night. When I woke, the utility company's circuits were busy. I found people in the streets of Tulsa happily bemused, singing songs, joking that in nine months there would be a wave of new babies. A neighbor threw grapes in the air and I caught them in my mouth and then it got dark.

"Were you a maid at that farmhouse?" I said.

She coughed. "No."

Adaptation. She'd been out there by herself, watching us, watching what I did.

I wanted her to ask me if I'd ever done anything worse, because I definitely hadn't.

"Is Charles the boss?" I said. "He makes the rules? He strong-arms all these farms around here?"

"All this land you can see is ours. No, he isn't my boss. I listen to Elizabeth."

They just wanted to hear me say I was a killer. They thought saying it was bridge enough for me to cross.

"I really am sorry," Xochitl said. "I didn't know it would be like that. I think Charles has been harder on pilgrims lately and I don't like it."

"…"

"But you have to decide right now. You push me out of the truck or you don't."

My stomach felt a little better. And my lackey muscles were strong.

"I'm no pilgrim," I said, quietly.

I didn't have to be loyal. I didn't have to commit to anything until I understood what kind of setup they had. I told myself I'd just see.

So we drove west to scavenge, an activity I understood.

We went through a few microscopic deserted towns, past a gas station whose reserves had long since been dug up. We stopped a few times to check abandoned cars but their gas tanks were all empty. Farmland was over: now we drove through craggy hill country forsaken for way longer than five months. Xochitl's paper map said there were towns further southwest.

"I was lucky," she said. "I found the farm when there weren't as many people. It was less than a week. I was a hitchhiking *mojada*."

"Where were you hitchhiking?"

"It's not where I was going to. It's where I was going from."

"…"

A road sign was spray painted with side-by-side Greek letters: alpha and omega.

"First and last letters," I said. "Beginning and end."

Xochitl had hidden a second gas tank, empty, beneath the trash in the bed.

"No soldiers have visited the farm yet, even after five months?" I said.

"Not yet," she said.

We drove a while longer and saw smoke to our south and steered toward it. We got off the highway and found a small commercial district with people walking around in the sun. A few cars were creeping in the streets; someone had fashioned homemade stop signs for every intersection. I'd seen places in worse shape. We parked on a side street across from a carpet store and got out. Xochitl had a length of garden hose and she asked me for the truck's key. Cottages here demonstrated signs of life: clothing on lines, newly split logs, bean gardens, casserole dishes for rainwater collection.

We walked and the top of Xochitl's head came up to my shoulder.

In one yard a teenage boy was minding seven or eight small children. They were playing Red Rover, bashing through each other's lines. Xochitl said, "Are your parents home?"

"No," said the teenager. He was black, all the kids were black, and they looked away from me. They were disappointed to be interrupted and I stepped back into the street and lowered my chin.

"Where are they all?" said Xochitl.

"Working," the teenager said.

"What do they do?"

"…"

"It's all right."

"My father's coming back soon."

"We'd like to meet him," Xochitl said. "I see this house has a generator. So you have a refrigerator and lights. That's good. You and my friend can talk, why don't I take these children inside?"

"No," said the teenager. "It's my job to watch them."

"I'll go inside anyway," she said, and signaled to me.

"Our families have some cattle. They're out feeding and watering the cattle." The little kids were silent.

"Not many cattle farms around here," said Xochitl. "You wouldn't lie to me."

"A man had them on a big truck," the teen said. "He traded us for some gas."

I hadn't moved. Xochitl walked toward the cottage's front door and everyone watched her. Something seemed wrong.

"Is there anybody in there?" I said. "Hey, kids, is anybody in this house?"

"…"

"Tell me: what grade is everybody in?"

"Mama Josephine is in there," said a little girl. "She's

sick."

Xochitl stopped. "Is there a lot of trading in this town?"

"We're poor," the teenager said. "Please. Please don't take anything from us."

Something moved in the front window; Xochitl saw it, too. I sure wasn't packing a weapon. "All right," she said. "You guys stay here, I'll be right back." She spread out her hands and stepped to the door, tried the knob, walked inside.

I watched the house. As days and desperation progressed, surely there would be less peaceful exchanging a bit of labor for food. A few weeks before, we'd heard a rumor that this whole crisis was intentional: part of a big-business takeover of government, oligarchs battling for control of various institutions and utilities, something like that. Was that any crazier than some large-scale equipment malfunction? I held my breath.

One of the little kids screamed and it scared me so badly I fell to one knee.

It was a girl who'd stepped on an anthill. The kids lorded over it, excavated with a stick.

"Second grade," said a little boy. "And first and Isaiah is in third. But we don't go to school anymore." There definitely were multiple places where militias had forcibly taken water and gas and food. I'd seen them. How long would it take before they reached this town, or Xochitl's farm? The teenager and I looked at each other like opposing lieutenants.

It took a long time, but eventually Xochitl came out. She still had the hose, but nothing else. She inspected the generator at the side of the dirt lawn and shook her head at me. We said goodbye to the kids and kept moving. She said, "An old woman is almost dead in there. I didn't remember all the words for last rites."

"Are there really parents at all?" I said.

"'May the Lord in his mercy help you and the grace of the Holy Spirit raise you up....' I didn't know any more than that. Her pulse is very slow."

We walked around town. People in the streets or on their lawns were wary of us, as they should've been.

We crossed the main thoroughfare close to where we'd parked and saw a house apart from the others, partway up a bluff amid scrub oaks and patches of creeping thistle. A big Confederate flag flapped above the driveway. It was the kind of place Clooney and Majido would've targeted, too. A guy in a camo jacket answered the door.

"We have gas to trade," Xochitl said.

He was bearded and hugely fat, with a mole on his cheek and different-colored eyes. He said, "You do, huh? Come in." His front room was warmed by a fireplace but smelled like sewage. We passed through a kitchen. I saw he was holding a video-game controller. "People in town tell you to come out here to trade?"

"Yes," said Xochitl. "They did."

He kept waddling, through a living room whose TV displayed a pixelated and splattered body, frozen mid-death. Music came from upstairs: soft piano repeating three chords. We stepped out the back way and he lifted storm cellar doors and revealed a bunker. From ground level we could see rows of shelves, stocked with thousands of food items. I turned and the man had pulled aside his jacket to show us a gun in his waistband, straining against his hairy gut. He said, "Why don't we go inside and talk it over?"

We sat in his living room. The piano sounded live, but certainly wasn't. There was a beer-can pyramid and a spotless fluffed-up bearskin rug. "We have a fifty-gallon tank," Xochitl said.

"She does all the talking, huh?"

"Most," I said.

"All right," said the man. "What do you want for it?"

"What kind of generator are you running?" she said. "We have pure diesel."

"Four-hundred-kilowatt John Deere. Chugging away out

back and you don't even hear it. Nobody has enough gas, though."

"We do," said Xochitl. "And you've got food."

"That I do. Where's your truck?"

"Down in the town. Smarter to make a deal first, right? What's your name?"

"I'm William. Billy. I can give you fifty cans of food, and you can choose whatever you like."

Xochitl smiled. "A gallon per can, Billy, that's not a very good price. The people in this town said you were a serious man."

"That was nice of them," he said.

"The price is three hundred cans. There's a lot more food in the world than there is gas."

"What kind of truck you driving, you can make off with three hundred cans of food? What kind of army you got to protect 'em?"

"Big army," she said. "Big, scary army."

Billy stood and his camo jacket flapped and he pulled out his silver gun. "Strange goddamn times. Strange coming into my house unarmed, announcing what you got. You are unarmed, am I right?"

"Civilization isn't done yet," said Xochitl.

"Well, okay. In that spirit, I want to offer you both a cold beer. Takes the edge off hunger, is what I find." He folded in front of a mini-fridge. "Three beers coming up. This is a good Christian household. But when the door-to-door people used to come, selling encyclopedias or trying to tell me about the Hare Krishnas, I won't lie: I shot out a tire or two. I've got a reputation in these parts. And I think maybe the townsfolk are having some fun with you, sending you here. Three beers."

"We didn't come up here to be threatened," she said.

"No, you came here to rip me off. Two hundred cans."

"I need to think about it," she said, looking at me. "May I use your bathroom?"

Billy opened a beer and handed it to me. "We don't waste a precious flush on strangers." He laughed. "You should see your face. It's down the hall."

Xochitl exited making a private quack-quack hand gesture meant for me. Keep him talking.

"This is great," I said. "It's the first beer I've had in a long while. Thank you."

"Don't know how you stay sober around that one," said Billy. "She's a ball-buster."

"…"

"Oh, I don't mean anything. The cock wants what it wants." He drew down on his beer with one hand still on the gun. "I guess you came along at a good time. Knowing my luck it'll be a cold-ass winter."

I said, "So we'll be helping each other."

"I did all this prepper shit, most everything the Internet said, but I dragged my heels on fuel. It's a pain in the dick to store gas, right? I had twenty-pound propane tanks on the front lawn and someone took 'em, first couple days the power was out. What could I do? Could've gone rampaging through town, I guess, but at the time I figured it'd only be another day or two."

"Yeah."

"You know what all this is, right?"

"What is it?"

"Well, it's the revolution."

"…"

"I'll admit the liberals had one thing right. Wealth inequality and all that. But you know where wealth inequality comes from? You make this massive *thing*—this huge government that's reaching everywhere and reacting to every problem by writing a thousand rules for it—you ensure there'll be corruption. Makes it easy for CEOs to earn a thousand times what his factory worker makes. Spend on a gigantic military, more corruption there: your three-hundred-dollar screwdriver. And put everybody to sleep with reality

TV? Well, maybe they were sleeping but they woke up, that's all I can say."

"They did?"

"I got a ham radio in the shelter. Been talking with people all over the place. This whole thing, it's the masses rising up to control the means of production, right out of the little red book. Except it's that old joke: 'What do you call a liberal with an IQ of 130?'"

"..."

"A foursome."

I said, "When you talk to people in other places, do they have electricity?"

"Here's one for you. Just imagine how many natural gas lines have exploded. Imagine who's got their finger on nuclear power. Exactly what I want: lefty revolutionaries taking a vote whether or not to stop the reactor core from melting down. 'Sorry, Wavy Gravy, that's ten hippies in favor of shutting it down, but the other twenty want us to do a study first.' If half the world has literally gone up in flames, how would you know? But all right. Enough about that. I have something to tell you: and I'm afraid it's bad news."

"..."

"It turns out I'm not giving you any food." The screensaver on his TV flashed to black.

"You're not."

"It's every man for himself." Billy pointed the gun at me. "Hey, lady! Yoo-hoo! Come on out of the powder room!"

"Cut it out," I said.

"Your bitch takes a long damn shit. Unless it's ragtime! Is it ragtime in there? Please be nice and flush twice! I'll tell you one thing: you should've come here armed. You would've needed a lot of guns to take what you were after, but still, it's just common sense. You were never gonna last much longer in the new world. And now what's gonna happen is: I'm gonna hold onto one of you, and the other one's gonna go get that truck with the diesel in it, and if they're not back in ten minutes, I'm gonna kill the one who stays, which given who wears the pants in your family I have a feeling is gonna be you."

My hands went up. "She wasn't kidding. We're traveling with soldiers."

Billy laughed. "No you're not. Okay! Time's up, sugar britches! Come on out of there!" He was still trained on me, finger on the trigger. He walked me down that hallway, toward the bathroom. I couldn't hear any more music. "Hey! Get out here in three seconds or hubby gets a bullet!"

"…"

"This is adorable, because either she thinks I'm bluffing or she's okay with me blowing your head off. One!"

I was trapped at the end of this hallway and I tried to squeeze past him, but he elbowed me back.

"Two!"

I looked into the muzzle and I flashed to the boy in the soldier's suit: what had been the mechanics of that, he'd swung the gun my way but he must've hesitated—he must've been showing mercy—because there really should've been no way I had time to grab his uniform and pull him toward me, if he'd really planned on shooting me, too.

So why hadn't I just disarmed him?

"Three!"

A car horn sounded. It came from inside the bathroom. Billy pushed the door: it wasn't locked. He swiveled his lard into the doorframe and the gun left me; bathroom curtains ballooned in a breeze: a window was open. Xochitl was not present. I thumped him with my shoulder and wrapped my arms around his oozy back, he fell into the small room with a galumph that sounded like the floor and walls would give, I pulled the bathroom door shut and held it, he pulled, we wrestled with the knob but I had better leverage, I held it fast and he gave up pulling and pits of light appeared in the door and also the wall behind me and I couldn't figure it out but then it was obvious he was shooting at me through the door.

I got down, still gripping the knob.

Then I heard different shots, out the window. I high-tailed it: in the kitchen I stole a box of ammo and an unopened jar of peanut butter and ran through that foul-smelling front room to the lawn, then around to the back where Xochitl had driven the Tacoma and was siphoning gas from Billy's generator into our second tank. Billy had fired all his bullets and was shouting down the distance Xochitl had jumped, unwilling to make the leap himself.

"Piece of shit!" Billy said. "Piece of shit! Piece of shit!"

"Tell me the plan next time!" I said. "Are you hit?"

"Are you?" she said.

"Fuck you!" said Billy. "Fuck you! Fuck you!"

"Billy," said Xochitl, "how much of this gas do you think should we leave you!"

"Fuck you!"

"'Take it all?' He says take it all. That's so generous of you, Billy!"

"Don't do it!" Billy said. "Don't do it! You're murderers! You're murderers!" He threw his gun down at us and pulled his top half back inside the house.

"Time to go," I said. We left the hose. And in the moment before Xochitl started up the engine again, as Billy was presumably bumbling through his house, I heard a new sound. It came from higher than the bathroom, one floor up, and fell down on us without mercy. It helped me place the septic smell in that front room. Someone else was standing in an upstairs window, trying to see what was happening and joggling something in her arms. She held a crying infant.

We stopped laughing, we stopped smiling, and we drove off.

4

They assigned me a cot in a tarpaper shack down the hill, half-a-mile from the farmhouse. I bunked with four other men and a woodstove that did little more than leak smoke into the room. When the cots were set up, there was nowhere to walk. Three of the men worked the fields and bore a circus hay-and-feces funk; they were Morales and Conrad and Bob, and they were awake and asleep early, accustomed to transient work. The other man, Kimo, was six-foot-six with Grecian-urn arms and a broken Polynesian nose, tatted with a collar of skulls and in the process of crossing over from athletic to overripe. He looked like a bulldog chewing a bee. He was an ex-con and, basically, seemed like the farm's bouncer. After the others were gone at dawn, Kimo would tell me chapters from his story:

"I was abused. It was my uncle. If he showed up traveling the road, boy, you know I hope they decide to let him in because then I could kill him slow. I was a bodyguard to prove to myself I'm a man. Why didn't I play football? They asked me to play but instead I dropped out because Spider said so. 'Just be big, you got my back, don't smile, but don't worry about nothing, nothing ever happens.' Well, something happened and I did a five-spot.

"Spider knows a guy, says he got a supplier who won't pay him back. So as a favor, Spider says we'll go get the money. And the guy says don't even bother, this supplier is crazy, he don't care if you break all his bones, but Spider goes no problem. I wish he told me what the plan was…but he never told you, it was a one-way street with Spider. We got there and I busted in, and the supplier acted scared and promised to pay. And Spider didn't hit the guy, he didn't touch the guy. Spider looks at me and he hands me over his gun and his phone, and he told the supplier to get on his knees. The guy got on his knees.

"Spider told me get ready. He was a one-way street, boy.

"He took down his pants and his underpants. He told the guy open his mouth. And of course the supplier didn't want to, but Spider said he had two choices and one was a bullet. So the guy did it. And Spider told me take some video, and I did it. And Spider said you and I both know you ain't gonna bite down. He thought I thought it was funny. He made funny faces for the video. I stopped and went outside and Spider came out, too, and now the guy had to pay up or everybody would see that video.

"But I don't know if he paid. I stayed home and I couldn't stop thinking about it. I guess I understand how you can do some things, but other things, boy. Spider called and called. I didn't sleep, and then I went to the cops. But they tricked me. I know better, but they tricked me into talking and I got a five-spot. Spider went away for longer. I'm lucky there's no Internet anymore or he'd come kill me."

I worked with Xochitl. We drove out every day; we were the farm's emissaries. Mostly we did legit trading, and I guess I was her backup. You didn't get much gas for a vegetable basket but the farm had produced a lot over the summer. People said there were places where paper money was still currency, but we didn't live near those places; maybe you could add a hundred dollars as a kicker to get a trade done, but that was rare.

In those early days, we tried not to steal. Any whiff of possible confrontation, and we agreed to move on without actually mentioning our first heist, but the memory weighed on us: Billy calling us murderers while his baby cried. And since we didn't steal, our perimeter got unsustainably big. The drawbacks were self-evident: how much gas do you burn to maybe find more gas? Plus fewer than fifty miles out we found exit-area service stations that were being dug up by soldiers of one kind or another. Civilians in functional cars weren't unheard of yet, but we couldn't risk a tail back to the farm. That night, Xochitl felt we were being watched and we slept in the Tacoma.

We were in service to the farm's four-pole multi-fuel generator. It was mounted on a concrete floor beside the farmhouse, inside that pink enclosure. Diesel was the prize; we could and did also use regular gasoline but the generator burned through it faster. The people who ran the farm were strict: electricity was for a few kitchen appliances, a walk-in freezer, some lights at night and the farm's well pump. Otherwise, it was frontier living.

And the nights started getting cold. It was terrible. Someone had tried eliminating our shack's draftiness by nailing up plywood and slathering seams with some kind of bad-smelling commercial sealant, but sleeping in there still required tucking my face beneath my pile of blankets. I dozed half-an-hour at a time, woke up suffocating. Conrad caught the flu and had to stay in bed and the others talked about him like he was dead. Nobody gave him medicine. Did you recover from the flu after the world ended? A day later, Bob was sick. The five us would lie in darkness, inches from each other, listening to the wind and the ailing men groan. They weren't my brothers. The only thing we had in common was fear borne of no better options. There was a fireplace up in the farmhouse; there was electricity. I wanted someone to speak up and hatch a plan to get me indoors at night. We wouldn't last another week like this, let alone an entire first winter in darkness.

I needed to learn who wielded the power in this place.

One morning, Xochitl and I ate fried potatoes and blackberries standing against an oak post fence, from whence dead grass receded into a patchwork of vegetable plots. Women were out there digging, hammering, gathering, shoveling, spraying; it was more chaotic than it sounds: the geometry was off, the plots weren't perpendicular to each other, nobody really chatted or commiserated, it felt like a farming ghetto.

I said, "Where does Charles sleep?"

In the couple weeks we'd been driving together, it had become Xochitl's custom to behave as though I were remedial. I *was* remedial. She sighed.

"I can't help it," I said. "It's cold. Is it women-only in the farmhouse?"

"…"

I said, "There are other barracks. Like the place they starved me. Who decides who gets to be warm?"

"Not me," said Xochitl.

"Who are the other new people?" I said. "Who here's newer here than me? Where do they sleep?"

"I don't manage the list," she said. "They say, 'Xochitl go find gas, go find a can opener, go find toilet paper.'"

"…"

"I like you quieter."

I nodded. A veiled woman carried a basket of steaming laundry. I had a rush of communal feeling, that these chores were being done around me. (Of course, nobody had volunteered to wash my clothing.) The woman was walking our way. I said, "All right, who gets a veil?"

Xochitl chewed.

"I mean why don't you get one?"

"I don't want one," she said.

"What do they mean?"

Xochitl said, "Why don't you ask her."

The veiled woman paused before us.

"Sorry," I said. "Never mind."

She was so skinny, and her fingers were scratched and blistered. Her veil hung from a hooded cowl and concealed her face down to the point of her chin. She could see out, but there was no seeing in. She seemed to be looking up at me and condensation frothed between us. "Ask me what?" she said.

"He wants to know about your veil," said Xochitl.

The woman's head didn't move and I assumed I'd made a terrible gaffe. We stood there too long, just an intolerable pause during which I felt my permission to stay on the farm was in danger of revocation. It might've been ten seconds. Another woman passed by, not veiled. For days I'd counted the men I'd seen here: nine, maybe ten, though I hadn't met everyone, and I hadn't been inside the farmhouse since the first night. But it seemed genuine and by design, this gender ratio, and it made me feel provisional, as I surely was.

When I didn't actually ask a question, the woman said, "Well, I guess have a good day," and left us.

Xochitl wasn't pleased. She said, "I expect a very quiet drive today."

"There's a rule against making friends here," I said. "Inversion of the way things were. Men need to know their place."

She smiled crossly. "No, just don't be a fool."

"I'm not clear what was foolish."

"Make friends. Don't make friends. Just don't treat people like they're strange, and you're the normal one."

"You didn't wonder why people wore veils when you first got here."

"I did. I waited for somebody to tell me."

"I didn't mean disrespect," I said. "Just: the world has enough mysteries."

"They wear veils because Elizabeth does."

"..."

Things stayed unsettled between us that day. We drove west, in silence. The towns here were populated but quiet, more links in the chain that had snapped or was in the process of snapping. Clooney's habit had been to stop and chat with strangers, hear their thoughts and recommendations. But we'd had nothing more to protect than what we carried.

Elizabeth. Dear Leader. I wanted an audience. No, that wasn't true, I didn't. That wasn't me. I wanted Xochitl to make a plea for warmth on my behalf. I watched vacant franchise restaurants flip by in the passenger window. I hadn't yet seen Charles or Fein again. The unfairness of my starvation those first few days returned, Xochitl was an extension of that bad treatment and I fantasized about finding an empty eighteen-wheeler, ditching my so-called partner out here in no-man's land and returning to steal the farm's entire gas supply.

That would show them, and finally get me back into Tulsa.

When we returned that night, Xochitl grunted goodbye. I picked up a paper bag of mixed greens—my supper—from in front of the house and spent the walk downhill imagining everyone inside the house dining gloriously.

Kimo was smoking a cigarette outside our shack. He said, "They got someone new."

"Okay."

"I know him. Well, I don't really know him."

"..."

"He's not like us. But I guess maybe they want him anyway. I don't know why." He was blocking the door.

"I just want to eat and go to sleep, Kimo. Before it gets too cold out."

"For me this place is great," he said. "It's the best place I ever lived. What was it like where you lived? Ha, I don't miss my bank account very much."

"Kimo."

" . . ."

" . . ."

"Charles says to watch you," said Kimo. "He said tell you they got someone new, and then watch you. And don't let you go out again until morning. He thinks you would do something."

"I figured you were already watching me. I figured that's why you have to stay down here, to keep close watch. Please just let me go inside."

Kimo inhaled and his face glowed. "I like it if we get new people. I didn't like what they did to you."

" . . ."

"Do you really not care what they do?"

I thought about it and stood beside him, leaning against the shack. There was no moon.

"Before everything broke," he said, "I told you some of the things I done. You didn't tell me anything."

"They got it wrong with me," I said. "I tried to tell them."

"You were just good."

"I wasn't anything. I was the most neutral person in the world. Yeah, you're right, I lived in a nice part of town, and I had money saved."

" . . ."

"I never spent it, I just kept adding to it. Sometimes I saw a telethon on TV and I cried about the sick children, and thought I should send a check, but I never did. Or...I probably did sometimes. I can't remember."

Kimo said, "When everything broke, people stood in line at the ATM. Everyone knew it didn't work, but they stood in line." His cigarette went out and now it was only his voice. "One guy told me it was God turning everything off to show the wrong track we're on. He made some good points, but I didn't believe it."

" . . ."

"Charles is the boss, but I learned my lesson. I'm not listening to the boss anymore when I think it's wrong. Come with me?"

We walked. My eyes adjusted and I could follow the back of Kimo's sweatshirt, big and white as a sail. The fields were wet and my toes became soaked and freezing. How many acres was the farm? How big was an acre? It went on; there were other small houses at long intervals, dark against the dark horizon. We crossed a paved lane and after so much soft ground my legs almost couldn't take those few hardpan paces. Then we stopped and he had a flashlight and illuminated a barbed-wire fence. I said, "What am I looking at?" The light skimmed down the line until it found a spot where the wire had been cut.

Kimo said, "Somebody did this."

My face was hot. "It wasn't me."

"I know. It's cut bigger on the outside."

"…"

"I wanted to show this to you first," said Kimo.

"What does it mean?"

"Come on."

We slopped along this perimeter, the fence continued, we seemed to be at the farm's easternmost edge. I wanted to ask whether the barbed wire predated five months ago, but appearing extra-inquisitive about the homestead's defenses seemed like poor strategy. An incursion could simply be a starving family boosting a handful of vegetables, or it could mean something direr. I remembered Tulsa: four weeks in, a polite guy wearing a military surplus jacket had knocked on everybody's apartment door and explained we had a day to get out before someone forced us out; my neighbors had shouted and laughed at him and he'd taken it like a bureaucrat, moved to the next block. The following day hundreds of mismatched fighters clomped in. None of us stonewalled. We inspected their snarls and assault weapons and carried our possessions beyond the city limits as losers have done for millennia, provided their conquerors were merciful. I looked at the children's faces. They were all of us. I didn't like kids, but even I could see that.

"I think it means there are people who want to get in," Kimo said. "More people than just pilgrims."

We hiked more: dew-soaked and uphill. I said, "I can look for stuff to repair the fence when we're out tomorrow," not knowing what such materials would even be.

"I miss music," he said. "But the electricity is too important for it."

I knew this was an opening to ask him what kind of music he liked. I could tell he wanted to be my friend. Instead, I said, "Have they let anyone else onto the farm since me?"

"I don't know. They don't tell me very much because they don't think I'm smart." Kimo stopped walking and I bounced off him. Softly, he said, "There they are."

And here were the interrogation barracks I remembered, small and square, illuminated now by a car's headlights. Two men were talking hands-on-hips: Charles and Fein. I said, "They have someone new inside?" and Kimo said, "Yes."

We waited. Life was so much more physical now. Cold and wet, tensed to pounce.

"What do you think happened to the power?" said Kimo.

"..."

"That guy I told you about, who said it was God that done it. He was a priest. My uncle used to say if you're a hammer, all you see is nails."

I watched my former jailors. Charles opened the barracks door and pushed Fein in, and Fein pretended to struggle. They both went inside and the door slammed shut.

"They don't trust me to be the actor," Kimo said. "Sometimes I get to be the mean one at the beginning. They want to know what he saw when he was out there, and they want to know who saw him."

And then? Did everyone interview for admission via torment? Did some pilgrims skip the formalities and steal produce via that cut fence? What happened if they were caught?

I said, "They asked me the last time I'd seen soldiers."

"Yup."

We waited in the trees for a long time. I said, "Kimo, do you know Elizabeth?"

"No. Charles says stay away."

It took half-an-hour more, then Charles came back out carrying the five-gallon water jug.

We still waited, and finally Charles drove away. We approached the barracks door; Fein was in there monologuing. I couldn't make out the words but his inflection was the same priggish paranoia. I just stood there. They were about to start torturing someone else. I guess I don't know what I was thinking.

Kimo pounded the door. He said, "Hey! Hey!"

Two voices were immediately closer. Fein ad-libbed some rescue-me dialogue. The other guy just said, "Help!"

Kimo said, "Quiet down!" But Fein wouldn't, for obvious reasons. "Stop yelling so you can hear what I'm saying!" It went on for a while, Kimo slapping the door, voices jumbling inside.

Then I heard myself talking. "He's in on it! He's one of them! Don't listen to anything he says!"

It was temporarily quiet. One of them said, "Who is?"

I said, "This isn't real! Don't be afraid! It's just some messed-up test!" Kimo clicked his flashlight again and made funny eyebrows, like he was surprised I had some gumption in me.

"Who are you?" said the unfamiliar man's voice.

"We don't have a key," Kimo said, "just wait 'til morning."

"When's that?"

I put a hand over the flashlight and said, "Battery life,

Kimo," trying to make it sound like a joke.

So we waited for hours in the dark. And the way to avoid the flu was *not* to sit around all night in the cold, shaking too badly to sleep, recalling my first few days on the farm: behind that same door, starving and terrified. Kimo just lapsed into snores. Knowing Fein was in there stewing helped.

There had never been such close links between a moment's decision and my personal survival. Billy or the boy trying to shoot me, yes, but also taking a wrong turn into captivity or eating pestilential food or staying out in the cold to make a point.

What in my prior life couldn't be undone? What decisions had been inescapably final? Everything had *seemed* dramatic, every story I wrote or read had made the case for its own essentialness. Now I shivered with part of me disbelieving the facts: that I probably had the flu virus in me and that my behavior—sitting out here freezing—was helping it along. I stupidly believed I would endure because I always had.

Well, I did endure. Lesson not learned. Dawn warmed us; Kimo had Twinkies in his front pocket.

Charles returned in the car alone.

"I know what you wanted," Kimo told him. "But it ain't gonna be that way. We're not gonna be terrible to people anymore."

Charles was displeased by our tidings of reform. "Don't give me this shit," he said. "It's not your job. It's not your decision. There are things you don't understand, Kimo." He looked at me. "You I'm not surprised by."

". . ."

"You think you know everything. I can tell it by the way you talk, the way you're smarter than everybody you meet. People around here think it's simple as, 'Just stay real quiet, nobody will ever find us.' And then they don't want to know what goes on in this room. They don't want to know what direction this whole thing can take. You think there aren't farmers living up and down these roads who'd love to talk all about us? You think there aren't people ready to give us up and see us get our cushy lives taken away?"

But of course, I wasn't living any kind of cushy life. I wanted what they had.

"Trusting people means you have to trust them," Kimo said.

"The new guy in there can't stay now," said Charles. He squinted in the sunrise. "No matter what might have happened, no matter what use he might've been, now we can't test him, so we can't trust him. That's all you've done."

"…"

"And he's soft anyway. I don't know how he got this far." Charles had the leather holster and the tattoo and the autocratic privilege and the smugness, he was tough and too specific, like it was an act he was sorry to be forced to play and in which he couldn't afford to show a crack.

He unlocked the door and we stayed outside. The prisoner came out blinking. He was tan and upright and handsome, and he staggered my way and deflated against me. Fein strolled out behind him wiping his hands as after a job well done.

"Got some bad news for you," Charles said. The new guy was playing it up a little, rasping and whimpering.

"Now hold on a minute," Fein said.

"Please," said the man. "What's happening?"

"I won't do this anymore," Kimo said. "It's not right."

"There's no other way," said Charles. "How many people you think we can feed?"

A woman sang, far away but closer than I expected. She sang "Killing Me Softly" and it was the kind of blithe nonsense patternmaking the new world would taunt us with: no more portentous than the sun posing moonily through a mask of pines. Us and Them and We and They and Ours and Theirs and it was true, it was a lot easier to be Kimo in that moment if you believed this change wasn't forever.

Fein folded his arms and put a hip against the pollen-marbled car, and he said, "Now hold on. I agree with Kimo we can make an exception." He drew an arrow on the hood, pointed the dirty finger at the man in my arms.

5

He was a professional football player. He'd been a punter.

"Who cares," Kimo said to me. "Who cares *why* they let him stay? I'm just happy they did."

But dammit, I didn't live here. I was passing through, right? Well, I didn't know. I hadn't wanted the new man—Jon Scoggins—to suffer as I'd done, but in retrospect even that felt like a pose. Did I really care? I only knew I hated and feared Charles, and I needed to get out of that damn shack.

Scoggins slept a night and a day in Kimo's bunk and gladly ate what they gave him. Fein was a big football fan and wanted to hear the punter's locker-room stories. He argued it was good for morale; presumably he meant *his* morale.

Scoggins was an actor. Maybe he was a literal actor; maybe he'd done aluminum-siding commercials or starred in action movies. But I just mean his whole gestalt. He wasn't quite friendly but he did a great facsimile. He looked at you the way a person who's interested is supposed to. He wanted to hold court but realized sometimes that might come across self-centered, so he'd demur over and over, asking if we were sure we wanted to hear his next tale. When Kimo talked about Spider and jail, it was actual self-loathing. Scoggins issued artificially rueful declarations that he'd never made All-Pro.

To others, he delivered funny stories of being pranked with Icy Hot in his jockstrap, and thinking a TV crew wanted to interview him when actually they were signaling to the quarterback, and missing the team jet because a herd of cattle decided to block his car. But he could tell his likable act didn't work as well with me, so when we were alone in the cabin he'd say, "You're really smart, I can tell my charm offensive is lost on you. Sorry: it's a defense mechanism when I'm intimidated" or: "Whenever my bullshit gets too thick, you have to promise to pop me one." But he didn't mean it, that was more acting. He had to win you over and it was hard work.

His presence threw things off. Several of the women, including a couple of the veiled, ventured down to the cabin during the day and cackled at his yarns. This lasted a few days, during his convalescence, though I didn't know exactly what he was convalescing from. (Conrad and Bob had finally admitted how sick they were and Fein said they were in the house getting better.) Scoggins sat up in bed like an archduke and held forth, gesturing with giant bronze hands, pausing on laugh lines. I left in the mornings and came back at night and a new shift of admirers would surround him. I asked Kimo what job Scoggins would eventually have. I suggested he could be the farm's TV weatherman.

I found a full vodka bottle hiding in a bin of baby sandals, deep inside a shuttered shoe store, and I concealed it from Xochitl. That night, Kimo and Morales and Scoggins drained the bottle and I watched them. Kimo told a story about getting his jaw broken by a prison guard, and I watched Scoggins pretending he wasn't desperately waiting for his turn to talk. It was unclear how much English Morales knew.

"For a couple weeks," Scoggins eventually said, "we all still came to the team facility to work out. Dallas was dark, but us big dumb jocks needed to tend our muscles. I mean, who am I kidding, I kicked a few balls and practiced my golf swing, but whatever, every day our position coach would come out and tell us we were a day away from the electricity coming back on. That's what they were telling him. All anyone really thought was: it's a good thing it wasn't during the season, because the networks wouldn't be able to get a satellite signal to broadcast the games. What mostly stressed us out, what the coaches kept saying over and over, was: everyone else in our division lived in a city where the power was on and life was normal and they were training as hard as they could, so if we didn't stay super vigilant we'd be screwed in the fall.

"Little by little my teammates stopped showing up, but the rest of us worked out like usual. A couple years ago everybody got a stomach bug—people stayed home and it was half-a-ghost-town—so people just pretended that's what it was. But the coaches stopped telling us what they'd heard. Then the coaches stopped coming. My house is five miles from the facility and I didn't have to worry about refilling the car for a while, so I just kept showing up. But the conversations changed. The airport was closed, and a couple guys drove out of town to check on their parents. Three weeks in, they shut down the facility. To let you know what kind of idiot I am, two straight days I woke up and drove in anyway out of muscle memory. Most people just accidentally flip a lightswitch for a couple days.

"My house is a McMansion on a golf course, and we were probably a magnet for attention. My wife worried all the time about getting looted, she was extra-sweet to everyone in the neighborhood, she stopped people on the street and offered them food, she went door to door to make sure everybody was doing okay. It was smart. I was so committed to everything being okay. People still played golf and I sat on a lawn chair in the back yard and waved as they walked down the 15th fairway. I walked to the park to throw a ball around with some kids. Police kind of had the neighborhood surrounded just in case. I mean, I was still going to the grocery for weeks after! And everybody would tell you the lights were supposed to come on tomorrow, and I just have this picture of myself cruising along totally denying how serious it could turn out to be."

The bottle made another lap. Scoggins was smiling less, and telling it to the shack's far wall. He continued:

"My brother showed up, middle of the night. He lived in Austin and he drove up and he was jumpy as hell. We weren't close and he blamed me: I was the superstar our mom and dad were proud of, he was the fuck-up who'd been to rehab. My wife woke up, we acted happy to see him, but when he gets me alone he's like, 'I've got to show you something,' and his truck was filled with gas cans. A hundred red-plastic gas cans. And my brother goes, 'It's the end of the world and I need a place to hide these.'"

Listening, I kept my face even. Kimo said, "It's not. That isn't what it is." But he said it slow and drunk.

"My brother said if the power didn't go back on soon gas will be like gold. I asked where he got it and he wouldn't tell me, and I was so stupid. We were fine, we were part of a community and we could've made things work for however long we needed. I should've said no. My brother didn't even know what truth even was. But I thought about my parents, who've been gone a while now, and you're supposed to take care of family and besides I was so deep in denial. So I said fine, let's stick the cans in the basement. Next morning he's gone, his truck is gone, the gas is still there. To a smarter person than me, fireworks would've been going off in their head. I just tell my wife not to go into the basement.

"Very next day, a cop I knew knocked on the front door. They had a tip we were hoarding."

"Aw, no," Kimo said.

"Part of me thinks, 'So what if we're hoarding? Isn't what that people do?' But this cop—I know his wife, I know his kids—but he's all business. He said it's frowned on, the police are trying to stop trouble before it starts and as soon as someone finds out what we've got, how much we've got, there'd be trouble. He said they couldn't allow it. How'd they know? Did they stop my brother on his way out? I never found out.

"I didn't have a gun and even if I did, you wouldn't bet on me in a shootout. So I admitted it. I took the cop downstairs and showed him the cans. He was calm and said he could help. We should get the gas out of our house that night. He said he'd take it to the station. Of course I knew what was probably going on: he was taking it for himself. But what were my choices? He came back with a couple friends and they marched the gas cans right back out. I said, 'Does this mean the lights won't be turning back on?' and he said, 'Oh, I'm sure they will. Any day.' *At least we're back where we started*, is what I was thinking. People who lived around us were still being pretty cool. Nobody was starving or anything. People were sharing. And as we're standing out on the driveway in the dark, like it's nothing, this guy I've known for five or six years says, 'Does your wife know about the gas?' I said she didn't know anything, which was true. And he said, 'I'm supposed to kill you.'"

I looked at Scoggins and my stomach's bottom couldn't help from dropping. He'd begun talking airily; now he was sweaty and confessional. He'd pivoted, wanting to be known, and had decided to pick that particular lock with the truth. Or had he just figured out how to hook me?

Scoggins said, "That's not something I ever thought…. I almost laughed. When your favorite TV show, the one you binge with your wife, when that's happening on your own driveway. I tried to talk him out of it. I told him we'd pay whatever he wanted. He said he didn't care about money, he had to make sure nobody else knew the gas even existed. *His fucking hand was on his fucking gun.* He said there were two choices, I could get in the truck or get my throat cut right here. There wasn't time to do anything. I got in. I asked if I could bring my wife. They said no, and I thought they were taking me somewhere to put a bullet in me. But they drove way north into Oklahoma and pushed me out."

"…"

"I hitchhiked back and I walked when I couldn't get a ride and it took a few days. When I finally got back to my neighborhood, the country club was barricaded. There was always a military base nearby, and now there were patrols. People were getting moved out, I'm pretty sure people were getting shot. I waited for it to get dark and snuck in and got as close as I could. There were flashlights moving around in my house. A lot of them." Scoggins was half-crying now, either pitiable or virtuosic. "I went from hoping my wife was in there to hoping she wasn't. I decided to walk to my sister-in-law's house. I knocked on all the doors and nobody answered and I broke a window. Nobody was home. I slept there but nobody came. I left a note telling them everything that happened. God, I didn't want my wife to think I'd just *left*. I thought about staying, but there was no food so I got out. In the note I said go north. Find a car and get to Oklahoma City or Tulsa. But they're both shitshows. You can't even get in. Would you believe they've got a tariff set up in Tulsa? I heard you have to bring a huge amount of gas or they won't even let you in."

His story done, Scoggins drank deep. I made my face look like a surprised person's face.

Then Morales staggered outside and I followed him.

It was the coldest night yet, probably low 30s, and moonlit enough so I could see Morales relieving himself across the path, on a row of picked-clean Brussels sprouts stalks. He was wreathed in steam and sighing, and I paced around. I believed Scoggins's story and whatever nasty pleasure I felt knowing a millionaire suddenly had injustice thrust upon him was nullified by the cold. If I'd never come here, if I hadn't followed Xochitl: where would I be? Would I be this cold? I never had opportunity to speak with anyone on the farm other than these shack-mates and Xochitl. I didn't know whose edicts kept me down here: edicts about who slept where, who ate what…edicts that made literal bedfellows out of me, the millionaire punter, and this farmhand doing the thing maybe I wanted to do out of defiance, except I hadn't been drinking, I was dry. Injustice, yes, and I laughed at myself. Morales tottered back my way and he was saying, not to me, *"…ambos caerán en el hoyo."* I figured he saw me foppish, because that's how I was.

When Morales had gone back inside, I thought I heard hydraulic brakes. I walked further out into the fields and searched the tree line for a truck's lights. But it was too far to the main road and I couldn't see. My feet were wet again. It was dead quiet: no vibrations, no engine. But it could happen any time: the paramilitary breach. These farm people were sustaining themselves and how long would that go unnoticed? I'd seen a lot. If they could clear out whole cities, what were a few loops of barbed wire?

I heard a man's laugh.

It came far from this field, north, the direction of the farm's dirt pass or perhaps beyond. I wasn't brave. But I wasn't going back to that shack to be slaughtered in my half-sleep.

I snaked through a harvested wheat field and heard voices: I wasn't crazy. The exit was that way, I'd regret leaving the Tacoma behind but I was never getting back to Tulsa like this, scavenging for fertilizer and books and scissors and letting them keep me in cold storage. It seemed possible I could start again, walk out and find someone else to latch on with. But I couldn't fully make the decision to bail; I kept moving toward the voices.

Two figures, less spectral than derelict, moseyed up the pass toward the farmhouse smoking and chuckling: kings of all they surveyed. One carried a stack of empty crates. If they were militia, they were awfully casual about invading. I tried to listen but the sounds were all vowels. It had to be Charles and Fein, but I couldn't be sure. I remembered their voices well enough—I heard them in dreams—but they got quiet passing my crouching spot in the husks, and everything was tinted deep blue. I thought I should follow them, find out what they did at night and where they did it. But they were gone and I stayed there silent for several minutes, telling myself I was waiting to see if anyone else followed.

I returned to the shack and everyone had passed out.

More days and cold nights went by. Xochitl found me a winter coat in the farmhouse, and I slept wrapped up in it. We drove east and not for the first time she joked we should visit the famous country music theme park to see what the outage had wrought, but it was way too far. We took a rural road that unspooled through miles of country nothingness, no towns, just tiny forlorn stone houses topped with sheets of corrugated tin. We passed roadside paddocks with optimistic ranch monikers carved and burned in archway lumber, and sometimes riders were grinding away therein, still breaking and training horses, and sometimes they waved their hats. A yellow sign advertised state vehicle inspection services. We crossed a truss bridge over a lake and found signs of life at a Ski & Sports store. Folks were hanging around, reclined on their tailgates, laughing and smoking weed. It was a dirt-lot vacation scene and they welcomed us to join. I left Xochitl and snaked down through dying wild rye and balding oaks to a muddy strip of beach. A boat launch was filled and unmanned. I stripped and swam and froze, by way of a thorough scrubbing. I heard another car's tires thump across the bridge.

When I returned dripping to the Ski & Sports parking lot and its dozen kayaks in a row, Xochitl wasn't there. I stood at the Tacoma pretending I wasn't scanning for her. The stoned hillbillies told me she'd gone inside with a guy. I accepted an offer of a campfire-baked potato. They asked where we were headed and I made up a story about wanting to see the

Atlantic Ocean. I burned my mouth on the potato and traded a gallon of gas for a battery-powered radio, to give to Kimo.

Xochitl returned wiping away a dreamy smile.

It was October 27th.

It seemed like the Scoggins incident—interrupting his inquisition—would be forgotten. The punter worked in the fields and slept in the shack. There were fewer visitors, though Fein was there many nights and they walked off together into the dark and I stayed behind with Kimo and Morales knowing that things were happening without us. It was easy to believe this routine was forever, when it had only been a couple weeks. I saw myself across multiple days: there I was again, getting up shivering, looking at Scoggins asleep drooling on his pillow, convincing myself to be thankful I had someone giving me food, someone putting me to use. Was I really so passive? Absolutely, and saw myself doing it: inhabiting the exact shape other people had drawn for me, and therefore angry all the time, but also biding. Something would happen.

But would it? Was I really playing the long game, same as I told myself while watching years evaporate rarely making friends, pretending to be friendly on grocery checkout lines but hurrying away relieved for the interaction's end, dreaming of companionship but never interrupting righteous solitude long enough to know if I could make it happen? I drove with Xochitl and the silences were punishing and I thought in a year I'd be doing the same thing, trading or plundering like this, living under the same conditions with the same tradeoffs, because that's just how things were.

Then one night Charles rambled down the hill and told me my trial was the next day.

6

They gave me directions through different trees to a different barracks, from which cots and linen had been removed and in which a folding table was assembled. Charles and two women—one veiled, one not—awaited me. They asked me what happened the night of Scoggins's internment and Charles didn't wait for me to answer.

He said, "The defendant came to us pretending to be some poor lost gentle soul and had hard feelings after we scrutinized him. I warned bad behavior would have consequences. He knew the rules and got in the way, more than got in the way: took pleasure in sabotaging our methods. And so he gets the boot."

The veiled woman sat in the middle. The others waited for her to talk. I was standing. I was supposed to feel anxious, I probably did feel anxious, but for me these were customary tenterhooks and so if it's possible to be comforted by the parameters of someone else's power, I guess that was me: privately at ease with the feebleness of my squirming, secretly never wanting to be the sled dog whose harness has snapped loose.

Yet how silly would it be to behave like it's *Lord Of The Flies*, and then have the lights come on tomorrow?

The veiled woman said, "You should probably respond."

I didn't. I didn't say anything. Many replies went through my head and I couldn't pick one. Maybe it looked like defiance, and I could see Charles's shoulders bow up. I liked to believe improvisation was a strength of mine, but here I was staring at this woman who wore a black sweater, jeans and a pillbox hat whose veil was dark mesh, and who probably wasn't charmed by the humility of my silence.

"There's a reason he's here," said the other woman. She was past fifty and her lower lip curled down. "Charles, you made a case for muscle. Someone to protect the farm, you said. Someone to go out and trade. And within a short time you've lost faith in your own decision? It seems to me the same logic you used to convince us now applies to not turning him loose."

"Sonya, that's not—"

"You told us the danger of someone invading this place goes up if people in the surrounding areas have reasons to resent us. If we're casting people back out into the world, if we're telling them, 'Sorry it didn't work out, now go fend for yourself,' isn't that a reason to resent us?"

Charles said, "So nobody can ever be forced to leave, for any reason? We haven't had to deal with much in the way of crime yet, but now here it is. What if he'd raped someone? I assume there's something he could've done where you'd be ready to kick him out."

Sonya pointed that lower lip at me, squinted one eye.

Charles made his mouth fussy and he said, "Trust me, we just cannot have this," and they both looked at the woman in the middle, who seemed to be looking at me.

The veiled woman said to me, "You've been helping keep the generator going. We appreciate it. You're here to fight if we need it. We appreciate it. But that's not why you get to stay."

Charles flopped his arms and huffed a sigh. Sonya's expression didn't change: she was gauging my reaction. I realized I didn't know what my reaction was.

"It's my opinion," said Charles, "that having this kind of person here adds to the possibility of dissent and discontent in far greater measure than whatever damage he could do if he were no longer here. I'd be happy to blindfold him and put him in a car and take him a hundred miles away and throw him out into the dust. I'd happily make an exception for a second car to be taken out. In my opinion it would be a good use of gas."

I didn't actually know what I wanted, but it was easy to prefer things Charles didn't.

Sonya said, "You broke him, you bought him."

"It will come back on us," said Charles. "I could tell the first minute I met him."

I almost said, *I saw you walking around with Fein in the middle of the night.* But what did that mean?

"Put him to work," said Sonya. "Get him working on your defenses."

People were off in this tiny corner of the world, politicking, strutting and fretting. They had a decision-making council. They had debates. It was inevitable, Clooney knew it, which is why we'd never kept still: he liked people, it wasn't an act, but he didn't trust them to keep it simple. The more they stockpiled, the longer the committee meetings. Then again, where did our vagabond ways get him?

The veiled woman said, "Charles, Sonya, would it be okay if I talked with him one-on-one?"

The others left. Charles paced out bowlegged like a buckaroo.

"I still can't imagine this is forever," the woman said. "Anyone who's sure we'll never get electricity working like it used to…what's their explanation? I think it would have to be technical malfunction. The lights went out because something broke. But they never say what could've broken so badly in so many places that it can't be fixed."

I said, "You're Elizabeth."

Her veil puffed out. "I still wake up every day thinking this is the day everything goes back to normal. But then it doesn't happen, and maybe I get a little more convinced it must be a willful act: somebody intentionally withholding electricity. We have people in this place from hundreds of miles away, and everybody's story is the same: lights out. Some will say they've seen dams or solar farms held by unaffiliated-looking soldiers. Some will say they've been to electrical substations that were empty and dark. I say this: if somebody's withholding the power, I think that's worse. What are their demands? Why has it been so long? Yes. I'm Elizabeth."

"…"

"People seek security. It's natural. I'm not telling you anything new. And this is the postmodern crackup. Who didn't watch zombie shows on TV? Who didn't see a hundred movies about the end of the world? We all carry around a picture of the mistakes people make during civilization's downfall, and here we are, making them all: inventing rules, keeping pilgrims out, guarding our food, making deals with violent people. Such as yourself."

I said, "I heard it's electromagnetic pulses."

"You are what you can't stop doing," said Elizabeth. Maybe her voice sounded like older woman's: it faltered as an aged person's might. "But I admit I don't know how else to do it. How can I disagree with Charles? How can I argue there isn't scarcity? People who stumble across this farm: of course they could screw us over. Take what we have. Hurt us. Take control."

"…"

"Oh, we should've made an exception for you, though. We should've let you right in. We should've just known you were a good egg."

"Why do I get to stay?" I said.

"I think there's already a nostalgia here for the way things probably never were. 'Remember when people on the farm were really good to each other? Remember when we didn't always have to be on guard?' The first few people on this farm liked to imagine this was a chance for a social experiment. 'How should we build a civilization from scratch?' But there is no scratch, there are just thousands or millions of people going hungry and they're not interested in Plato or James Harrington."

Talk-talk. That was Elizabeth.

Oh, but I wasn't so cool. I told myself nothing could touch me and I had to focus solely on myself now, but I also was beginning to feel intoxicated because she spoke to me as if I were smart and who doesn't like to feel smart?

I said, "Why do I get to stay?"

"My sister likes you is why," she said.

"…"

"But no more of this. Just no more acting like a petulant kid. Charles is blunt but I believe correct: to pretend we exist in total isolation is dangerous. I'm the first one to agree I don't know everything that's going on out there. 'Something there is that doesn't love a wall. That wants it down.' Are there really militias roiling and churning around out there? Well, I know there are! It seems such a cliché, it's hard for me to believe it's real."

"It is," I said.

"Somehow the power will come back on, because if it never does…it's too terrible to think about. So we hope for the short term, plan for the long term. And you and Xochitl are part of our defenses. You're our only face to the world, as well as a budgeted gasoline investment. It's a difficult equation, trying to be ready if someone comes. And all this says nothing about keeping the people here working and optimistic, which is what Sonya and I do all day."

"Did Kimo tell you he found a fence that was cut?"

"He did."

"And what happens when someone decides to invade?"

She carefully tore at a hangnail on her thumb. So much

was projection, the fundamentalist mystery, when the face's cinema was closed down. "Let's first say I like hearing you be concerned about it."

"..."

"Because I've personally known you about fifteen minutes and I find you inscrutable."

I resisted the urge to point at her veil and tell her I felt the same way.

"What happens is: we listen to Charles."

Now I couldn't stop volunteering thoughts. "It really could happen any day. I don't know what you've seen. I don't know what Xochitl tells you. They're out there. They'll come."

"It's not a dictatorship," she said. "My word isn't law, and I can't promise what Charles will or won't do. We have freak-outs. We have people who get depressed and say they can't work. But so far we *haven't* had violent crime, we *haven't* had revolt. I want to hear you say you're not going to do any of those things."

"I'm not."

She nodded and I thought maybe she'd avalanched me with words because she could tell I was sensitive. I did occasionally like to flatter myself.

I knew this was an opportunity to ask her about sleeping someplace warmer. I should've done it. I should've said I represented the working men from my shack, I should've turned this into union negotiations. Finally here was Elizabeth, whom I'd been blindly resenting for weeks.

But I faltered. I hated them all and wanted all their gas. Then I thought about everything they did to keep each other alive—these systems, these mechanisms, these methods—and I loved them a little again. I was perfectly apart from them. It was just me. I was afraid to complain.

I walked out of the barracks. For the first time I thought it was weird there were apparently no children on the farm.

Someone was standing out here, looking up at the trees.

It wasn't Sonya or Xochitl. It was a very skinny woman whose fingers were badly blistered. She was singing these words: "Sweet sweet sweet sweet fire in the street." I recognized her voice from a few mornings ago. I didn't know if she knew I'd exited, because she still wore the cowl and the black veil. This was the laundry woman I'd met: Elizabeth's sister Maribel.

"I was a professional singer," she said, and then she laughed and said, "No, I wasn't! I just had a rush of guilt because one day you might be able to Google me." She was a bird-boned, five-foot woman whose handshake felt like nugget of ginger. She said, "Naughty boy, you got yourself in trouble."

"…"

"I'm naturally blonde under here. Oh, I'll just show you." And she lifted off her cowl, squinting. She was soft in the cheeks and under the chin, eyebrows darker than her hair. "I schedule the generator," she said. "It's one of my jobs. I wasn't a singer, I was a skin technician in St. Louis."

I said, "What does a skin technician do?"

"The office had this bed with LED lights coming out of it, and ladies used to pay $200 to come lie on it for an hour."

"I interviewed a guy about his company that made cat grooming tools."

Maribel seemed to consider putting her veil back on. "I know I'm washed-out now. My coloring. Whenever a new girl arrived we used to ask what makeup she was carrying with her." She pretended to read an unseen label. "I'm just kidding. We didn't do that."

"I get the gas and you use it."

"Yup."

"What a team," I said.

"I was wondering, do you want to eat with me tonight up in the house?"

"I do. Very much. Yes."

She was melty-looking, pale, and the strangeness

between us wasn't romance, she couldn't possibly have mistaken it for romance. She wore a pearl on each earlobe. She said, "I think you're handsome."

"Tonight," I said, pretending to get my bearings, pretending I knew in which direction I was stumbling away. Who hadn't heard shrill collegiate discussions about how the world would fare under female stewardship, without testosterone and figurations of manhood getting in the way?

Four months prior, Clooney and Majido found me in a Tulsa suburb. I was in the old-timey, pickup-strewn downtown, listening to a live Dixieland quartet, boiling water alongside many other volunteers, and also hearing an older gentleman explain why gas stoves and their pilot lights hadn't stopped working even while electricity was out, which amounted to residual natural gas in the neighborhood distribution line. I was down on a knee filling one of a hundred thermoses, and the sun went away. Someone stood over me: Clooney. Squinting even with his face shadowed, as though to wring out yet another ounce of charisma. Would I be willing to trade some water for a package of steaks? I told him it wasn't my place to trade, but also that uncooked steaks weren't particularly attractive a month post-refrigeration.

"The steaks are cooked," he said. "They're on ice."

I never found out whether this was true. It probably wasn't. Clooney was a b.s. artist and I liked him so much, right away. Majido wore long-sleeved clothing and his ridiculous fishing hat with a gaiter draped over his neck; he had a rifle and a frown and served as squire to the great man. Clooney asked if I was part of a government assistance effort. "There's a reason they call it Foolishly Expecting Meaningful Aid," he said.

This was June and *hot*. By now people understood that nobody was swooping in to deliver food or medicine. There were meetings on Main Street, or you could walk down the block and go to a competing confab on Dallas Street. Young strong men who hadn't immediately hitched up with the kind of militia that had forced us out of our homes—maybe because they had young families, maybe because they just didn't believe things should come to that—prowled and paced and planned. There were so many plans, and towns like this one attracted refugees. There were no deliveries, or none that stopped for us; people still saw trucks on I-44 heading for Tulsa. We should farm. We should build up a force to re-take the city. We should find the solar ranch in southwest Missouri that might still be producing electricity. We should organize informational expeditions to Oklahoma City or Atlanta or Washington. People were still okay. Nobody was violent there, and nobody tried to steal supplies we all agreed should be parceled out to everyone. I slept on an air mattress in a pizzeria.

Clooney wore his safari jacket and rolled up the cuffs and ate the canned beans we gave him. He and Majido hung around: Clooney talking, Majido quiet. It was easy for me to believe that the real outrage was having been forced from my apartment, because some of my former neighbors were here, too, and that's what we all said. Not that something had broken, or that someone had shut down the world, but rather how much more comfortable and easy to take this would all be without the injustice of having been dispossessed. Clooney had found a copy of *The Road* and read passages aloud, and most everyone else told him to shut up but I couldn't get enough.

I didn't know where he slept. One night there were awful thunderstorms and hail and he came splashing into the pizzeria and we gave him towels and cigarettes. When everyone else fell asleep, he kept talking.

"Sitting still is the problem," he said. "You could say it was a problem for me way before last month, I tend to be a little overactive anyway. But now it's a poor lifestyle choice. I agree with the Hoskins boy, or that other one, the one who says get off our asses and at least be active participants. But they've got the wrong idea, because there might be hundreds of millions of people living the same nightmare and nobody can take care of us all. Maybe it's just in the Midwest. But how long have we suspected the rest of the country would be happy to see us fall off the map? My point is: no matter what it is, no matter what caused it…it's cold-blooded for me to say, but the only way to go about surviving is branch off into a smaller group. Pretty soon there's not going to be any way to take care of this many people. I remember something I read about survivalism taken to the next level, survivalism for billionaires. Supposedly there's a doomsday complex in Wichita, been storing up for years. Built inside old missile silos, life underground, ready for anything. I have to believe anybody who paid for that little escape is enjoying it now, and it's sustainable: raise their own fish, hydroponic vegetables, solar-powered generators. Of course, they also supposedly had security and snipers, so you couldn't just waltz in. But you're never finding a solution like that while trying to solve the problems of a thousand people."

"…"

He drank from a pearl-plated flask. "That's just an example. But it's the point, though. Any time we spend *not* thinking about a potential end-game solution—no half-measures, no stopgaps—that's wasted time. If it's rounding up an army to overtake a city, okay, but you better be sure that place has got what you need. I prefer a less violent solution. It suits my temperament, a more flies-with-honey kind of thing. Where are the other bunkers, what clever ways can we think of to infiltrate? Long term, maybe get to a better year-round climate, and also now that I just mentioned fish, maybe get a boat. That's an avenue of inquiry worth exploring. Remember I said that, okay? What would it be like on the Pacific coast, someplace like San Diego where shelter is less of an issue, what kind of vessel would you need to fish and be self-sustaining? We'd all rather have someone else do it for us, ha-ha, but the days of not getting your hands dirty are gone, alas."

What did Clooney think happened to kick off this crisis? "Conservative white male grievance, of course," he said. "Anti-government forces, heavily armed, acting on the propaganda that's been powering them for a half-century. Never did quite understand the far right. You don't believe in wealth redistribution, you hate immigrants, you think no government is the best government…and you still shop at Old Navy and buy iPhones made by slaves in China, you take college financial aid and food stamps, you don't exactly refuse federal money for a bridge or a road in your town. But of course it was never about any of that, right? What civilization doesn't have cynical old men stoking up stupid young men to do crazy things?"

He wasn't the only one I heard say things like this. The pizzeria leaned left. But he was smart without being aggressive about it, with a gravelly voice and an inclusiveness that made you believe you were changing his mind about some things, though you probably weren't. I wasn't the only one who felt this. When he wasn't reading aloud from a novel about people walking around in a nuclear-charred wasteland, Clooney solicited smiles and consensus. Little things: volunteering to forage for edible greens like dandelions and wild asparagus, the trick of taking a cold shower after an allergic reaction or using a beer-can shim to open a combination lock, telling stories about the Greek gods to gatherings of little kids, playing a guitar around campfires. Or big philosophical things: there was an endless supply of rednecks who called our circumstances the natural result of too much debt, refusing to shut off the Social Security and Medicare teat, so that someone must've printed too much money and this was just an economic collapse that looked like a technological one. To these guys, Clooney would calmly say, "Which is it? Is the government hapless or diabolical?" or he'd quote D.H. Lawrence (and *tell* everyone he was quoting D.H. Lawrence): "Doom! Doom! Doom! Something seems to whisper it in the very dark trees of America."

He and Majido had been around for about a week and I looked forward to the next day, the next lecture. What in someone else might've been supercilious was, in Clooney, endearing. One morning a mother came unglued because her son had wandered off and Clooney volunteered to look for him out on the country lanes east of downtown, volunteered Majido and me. They gave us someone's white Tacoma pickup filled with gas.

To Clooney's credit, we did look for the kid. We drove around winch factories and concrete casting facilities trying to find a solo boy matching his mom's description. There were plenty of folks around. People sitting on their burned-out lawns in front of tiny brick houses waved when we drove past. Teens skateboarded around a rusted camper van. Seniors out front of a care center did calisthenics. We drank bottled water and ate peanut butter crackers, parked in front of a campus for developmentally disabled Oklahomans, the Tacoma's air conditioning going hard. It was sobering to imagine what was happening to the people on that campus. Were any of their caregivers still giving care?

"Smaller bites," Clooney said, and he didn't mean the crackers.

"How much longer we pretending to look?" said Majido. The three of us were pressed together in the cabin.

"Never give in to cynicism," said Clooney. "That boy is definitely somewhere. That's a fact."

Okay but Majido and I weren't sure what good that did us, and I figured being out here was just a ploy to get a couple hours of a/c. But Clooney got out from behind the wheel and slammed the driver's side door, and we fumbled out into the heat to walk behind him. He cut down a single-lane road marked Dead End. An unhitched trailer bore a dozen rotting sheets of plywood, and had a jack under one of its wheels. Clooney inspected the tiny ranch house to which the trailer seemed to belong. Majido in his fishing hat and long clothes and embroidered boots walked to the neighboring houses and the one across the street, peeking in as many windows as he could find. He nodded to Clooney, who stepped on the brown lawn and put his safari jacket's elbow through the glass door, then Majido was standing behind me with his rifle and I had no idea where he'd gotten it; I was so stricken or dreamy it didn't occur he'd brought it with him. I figured he'd found it on the ground. Majido was covering Clooney, militarily, and Clooney said, "Hello? I'm coming in!" and they waited for the house's occupant to make a move.

Nobody did. They went inside, called for me to join. The house was gray brick and blue paneling, little more than doublewide-sized but painted and trimmed and orderly, with a basketball hoop above the garage.

It didn't smell good in there, and the refrigerator was filled with blackened items no longer fit for human consumption. But there were plenty of food boxes in the cupboards. Majido filled a laundry basket. Clooney said there wouldn't be any guns or fuel, but we should look anyway. The two bedrooms were suffocatingly hot but clean and ordered. NASCAR posters and nice electronics in the living room. I was looting! The neighbors with whom I'd beat my retreat from Tulsa, they held themselves above such misbehavior and I did, too: civilization broke down when people decided it was broken, and not being villains was how we could be better than the quasi-soldiers. I rummaged through a closet and stole an old backpack, a new packet of D batteries, a few shirts and some nice aviator sunglasses I'd eventually lose dismantling the nylon tent we'd not yet pilfered.

We carried our spoils back up that street. I didn't see anybody. Majido had his rifle in the laundry basket and I felt ridiculous, that this was what things were coming to, we were doing the thing bad guys did in apocalypse movies. Clooney said, "You can relax. They weren't coming back."

We drove around town for a couple more hours and Clooney was a savant finding forsaken homes and avoiding conflict. He made it feel like we were on a shopping spree. In the final place, closer to a nice neighborhood to the north, I was sure we were being watched but didn't say anything: that place was creaky and creepy and a thousand degrees, and suddenly it was obvious these houses weren't permanently forsaken, their owners *were* coming back, and these weren't victimless crimes. The limits of my capacity for self-deception kept sneaking up in the ticking quiet and tapping my shoulder.

We headed back to the Tacoma with our plunder. The sun was still high. I'd lost track of where we were relative to downtown, where people were waiting for word about the missing child. Loading the pickup, I thought about the mechanisms of society, I thought about the units of life: day and night were ridiculous planetary accidents around which we build meals and occupations and the counting structure that binds us to mortality. I got in, sweaty, the dope who had to sit in the middle, and Clooney touched my left flank and Majido my right…and directly out the windshield I saw the boy we were supposed to be looking for.

He was walking by himself, eating candy. I recognized him and he recognized me. He did a comic double-take and finished crossing the street in slow motion, as though it would make him invisible.

"That's him," I said.

Clooney rolled his eyes and sighed. "Are you sure?"

"Yes."

"He doesn't want to get found," said Majido.

"…"

"And anyway: it's safe enough out here. Let's go."

The boy strolled down the sidewalk behind us, pace unquickened, trying to escape by means of composure. Now I understood what we were doing, why Majido wanted to leave the boy to his fate. We weren't bringing the stolen food and clothes and battery-powered items back to the larger group, and we were stealing the Tacoma, too. In a day of

worldview adjustments—in a month of nothing but
worldview adjustments—I continued to feel dumb and slow,
but as dawn broke over my brain I was also flattered. I had a
surge of esteem for Clooney. It would've been his idea to
include me; Majido would've expressed reservations. I said,
"Why me?" and Clooney stuck out his chin and said, "I can
tell your power rests with loyalty."

That's the way he put it.

He started up the engine and the a/c blew hot then cold.
Everything was like that now, the total victory of cross-
purposes. Majido knew him well; he actually groaned a
moment before Clooney said, "Dammit, it's *not* safe enough
out here. It wasn't safe for a little kid even before all this."

So we drove after the boy and he heard the engine and
looked over his shoulder and sagged. He climbed into my
spot, and I got in the Tacoma's bed and watched them
through the rear window; they needled the boy until he
cracked up laughing. We crossed over the interstate, past
malls where many folks were still slinking around in their cars
testing the limits of their new lives, but we stopped several
blocks before the downtown camps began. Majido and the
boy got out.

Majido said to me, "You should take the kid the rest of
the way."

I climbed down. Clooney thumbs-upped me through his
window.

So I did it. We walked down Detroit Street and didn't
talk. The boy was maybe ten or eleven and looked tired and
ready for a motherly reunion. I was sweaty and sunburned.
He wanted me to talk to him but I could only think about
what came next, whether I'd walk back to where I'd last seen
the Tacoma and whether or not it would still be there.

7

The same morning, after my trial, I was spinning up the quarter-mile dirt pass thinking how fun it would be to say nothing about my dinner invitation all day, then just *be* there at a well-appointed banquet table as Maribel's guest, grinning at Xochitl's disbelief and wordlessly indicating where Charles could shove his objections.

Then Xochitl said, "Pull over!" and I stood on the brakes.

We were close to the highway and she scanned west for a minute, and handed me her binoculars. I panned around until she said, "Against a birch. Are you blind? Just standing there."

I saw. A shadowy figure, probably male, his back against a tree. One knee up, a foot against the tree, lighting a cigarette.

"Don't move this truck one inch," said Xochitl. But that was silly: the Tacoma had kicked up a dust column that rose behind us like a speech balloon. We passed the binoculars back and forth, waiting to see if the guy took obvious notice of us, or if anyone joined him. "Pilgrims come up and knock on the front door," she said.

"Could be someone they already turned away."

"…"

Maybe the farm was just too sprawling to be defensible. Kimo's punishment would be a demotion to full-time fence duty, putting up more barbed wire coils somewhere out there on the periphery, but barbed wire wouldn't be an impediment to intruders with bad intentions.

"We drive past him," Xochitl said. "I want to see what he's wearing."

I didn't move us, and she didn't insist.

It was foolishness. This wasn't how it wouldn't happen.

The man walked into the sun, meandered like a person miming drunkenness. He knew we were watching. I was about as effective as the barbed wire; what the hell was I going to do when someone really did invade? The guy wore dark pants: possibly uniform pants. Xochitl placed the binoculars back into her bag, put on her sunglasses and slid her feet onto the dashboard. She wasn't very nice to me. I drove and we found no gas and nothing of value. Returning at dusk I wondered whether we'd bother setting the clocks back in a week.

"Good night," said Xochitl. But I followed her toward the house and she made a face and opened her hands as if I were about to be someone else's problem.

I stepped inside and moved past the cold dinner bags that were my usual disbursement. Nobody blinked. Was I allowed in the farmhouse after all? Had I been allowed all this time?

I smelled food. Dozens of candlelit people were here, bodies angling around tables and each other, a communal and casual routine reengaged: no big central table, something like a frontier unburdening or group exhale. The feeling was: oh, wait, maybe I've been incorrect all these nights, maybe all this time I *was* invited to come eat with the group. They had steel trays filled with vegetables and homemade pasta and cornbread, just step right up to the buffet. Women and men had plates and were already eating in groups. The central room with the fireplace was one room over and people were eating there, too. Everyone seemed tired but happy. Some of the women wore veils. The men were mostly people I'd never seen, and there were more of them than I expected. It all seemed weird and Amish.

"My beloved!" Maribel said, but she jabbed my ribs with an elbow that had been sent through a pencil sharpener, and her tone was no less puncturing. Her cowl-and-veil were back.

We ate with another couple: a farmer and wife who'd been married twenty years. They were tan and wind-burned, ate with their heads down, and didn't say much. Maribel talked a lot. I had three full plates and ate like a rescued castaway; I felt disoriented so I focused on the food, which was very good. Maribel slid individual bites under the veil. Sometimes she held the fork up in there while continuing to jabber away. I didn't understand anything.

"Time for bed," the farmer said, and the couple left their plates and silverware. The man guided the woman's shoulders around a doorframe

"She lost her glasses," said Maribel.

I nodded.

"Sorry they were a little rude."

" . . . "

"It's not like everybody doesn't know who you are."

I looked around. Nobody was sitting near us, and people in here were otherwise stacked tight. Plus they were all either stealing glances at me, or pointedly looking away. Somehow I was infamous. What a laugh the notion would've given my former traveling partners.

I said, "Tell me more about the skin-care bed."

She did: alternately expressing disgust and admiration for her former clientele's quest to look younger. She chattered on, and I won't lie: it was soothing to hear. It gave me cover. Eventually, most everyone finished eating and withdrew;

around us, a few people repaired clothing and baskets while two young women cleared plates and glanced at me as one might a desperado. Maribel liked the danger. She said, "Do you think famous celebrities are all gathered together on a secret island that still has electricity?"

Elizabeth joined us. She'd missed dinner and was eating a pear. She dwarfed her sister: taller, broader, arms lean and brown, shoes more sensible than the silver-bowed pumps Maribel wore. Nobody spoke and Elizabeth sat and pretended she was tipping over with exhaustion. Maribel's posture made her seem unamused, and some longstanding annoyance passed between them, whereupon Maribel took off her cowl. There she was, tiny features pointed down, sighing and palming imaginary sweat from her brow. *If you want to see what exhausted looks like.*

I said, "There are pear trees?"

"Yes," said Elizabeth.

"How is every little *thing*?" Maribel said.

"Don't be aggressive," said Elizabeth, in that old-lady voice that apparently came and went. "I don't mean to interrupt your date."

Maribel flushed.

"I've been thinking about our conversation this morning," Elizabeth said to me. "Charles thinks over the winter we need to be out there building real fences and guard posts, if it's not too late. And better scouting. I want a big magnetized map to keep track of troop movements." She laughed. "Listen to me. Who snuck my head inside this crown?"

"..."

"The reason I'm talking to you again is this," she said. "You should let me know if you want my job. I've also said it to Charles. Just let me know. I'm sure I'm making mistakes. And maybe there's something about a certain kind of person—let's face it, maybe a certain kind of *man*—who can't stand not running things. Testosterone does funny things to a body. If you feel strongly, take it. Or try taking it, and we'll see what happens. But if not, you're going to have to square sometimes I'm making a call. Sometimes there isn't time for putting it to a vote. And I'm a woman. You might not be able to tell." She pointed at her own veil. "But I'm female under here. I'm not asking for an oath of allegiance, but so far everyone here seems to agree it's the way things should be."

Maribel looked at her own scarred hands.

Elizabeth said, "Did you ever have a female boss?"

I did. I worked in a bookstore as a teen; the manager had once taken me aside and said she thought I could make a career in retail if I wanted, and the notion made me recoil. Also one of my freelance writing jobs, but she'd lived in a different city. "Yes."

"Excellent." She brought the pear beneath her veil and it returned to view one bite smaller.

Maribel huffed and crossed her arms and I heard myself say, "Did you always wear a veil?"

Elizabeth's head tilted. "I did not."

"Okay."

"You want to know why. So. Maybe I just like mixing up people's verifiable truth."

And she wasn't kidding. The silence that followed was disconcerting, and she wouldn't let me off the hook. I said, "I'm sorry. I don't mean to…."

"…"

"No designs here," I said. "I promise."

"I don't know you," she said. "And it's presumptuous to say I know what all men are like."

"…"

"But every woman on this farm has spent a life in fear of men, to one degree or another. And maybe we're falling into all the old traps but that's the one thing we *will* change. So project whatever holdover hatred you remember from your life before this happened onto me, onto this," again pointing to her veil, "and not the other women who live here. Because while this is horrible, this breakdown, you're learning something we've always known: being 'nice' isn't legit self-defense. It never was. It's smiling blankly past the person in shadows, praying he won't pounce. And in the end, the control we've always given up is what you're experiencing now: whether or not he pounces has almost nothing to do with you." She stood again. "And anyway what a relief," in a happier tone, "letting other people have jurisdiction. Good night. Oh, and I'm not making a joke: Tampax. While you're out there. We seriously cannot have too much Tampax."

"Elizabeth!" But her sister was gone.

It was fully dark outside and getting cold even in this room. Fein was here now, talking cordially with two women. I hated the sight of him, and wondered whether that would've been true even without his fraidy-cat act in those barracks. He listened to his friends and nodded, so reserved and self-contained. Then Charles and Scoggins came in from somewhere. It was odd. Maribel was talking and I was nodding, I tried to catch Scoggins's eye but he was preoccupied with watching Fein. They were all business. Scoggins, the archduke himself, ducked his head to make himself smaller than Charles. Fein got up and hugged his friends and the three men withdrew down a back hallway. I told Maribel I had to go to the bathroom and I followed them deeper into the house. I could see one of them light a candle and heard them clomping on hollow floorboards and I glided, knuckling the wall as I went. There was a back door and they stepped a long way down and crunched macadam, out into the night. There was no way to follow outside without being heard. I banged into a closet whose small window overlooked the backyard's beginnings and I saw the candle recede toward a barn's moonlit shape. It was quiet, I watched them go…then I jolted without knowing what was happening and smacked my face into the window: it was a sound, rushing water or ball bearings clattering behind me at once, and I looked back outside and saw the candle's small flame disappear. Then the noise happened again, some kind of rain stick or child's toy. I felt my way out of this tiny storage room and heard voices, my face was hot, I needed a story to tell a potential captor. But the sound turned out to be a woman in the main room pouring lentils back and forth between steel bowls. She grinned into the dust cloud she made, like she thought I might hurt her.

And I resolved that come hell or high water, I wasn't going down the hill tonight to freeze.

I found Maribel again and said, "Maybe you could show me where you sleep."

Her smile was anxious. She had very straight teeth.

People reclined around the big fireplace. Some kissed. Now I could hear the generator farting outside, from the opposite direction Charles, Fein and Scoggins had gone. She led me down a hall and it was cold again, then we came to a woodstove with a magnetic thermometer attached and more bodies under blankets, and then some bedrooms that were subdivided by beaverboard planks and Maribel ducked into one. Yes, there were many more people on this farm than I'd thought.

She lit a liquid paraffin candle. There was a floor-bound mattress, two milk crates' worth of clothing, a polymer water brick, a dusty crank radio, several chocolate bars and a fancy brass tray on which she'd gathered ointments and creams. Paper hearts were taped to a wall, the kind you might expect young children to make, except there were no children here. Maribel's eyes flashed garnet and she held her breath. I discovered myself close, her weak chin tilted back. I said, "Tell me about your hands."

"Oh."

"…"

She hung her cowl from a hook. "It happened a long time ago." She half-whispered in acknowledgment that other people were in this bedroom, in their own cubbies. I was able to back away and feel the air in here: not cozy but warmer than the barracks. Maribel had a legibility—shoulders back, so convinced she was witty and scandalous—that made me feel I knew her well and that I could never know her at all. "People never believe me, that it was because of jealousy. I swear it's true."

"…"

"I don't even know what burned me. Diana Joel threw it at my face in chemistry class and I blocked it with my hands. Acid or something."

"Really?"

"Yes. My family got a lot of money from the school. It's how Elizabeth and I paid for college. My sister used to tell people it was a small price to pay." She laughed and twirled; yes, Maribel danced across floors and courtyards wherever she was, whether she was veiled or not. She danced when there was no point, this silly sunbeam. "Diana found out her boyfriend was in love with me. I didn't do anything with him, though. I wouldn't do that. But she didn't even ask me first."

"Terrible," I said.

"I'm supposed to put my hands in bubbling water," said Maribel. "The natural kind. Elizabeth used to take me to Big Spring. We're from St. Louis, did I say that? But they're okay now. They don't hurt very much even without it. Sometimes they do."

We talked a long time, and kissed. Again I left to go to the bathroom. She joked about my hollow leg.

And I took a right turn and passed sleeping forms on air mattresses and recliners—so many people!—and I couldn't get my arms around the hierarchy, was real estate more desirable the closer one slept to the fireplace, or did these people yearn for cubicle-level privacy? Wasn't there floor space enough for the cold men in the shack?

Then I heard sounds from the kitchen, and that's how I met Ben.

He ran the kitchen. But he did more than run the kitchen! He fixed things, he knew things—how to skim milk, how to trap fruit flies…and also how to fix the four-pole generator or make a greenhouse—and it would turn out nearly everyone I'd meet on the farm held him in high regard. He was a totally admirable person. He was accustomed to holding people's attention, but he did it through self-possession rather than cracking jokes or raising his voice. Because he was cool. A lot of people effectively reported to him, because they wanted to impress him or because they honestly wondered about his opinion, not because of a formalized administrative structure. He was probably in his 50s. He didn't suffer fools, he wasn't condescending in his praise, he didn't try the old "Oh, I'm just the cook, ask someone else" line but he also didn't pipe up when he wasn't asked. Actually he was slightly withdrawn, happy to spend the time between breakfast and dinner prep (lunch was handled by what amounted to "subordinates") alone for hours tinkering with a pesky valve mechanism or pondering egg-production abnormalities. And when people saw him focused on a project, the bar for interrupting him was high although nobody ever said, "Don't bother Ben!" It was just something you knew from his manner. Basically, he didn't act. He just was.

In some ways, he was Charles's exact opposite. Charles had this picture of how a hard man behaved, to the point where actually listening to somebody else's ideas about security would be a display of weakness that would lessen his authority the next time a tough decision needed to be made. Ben just listened to people and nodded that he understood. He understood, but that didn't mean he agreed. Ben didn't care much about offending people but didn't go out of his way to do so.

Later, I'd have dreams that consisted of little more than kitchen conversations with Ben: we'd be sitting at his butcher-block side table, conserving instant coffee by mixing in wild chicory root, avoiding foot traffic in the rest of the kitchen and talking about wheat yields and winter temperatures and what a jerk Charles was. In the best of these dreams, Ben would be vexed by some complicated scientific or technical point, and he'd explain the situation to me, and together we'd work through the problem piece by piece without frustration and eventually I'd have a breakthrough but withhold it, wanting to extend the pleasure of speaking with him. He really was one of the most admirable people I ever met.

Of course, I didn't know any of this yet. I just heard sounds in the kitchen and wandered that way. Ben was there, a middle-aged African-American guy taking eggs out of a big staging refrigerator (there was a walk-in unit built into the back of the farmhouse) while three women scrubbed pots and plates at the sink. It was a Rembrandt in there, brown and lantern-lit. I imagined Maribel would be likelier to fall asleep the longer I stayed away, so I frowned and entered. Nobody cared. The women scrubbed. Ben held eggs up to the light and adjusted his glasses. I knocked over some unknown brass item that made a ridiculous crashing sound, and Ben asked me to come over and help him. Each egg was penciled with the date of its laying, and I picked out the older ones so Ben could place them in a bowl of water. The ones that sank were still fresh, the ones that floated were rotten, and the ones that tipped end-up needed to be used the next morning.

When we were done, ever on the ball, I said, "I guess that's all of them."

"Indeed," said Ben.

"Do you need help with anything else? I'm not sleepy."

"I think I'm good."

It was a farmer's kitchen: wide and deep with a high ceiling and cement floor. The young ladies at the sink were splashing each other and squealing. Ben sighed and laughed to himself. His face was narrow with a pronounced stubbled jawline, his cheeks were high, his temples were gray; he was noble without being frosty. I asked a question I prided myself on never asking: "What did you do before all this?"

He was spooning something onto a plate of seeds. He said, "A job too technical to talk about." He saw me watching him. "Mix coffee grounds with carrot seeds, makes them easier to plant and keeps the critters away. Grounds are amazing. Use them to keep ants out, get the onion stink out of your hands, deodorize a refrigerator, mix them with compost to add nitrogen to the soil. I guess what I'm saying is: any time you're out and about, and you find real coffee to bring back…."

"…"

"Yes, I know who you are," he said. "This is a small place. Not a lot of secrets."

"It's not so terrible," I said. "It's not terrible out there every day. We drove around for months. You just have to be smart. Every single person you meet isn't shooting each other on the streets."

"Not yet," said Ben.

"You, I can understand if they never let outside. Someone who can feed this many people. Elizabeth was happy to get you."

"I don't really know anything about cooking. It's just a numbers game and someone else's recipes. It's math. Anybody could do it."

Ben finished his seed mix and took a moment to smell the jar of coffee grounds. The dishwashers asked if they could be dismissed and he told them they didn't need his permission, but he did peek toward the sink and nod.

They left and I said, "People here have the wrong idea about me."

"Mm-hm."

"…"

"You're looking for advice?" said Ben. "How to change people's minds? You sure that's even what you want? Not being a killer, I'm not sure that's a thing to brag about these days."

"But you don't believe that, do you? You don't know me but…look at me. I'm not…." I chose my words carefully. "I'm not someone who just goes around killing. Who would believe that?"

He washed and dried his hands, never hurried. Obviously the water was cold and he seemed to take pleasure from it. "You're saying folks are just believing what they want to believe and refusing to consider new evidence? Shocking. That is truly shocking."

I said, "Veils and walls and torturing pilgrims. I guess there's a lot of made-up stories bouncing around this place."

He wasn't friendly and he wasn't unfriendly when he said, "Maybe it's temporary and maybe it's permanent, but things are different now, and I guess it's possible the rest of our lives will be spent in the darkness that comes before whatever comes next. But historical truth or fiction doesn't change the facts, and one fact of order over chaos is that people need stories."

8

And so yes, that place was built on lies, maybe because anything that more than one person creates is always built on lies. And even if that's uncharitable—even if instead of "lies" you'd prefer to say "misconceptions" or even "differing perceptions"—I won't claim it's a terrible thing. How could something as absurd as a new kingdom (or queendom) *not* have an understructure shot through with pretty distortions? The question really is: how good or bad does the lying need to get before the thing flourishes no matter the threats against it?

I woke before Maribel and met Xochitl at the truck. By now it went without saying that the tiny towns inside a ten-mile radius were entirely played out unless we were prepared to just start ransacking populated houses. And by the time we got close to the suburbs thirty miles northwest—by unspoken agreement avoiding the highway on which Clooney died— we'd seen several signs spray-painted with trumpets or ten crowns: an encroaching Christian apocalyptic imagery. In the parking lot of a general store we found a nice old guy sitting in his car and gave him the speech about not telling anyone he'd seen us and traded him some freshly milled flour for a few cans of fuel stabilizer. Most of the gas we would find or trade for had ethanol in it, which meant by this late date it was probably already gummy, which meant stabilizer didn't help. But sometimes we lucked out gumminess-wise, and also Ben was reportedly rigging a homemade centrifuge to polish old gas, whereupon adding a stabilizer would make sense. The nice old guy in his car said he had more fuel stabilizer than he did fuel.

This was zinc-rich country and also a place Bonnie and Clyde had bullied. That made me smile, wheeling around these streets with Xochitl. She said we should try an office park marked "OPX Logistics" across from a truck dealership. So we pulled up to a four-story building with smoked glass like the Death Star and three flags limp on three poles. The grass surrounding this place was dead and the lot was empty. The formerly automatic front doors were jammed open because OPX had long since surrendered its prizes. Nobody worked here anymore, despite the current world's obvious need for logistics; walking around an abandoned place like that was the closest things had felt to being *over*: the neutron-bomb feeling of vaporized meetings and agendas and productivity initiatives. I stole a box of staple removers, thinking maybe a savvy person like Ben could find a Rube Goldberg use for them.

Outside, Xochitl repositioned something in the Tacoma's bed and showed me, but I didn't know what it was. "Metal detector," she said, in a kinder voice than she usually used with me. "I was waiting to surprise you. Somebody on the farm found it in a pile of junk. And it works."

She drove. We wound through the suburb's oldest neighborhood, painfully slow, inspecting every house on each side of every street. We looked for curbside filler caps and examined house foundations for painted-over copper pipes that bent directly underground. I drew a street map and we marked six or seven possible candidates. Then we circled back and got out to knock on those six or seven doors. Most were still occupied and we played it friendly, offered to trade some vegetables, casually asked how their houses were heated. At two of the doors, nobody answered. Xochitl and I put on orange hardhats we'd found somewhere and walked around the first property but couldn't find what we needed. At the second, by a stand of oaks in the backyard, I found an inverted coffee can on the ground and cried out. It was rusted and ancient, and moving it revealed a vent pipe.

"Holy cow," Xochitl said. She fetched the metal detector and I grabbed a shovel.

After an hour of canvasing the ground, following pipes away from the house and also out of that backyard vent pipe—we were delayed by bleeps and squeals from some old coins—the metal detector closed in on what seemed like the right spot: the place where a below-ground storage tank for heating oil might be buried. Especially because the foundation pipes were painted over, there was a chance the house's former occupants had switched over to a different kind of heat, and left the old tank interred. And possibly full.

It was a job for an earthmover, but I used the shovel. Xochitl kept moving the metal detector around the yard and then into the hole I made. We barely spoke, but we agreed to at least satisfy our curiosity: find out what metal object was making the detector shriek while still avoiding neighborhood attention, and figure it out from there. It was late autumn and not warm but I sweated. I thought about cool overnight air steeping the morning tent and listening to another man breathe, knowing rations were scant but that the long generous day held solutions. And here I was, digging still. I wondered if behind the detachment I'd been accused of my entire life maybe an optimist had always been hiding out.

Then within the hole beneath my feet: the shovel drummed against metal.

I looked at Xochitl and she looked at me.

I scraped the shovel against a rounded metal plate, clearing, cleaning: it was big and it clanged like a hollow object. I pressed one foot against it and the metal indented then bent back. I tried to think what else it might be. It was shocking, I was shocked, because when you scavenged like this every day things rarely went so according to plan.

For a moment I thought, *If this thing is full, how will we ever transport that much fuel?* but then Xochitl was joyful, she jumped down into the hole and we danced.

For another long while I carved around the tank's shape in the coral mud, looking for a valve or aperture. There would be no moving the tank without a crane, but we could try and siphon its contents. As I dug, I played with the idea of not driving with Xochitl back to the farm, maybe splitting whatever fuel we found, maybe meeting Majido at our appointed date and time (but maybe not) and then maybe going back to what by now might've been actual gates in downtown Tulsa, toting tribute enough to gain entrance. They might have working generators all over the city. They might have power enough to be in touch with other parts of the world.

Xochitl brought me some water and said, "Maybe we should just cut a hole in it." I squeezed the blisters on my hands. Late afternoon's slanted sun projected stripes across the yard. Would it be betrayal to leave the farm behind? Would Xochitl even put up a fight if I left?

I stared at her and she didn't like it. She smiled and brushed hair from her forehead. Everything was so strange. Nobody had ever really actually said, *Okay, you and Xochitl will drive together every day looking for fuel.* We just did it; I'd just slipped into her hip pocket. I said, "Cut a hole with what?"

I dug more, and she heel-kicked away the earth.

And then I heard something, and I had a few moments of knowing something I didn't want to know.

It was a bird. A chirrup or a quack. I don't know these things: the classifications of avian thoraxes. But I knew this one didn't sound real.

I pressed a thumb against the hollow in Xochitl's

shoulder, angled her to take a step up and get out of our hole. She looked at me, first smiling, then—reading my expression—with dread. I went up first, and I felt something awful in the air, but this final hour of daylight blinded me. Part of me thought I was being ridiculous. The little brick house was hushed, shaded in blue. I didn't see anything new in the street. But something was wrong, the air was wrong, my feet shuffled on the brown grass and I watched the ground, trying to appear casual. Even if something was amiss it didn't need to involve me. But I felt small. I felt eyes in the trees. And I wasn't strong, I couldn't fight, I was as hot meat. Helpless if someone wanted to attack. Trying with my posture to indicate how little taking me by force would be worth, but knowing how close violation might actually be. Prey.

I felt hot metal go through me, but all that really happened was someone said, "Hold it there."

It was one man and maybe I could charge him, strike him with the shovel, somehow get out of this. But then it was more than one man. Other clicks, someone blowing a birdcall again, more shadows outlined against the trees. Now the one who'd spoken had an automatic weapon pointed at my face.

"Come on out of there," someone said to Xochitl and she did. They sat us against the house and removed our orange helmets. There were six of them. They wore clean clothes and had clean faces.

"If this is your house," Xochitl said, "we're sorry."

"It's not," said one of them. He was tall and bearded, but not in a backwater sort of way. They were all white and middle-aged; a couple of them wore hipster glasses. "They left last month. We saw you from over there," and he pointed next door. Wives and children were in the next yard, watching us. "Is there oil in that tank?"

"We don't know," said Xochitl.

"You've got a basket of fresh food in your truck," the bearded guy said. "Where'd it come from?"

Xochitl spoke to her feet. "We found it."

"Some of the neighborhood decided to leave," he said. "We've been making due." He kneeled to get close to us. "Do you know anything? Do you know what happened? Is it like this everywhere?"

"…"

One of them came back with a power handsaw. He wasn't sure if it still had gas, but it started up. The bearded one said, "Be careful with sparks. Whole thing could blow up."

The guy got in the hole and we watched his back and neck. He banged something with a hammer. I tried to get Xochitl's attention, thinking we should just run. But she wouldn't look at me. The handsaw made nails-on-chalkboard noises. I thought, *It's all right, I can find another tank, I can do this again.* The families were rapt watching this operation. None of them looked disheveled, but everyone was gaunt and gray.

The sawing stopped and the guy said, "I'm through!" and he lifted one bare arm into view and it was shiny and black as a sea lion. The men went crazy. They whooped and jitterbugged and high-fived. I tapped Xochitl's shoulder and gave her a gangster's come-hither head flip, but she stayed put.

The bearded guy came back and aimed his gun between my eyes. I flinched and turned away. He said, "This is *ours*. This is our ticket to survival and deliverance. We prayed and we told our kids to pray."

"Then we're messengers from God," said Xochitl but the gun stayed drawn.

At sunset they took us to a house a couple streets over and locked us in. Big teenagers with rifles guarded the door and windows, then one teenager came in and told Xochitl, "Get in that bedroom and take off your clothes," and he shook his rifle and Xochitl strode across shag carpeting and she threw a right cross and punched that teen on the side of his head. And the kid went down, and he whimpered and scuttled away, back outside. I gawked! But Xochitl made a strangled sound and it was her hand: I could see in the windowlight, the back of her hand was bent the wrong way and broken bones poked against the skin of her palm.

I called through the door for a doctor. Nobody said anything.

The neighborhood families were meeting to decide our fate. But this wasn't a militia situation! Fine, they had a right to what we'd found, the right to heat their houses with it or trade it for food. But they weren't killers. They were moms and dads and this notion that we'd all been slingshotted into some distant past or distant future where everybody was a damn savage…did everyone not see that it was melodrama? Probably the thing we'd all been fed for years—that life had gotten less authentic, that the way out of compromises and emasculations was a simple combination of meathead consumer products—made tiny slivers of people's brains crave it: they wanted "the modern way" to be irreparably gone. But families like this, who'd clung to their homes and lived as best they could, waiting for repair: surely they'd be circumspect.

Xochitl was in pain and she crumpled into a chair. She asked me to set the bones of her hand.

I did. I pushed my thumbs on her palm and it was like flipping circuit breakers inside a bag of mashed potatoes. She shouted and wept and I actually hugged her.

It got dark and there were no candles. I found a towel and wrapped Xochitl's hand. Some of her fingers seemed dislocated. We laid down on that scratchy shag in some departed family's family room. She cried more and apologized. "Only because it hurts a lot," she said.

"It's okay."

There were crickets outside. After a while she said, "You and Maribel."

"…"

"I know why. I'm not stupid."

"Do you and I talk about these things? Do we talk about anything?"

"I could use a drink."

"…"

I felt her hair against my arm as she rolled toward me. "You know. You know why I'm mean to you sometimes, right?"

"I really don't," I said, but I did.

"…"

"You saw me after," I said. "You saw me. I almost threw up."

"You crushed another person's face in," Xochitl said. "It's a very hard thing to forget."

I liked it. I liked that she wouldn't let it go. I dreamed about it. Actually, I often dreamed I *hadn't* killed him; I often dreamed that I was waking from a nightmare, so relieved that I wouldn't have to live with the sensation of my hand on that rock.

She said, "I know he shot your friend. But you had him on the ground and you kept…."

"…"

Her voice was low and sad. "At least tell me you'd take it back if you could."

"…"

"…"

"I would. Yes."

She shifted: her knee touched my thigh. My breath stopped, but she coughed to make clear it was an accident, and we both laughed a little. Now our heads were side-by-side and we spoke to the ceiling.

She said, "Charles will never let me carry a gun if you're with me."

"It's all right."

"But it should be my decision."

"A gun wouldn't have helped today," I said.

It was completely black. There was no difference

between open and closed eyes. I could hear something outside. It was a mother playing with her screeching child, fabricating delight, shouting, "Whoooooooooo!" every ten seconds. I felt irrational rage at the noise.

Xochitl said, "I should get a boyfriend but there aren't many prospects."

"Did you have a boyfriend?"

"I was thinking the handsome football player."

"..."

"..."

"Scoggins."

"Scoggins," she said. "Yes."

I said, "Why don't more people from the farm drive around these towns? It would help. More strangers would know they could trade with us, and that we'd keep coming back. Start a network. Good for them, good for us."

"Maybe they're afraid," said Xochitl.

"Yes," I said. "But also they like being special."

"..."

"The safer they think home is, the more justified they are staying there. They like that place. They look around proud. If the lights go back on, I wonder if they'd all stay."

"It's not safe there," she said. "It's also not safe to have them roaming around blabbing."

"So instead it's just us. Getting locked up in here."

"..."

I said, "Do you think the farm will end badly?"

The front door opened. Flashlights entered and we were blind. A voice said, "Come with us." They led us into a wet chill; I nearly tripped into a culvert. The darkness was absolute except for the lights these men carried at their hips. I smelled burning. I had to piss.

We were on pavement, going downhill. Up ahead orange light shimmered. We got closer and yes, the dark outline of a different house and behind it was a bonfire. Now I could see our escorts: a few of the teens and the bearded man. We rounded into the bonfire yard and saw children dressed in costumes: draped in bed sheets, decked out in princess attire, wearing painted cardboard boxes. The neighborhood had lost track. They were celebrating Halloween two days early.

The bearded man took us indoors to a dining room lit by two kerosene lanterns. An older man was here waiting.

"I'm Rudy," he said. "And that's Ray," indicating the bearded one. "Please tell us the truth when we ask you questions. We have people here who think you should be killed."

"We're not gonna feed you and we can't let you go," said Ray. He took a seat at the table beside Rudy. "I appreciate you finding that tank today. It maybe saved our lives. But we can't have you telling anyone about it. The neighborhoods all around this city, we all talk to each other, we're all friendly and civil and trying to support each other. But there are soldiers out there and everybody knows it. The minute they hear what we've got, they'll come."

Xochitl said, "But you aren't the people who kill," and my stomach turned a backflip because I'd thought the same thing, but who knew.

Ray said, "Times change."

"First of all," the older one—Rudy—said, "where were you coming from? You've got gas in that truck, and food. I've been all over the three-county area, there aren't too many places where people have fresh vegetables like that. Some folks around here had bug-out bags and thought that would be enough, fast forward these however many months and there aren't too many dogs left running around, if you get what I'm saying."

"We worked for that food," said Xochitl.

"By soldiers, Ray doesn't mean the government. Where the government is is a great mystery. He means militia, and there's a lot of those. I studied my Aristotle. *Horror vacui.* Nature abhors a vacuum. One thought is maybe you're the tip of the spear, you're out looking on behalf of one of those militias and the minute we let you go, you run back and spill the beans and they come take what we have."

"It's not true," Xochitl said. "We're husband and wife and we left our home to survive."

"And that home is where?" said Ray.

I said, "Tulsa."

Xochitl looked at me and the men looked at each other.

"We heard Tulsa is gone," said Rudy. "Wiped off the map."

"So you understand why we left," Xochitl said. She sat and I sat beside her, and she took my hand; her other hand was still wrapped in that towel.

"You'd love it if you could paint us crazy," said Ray. "You'd love going back to wherever and telling people, 'They've got fuel for the taking and they're totally fucked up.'"

"Language," Rudy said.

"People can't feed their families," Ray said, "and we've all been paying taxes our whole lives and the last thing I ever want to hear again is how the electricity all just *broke*, all of it at the same time, like it's one big switch. What kind of nonsense is that? Where's our tax money now? Government is a pyramid scheme, it can't actually take care of people when they need it. People running around, taking whatever they want. We can't let them know what we've got, so we can't let you go."

"It makes sense," said Xochitl. "Except you aren't killers."

"What else do you know?" Rudy said. "Where else have you been?"

Xochitl looked at me. "We left our house…months ago. There was no food."

"What else?" said Rudy. "Where did you go?"

Xochitl looked at her hands, was formulating some lie, and I said, "We've been driving up and down the plains and the Ozarks, trading where we can, sleeping in a tent, doing work and getting paid in food and gas. We've been doing whatever and it's been hard. What else do we know? We helped look for a lost boy in exchange for some beans and rice. We broke into abandoned houses. We found that metal detector in a pile of junk and were lucky it still had a charge."

Rudy nodded. "There are travelers and not. We're all in the same boat."

"We're not!" said Ray. "We have to be practical."

I said, "What happened in Tulsa?"

"We heard nuclear," Rudy said.

Ray said, "It sounds pretty: everybody trades and everybody gets what they need," putting his fists on the table, "but there's less of everything, every day. There's a boy here who needs anti-seizure medicine and the family is weeks from running out. Last time, we found a pharmacist who sold us every pill he had. Is someone out there making more Depakote? Are there other runaway pharmacists with more? How do we find them? Do you know what it means out there now on the street when you see an upside-down 'Wrong Way' sign?"

"…"

"It means children have been killed nearby."

We heard kids chattering outside this house, trick-or-treating around the bonfire for heaven knew what: rocks or maybe our stolen gear.

Rudy said, "Where'd you do the work that earned those vegetables? Who has enough produce like that they can afford to give it away?"

Xochitl said, "We don't talk about where we've been."

Rudy smiled and Ray said, "Dad, you're not buying this shit. They'll say anything to get away and we can't know where they go next."

"It's true," said Rudy. "We can't know."

"It's our oil," said Xochitl. "But we're traders. We'll trade it to you if you let us go."

Rudy stood, and his face lost definition out of the lantern

light. His boots thumped the wood floor. "I'm sympathetic," he said. "But even you have to admit: it's not yours to trade anymore."

Ray picked up his gun.

9

They marched us to a new house. They gave us no food or water, left us under guard. The house was cold and we couldn't see. I felt around for blankets or beds, but the place seemed entirely stripped. Xochitl and I spooned on the floor and from nothing, up out of the blackness and a moment before I began dreaming, she told me how she came to the farm.

She was a maid in Kansas City, and illegal: born in Nuevo Laredo and eight happy years in its catacombs, until her father did something stupid with Los Zetas and got his hands chopped off and delivered to the rest of the family. That was the end of good food and pretty dresses and the beginning of torment from a gold-toothed local dealer who wanted to possess her mother. So mother and daughter hid in an ice cream truck to cross the border. Mother died of ovarian cancer. Daughter dropped out of school and lived in an Independence Plaza tenement, cleaned houses, bothered nobody.

Then came the crackdown on illegals. Xochitl didn't watch news or pay attention to politics, so at first she didn't know what ICE was and thought her friends were overreacting. Then five people in her building were deported: one morning they were just gone, no criminal activity, no neighborhood complaints. Just ejected. But what could she do? Find an old white man to marry? She wasn't pretty, and the old white men she knew were all married to old white ladies and played golf and complained about dust on their picture frames. She just kept going to work. She met a beefy white guy in a trucker bar next to a contractor's office she cleaned; he took her home and it was her first time in a while, and the tactile surprise of another human's touch caused her mind to race and she made a mistake: the next time they met up, she brought him to her place. He said his name was Roger.

He was rough with her. He suggested they try things she'd never done. In the moment it could be exciting, but she wound up bruised. Her neighbor Valeria asked about finger marks on her neck and she found herself doing the stupid thing, making excuses, lying, though people could tell what was really going on. She talked herself out of love with Roger—they'd been going out maybe three weeks—and told him she wanted to stop seeing him.

Then Roger told her he was an ICE agent.

He may have been. He had a gun and a badge. But he didn't seem to do much investigating or enforcing, and was usually still sleeping when Xochitl left for work. He straight up threatened her with deportation if she broke up with him, so she didn't. She asked if he knew the fates of the people who'd been forced from her building, and he said he couldn't talk about it.

It continued for a year.

He was a big muscular redneck—Valeria called him *El Pulgar*—who acted like a gentleman in public and a psycho in the bedroom. But then he'd fashion new drapes for the window in her apartment that was brutally light at daybreak, and he'd spring for a night at the casino across the Missouri where they'd stuff themselves at a buffet and watch failed

American Idol contestants, and he'd rub her shoulders when she had PMS. He had nerve damage in one foot he said he got from a bullet, but he had no scar. He ate with his mouth open and had an ever-increasing bald spot and gnashed his teeth while sleeping. A thousand times Xochitl told herself she could marry him, and then he'd bite her shoulder so hard he drew blood or he'd leave her tied to the bed for hours or he'd sodomize her.

And always there was that deportation threat. He might not have worked for ICE but she was sure he worked for the government, and didn't think the distinction much mattered. He kept his own apartment by the hospital in Avondale and nights he stayed there Xochitl took stock, understood she was trapped, didn't know what to do.

Then one afternoon she walked up to Valeria's apartment for no reason she could remember, probably intending to borrow something as an excuse for company, and the door was unlocked and Valeria was on her hands and knees with Roger pounding into her.

She wasn't jealous. She felt free. He could simply move on to the next wetback and leave Xochitl alone.

That wasn't how it worked out.

Roger wanted to see them both—plus he had a third girlfriend somewhere else—and grew wilder: singeing Xochitl's skin with a lighter, choking her with rope, standing on her skull while pummeling inside her. Any time she complained, he pointed to his gun and badge on the kitchen ledge and told her what an exception he was making, every day he let her stay in the U.S. things became more dangerous for him, it would probably be best to turn her in. Valeria reported similar threats and Xochitl forgave her, or *said* she forgave her: privately she wondered whether her supposed friend might also turn her in.

His fingers were thick and always oily. His breath knocked around inside his chest. Whenever he was taking her from behind, she looked down at his unbelievably hairy ankles: it looked like he wore socks that ended before his feet. He made her cupcakes; he hit her with an electrical cord.

Valeria said they should kill him. Xochitl said she wasn't a murderer. (And, while saying this to me, nudged my arm in the dark.)

Roger's sweet times came at greater intervals. Xochitl took extra cleaning jobs to stay away longer, including moonlighting in a flour plant, every moment of which was also terrifying because she was nonunion and people on the night shift could see she didn't have the right employee badge and was probably taking a citizen's job. She thought it would be proper revenge on Roger to have someone else stab her in the back and get her shipped out. She didn't sleep much, winced when he touched her, cried at every other song on her phone.

Then the power went out.

Like everyone, she didn't think much of it. She took a bus to Union Hill where she had three regular clients. She cleaned, but didn't vacuum. She came back home, woke the next day, bused in to River Market. But now there were fewer people on the bus and it bothered her: she'd been in the States nearly two decades and only now realized the extent to which invisibility was her specialty. Every American princess's little-girl fantasy is to be plucked from the masses and pampered, but not Xochitl, not anymore: now the eyes around her were more scarce and thus more likely to see her and ask questions. And carrying her burdens past a policeman! On a half-empty street corner that usually teemed! Mortification kept presenting her with terrible new aspects.

That second day, she came home feeling sick, walking down East 9th gradually realizing people were out in their yards, pent up and shouting to each other and maybe looking for trouble. A daytime blackout magnetized everyone outside—kids dousing each other with hoses, yes, but also adults carrying around cellphones like Geiger counters or gathering in driveways, arms folded—and at this point she was flat paranoid: as though they could look at her and know she was undocumented, as though she were one more cruel turn from forcible restoration to a country she barely remembered. Which of course she was.

She arrived home panting and overheated. Turned the key, felt the swelter of her apartment. Dropped her burdens. Thought about dinner. Walked into the bathroom to wash off the truth. And probably she saw the thing, probably it was as simple as peripheral vision, but in the remembering she *felt* it: the sting of fact in the form of a dark looming shape. And then her skin was cold and her spine turned molten because she knew she wasn't alone in the apartment. She covered her eyes, uncovered them. It was still there and she didn't want to leave the bathroom but knew she had to, how far was it to the apartment door and back outside, maybe twenty feet but it was too far, she wouldn't make it.

There was sunlight enough in the bathroom to show a bleeding body hanging from the shower curtain rod: a naked woman spread-eagled, arms tied apart, neck broken, head pointed unnaturally down. The woman's legs were blood-streaked. The bathtub's lip dripped red. Xochitl got closer to the face. Hispanic but not Valeria.

She heard something down the hall. He was in the bedroom. He'd heard her come in. There was a raspy little chuckle and the scritch of bedsprings. There was no time.

She bolted and he expected it, was right behind, something touched her foot and she couldn't look back and she got a hand on the doorknob and he closed in and he brushed against the little bells coming out of a fake plant she found at a flea market and the bells were saying *run! run! run!* and she got the door open but his weight was against it and she kicked behind and made contact and his pressure on the door lessened and she got it open and all she could think was go up to Valeria's apartment and make sure she was still alive. She climbed the stairs and saw Roger come tripping out of her apartment, landing on one knee and grunting and seeing her and waggling his jowls like a mastiff, but she made it up there. She shouted to Valeria, please open the door, and thought: if she's already dead, so am I.

Valeria opened the door.

And they got it closed and locked before Roger could get in, but he had the key. Valeria said she'd heard a woman screaming below and assumed it had been sex.

They shoved a sofa in front of the door.

But he was coming. There was a fire escape. They got out; they had to jump. They did and it hurt. They ran.

He was up there, he saw them, it was awful. Where should they go? Just find someone, just barge into somebody's home and it's over. But they were running away from the houses and apartments toward the park and the back of a liquor mart and a chicken restaurant. Valeria shouted and Xochitl wanted to tell her to stop, it was a way for Roger to track them, but she couldn't breathe. It was still light out. He was behind them, silent and stalking, then she couldn't see him anymore. And it became impossible to know which way to run because he could be waiting around any corner.

In the moment, she didn't spend any time considering why: why now, why today, what had driven this man to the next stage. It didn't occur to her, except to think: *of course*.

They stopped. A closed auto mechanic. A vacant insurance office. A printing company with no signs of life. And to the south, the interstate protected by a fence. They'd backed themselves into a part of the neighborhood Xochitl didn't know well. She thought there were more apartments west. But to get there: an alley in shadows. Everything slowed down. He might've been behind them. He might've been waiting for them on the alley's other side. Valeria was sobbing and pulling Xochitl's shoulders, and they were in the shade. Something touched Xochitl's foot and her eyes hadn't adjusted and she prayed it was only a rat.

They moved further into the alley.

And as they moved it sounded like someone was laughing. It was a sound Xochitl would hear a hundred more times, in dreams.

She looked ahead and the opening out into the next street looked like a bright and distant rabbit hole. She stepped forward, dragging Valeria. The alley created wind gusts and those gusts smelled rotten, like decaying vegetables and new dung, an awful zoo smell. They tried to hear Roger, over their own breathing.

There came a sound of something trotting. Impossible to know whether it was a person or an animal, and whether it was coming into the alley or going out. What the stupid, stupid mind will do: assemble whatever data happens to be lying around into the possibility of awful truth, then make excuses when that possibility becomes actual. They edged ahead. Valeria's fingernails grooved into Xochitl's arm. A garbage can lid clanked.

"*Es un perro*," Xochitl whispered (as she whispered it to me, in Spanish).

Something scratched the ground *close*.

Xochtil got them walking, now she could see there was an old tire and a broken crate of rain-ruined paper. They were moving and dislocated, and they crept and she blinked and there was a face in front of her suspended in this darkness and it seemed like this face was exhaling all the terrible smells, and she ducked.

But the face was just a poster on the brick wall.

Valeria's fingers left her then reattached, the end of the alley was closer and Xochitl could see a street and a brownstone across it. Her terror flashed into an instant of hope and she reemerged into the light and was blind and Valeria said, "Roger! Please no!"

Xochitl stopped, gasping, shielding her eyes.

He wasn't there. Valeria had simply been unable to take the tension anymore. Xochitl could read the number on the brownstone: 1207. He wasn't there. The city made its medley of rumbles and sirens and pneumatic squeaks. Daylight. Rescue. The blackout didn't matter.

She walked out of the alley, controlled and saved on a filthy sidewalk, seeing things anew. 1207 had green grass and a watering can hanging from a nail. Just cross this cracked side street. They couldn't call the police, of course, but at least they could ask the people in 1207 for an evening's worth of protection.

She stepped down off the curb and felt a new breeze, very close. A sound, a whirl of colors, impossible to assemble until she staggered away: just a body and another body.

Valeria's voice broke. Xochitl couldn't tell which happened first: the voice or the other sound, the loud sound: a bright ping. Knowing nothing, Xochitl fell and rolled away from whatever had happened, and she felt a warm spray because Valeria was falling and in her fall she sprayed blood into the early evening because Roger was here with a garden hoe and he'd swung it and the blade had sliced open Valeria's face.

It didn't kill her. That required several more swings.

Xochitl sprawled on hot asphalt. She watched. She watched it happen, every swing. She couldn't even shout.

People came out of 1207. They shouted.

Roger snarled at Xochitl and the snarl said, *I will come back for you*, and then he ran. The people from 1207 shot a gun, but Roger was too far.

Valeria was carved up and spurting, a rag doll and a punch line to stories people had been writing her entire life.

One 1207 person arranged Valeria on her stomach, so Xochitl wouldn't have to see.

She never went home again. She stayed in 1207 for a week: they had food going bad in the refrigerator and a network of friends and associates still going shopping and to work and hanging on street corners reporting back, plus quite a lot of money, the source of which Xochitl knew must be drug related. She accepted their generosity without ever exactly learning anyone's name. She cleaned their house, dazed. It was hot summer-blackout living. Nobody felt compelled to conserve and the gas stove still worked. 1207 wouldn't have been air conditioned anyway. A couple of the young men complained about not being able to play video games but otherwise it was just sweaty and candlelit and fine, and a couple times a nice woman held Xochitl's hand when she woke sobbing on the kitchen floor. But the days and nights did get quieter. The distance no longer featured I-70's 24-hour fizz. Airplanes didn't pass overhead and neighbors on this street didn't fire up their beater cars, instead waited for gas station shortages to end. There was no music.

Xochitl didn't go outside. The police never came to investigate. The people in 1207 had taken care of Valeria's body.

Now, in retrospect, Xochitl wondered whether Roger had rampaged because he sensed how bad the electric crisis would be and how long it would last. Maybe the people at his job—people involved with the U.S. government—let slip the depth of disaster, and it had freed him from the burden of barely civilized behavior. Or maybe it just made him insane.

One night she heard someone trying to get into 1207 from the back porch and withdrew a carving knife from its drawer and told her feet to go get him, but instead she collapsed weeping in a kitchen corner. And it was one of the kids who lived in the house.

The next morning she said goodbye and discovered there were still enough cars around to hitchhike south.

That night in the abandoned house, curled with me on the floor in the darkness, waiting to discover our fate, she told me, "It was bad bad bad bad bad bad bad bad, then it was pretty good."

I hugged her tighter, for warmth.

10

The front door opened before dawn. One flashlight came in.

Ray.

"We're going," he said.

He didn't take us back to the bonfire house or toward the Tacoma. He marched us through a backyard and across a dry creek and whenever we looked back at him, he shone light on his weapon. Eventually the sky became mauve and I knew we were walking south. Our feet were numb and Xochitl cradled the towel around her hand. We tramped into a forest and it was colder in there. Life in its hooting way rose above us, as unperturbed as any Almighty could ever be.

"Your father decided to let us go," Xochitl said.

"He did," said Ray.

"So this is you doing this," she said.

"Yes."

There was no trail. We slowed, stepping deeper into years' worth of dead pine needles. I couldn't see where the trees ended: the horizon was all trunks and then the blackness of a place that never got direct light. Xochitl sounded cool: "What did your job used to be?"

Ray said, "I managed a call center."

"So pretty different than this," she said.

He didn't say anything.

It was slick in there. We were single-file, she was in the middle, we both kept looking back. He watched his own boots and us; his expression was worried. I might've been able to run, if only to get behind a tree and then another, make him find me. But Xochitl was focused on keeping Ray talking. She said he seemed like a man who loved his family. She asked how many kids he had, and how many times he'd fired a weapon at a person. He didn't answer until Xochtil asked why he thought the electricity was out.

"I was one of those people who thought it can't happen here," he said. "Republican, Democrat: small differences they pretend are huge differences because that's what people do, they need to make it 'us' and 'them,' they like when there's somebody to blame. That's what I thought. It's a conservative county, but whenever a neighbor told me how the liberals were un-American and wanted to bring us down, I said no, no more divisive talk, that's what got us in this mess in the first place. 'Don't believe everything you read,' is what I said, and I told myself I was a good Christian.

"They shut me up pretty quick, though, didn't they? The Democrats didn't like the way things were going and so they used the silver bullet. Shut everything down, I guess because they wanted to save the planet from global warming. And hell, I believe in global warming, of course I do. Never had patience for anyone who wouldn't listen to science. The question is what you do about it. Is it worth putting millions of Americans out of work?

"So something happened, something we'll all learn about someday. The wrong people got control, even if they thought they were doing it for the right reasons. And now basically we have a police state by doing nothing. Think about it: nobody's working anymore. It's a strike-in-effect, you ever hear of that? You can be sure industries everywhere are failing, and the government's doing nothing and there's no cash entering the economy because nobody's paying their mortgages or their loans, and I'm sure what we'll find out if this ever ends is the banks wind up nationalized, a lot of industries will nationalize, and there'll be no going back." He told us to stop and turn and face him.

His gun was on me. Xochitl was putting on the same disbelieving act but now I believed him and I slumped sideways as though to take a bullet in the shoulder, as though that would save me.

"What did *you* do before?" said Ray.

"Writer mostly," I managed to say.

"So…*pretty different than this,*" he said.

"…"

Then he approached Xochitl, whose hands were up. I said, "Don't."

"Did you ever do that thought experiment?" he said. "What would you do if you could go back in time to stop something evil from happening? Like 9/11 or the Oklahoma City bombing. What would you be willing to do?"

"…"

"I don't think you have any idea how bad things are gonna get."

"…"

"Tell me where you live," he said.

Xochitl's glowered at me. *Shut up.* I bit my lips.

Ray put his hand on her shoulder and gently pressed her down, first to her knees and then all-fours. I backed against a tree.

"Tell me where you live," he said.

Xochitl looked up. Of course she was thinking of Roger, of course she was. And maybe she'd overstated how scared she'd been a half-year before, or maybe that experience or the intervening months had hardened her, or maybe she genuinely didn't believe Ray would harm her, but she was calm. Where I'd previously only known her as something of a psychic tormentor, driving around in all that judgmental silence, now I admired her.

"Tell me where you live," he said.

She wouldn't.

She said, "Be careful when you're trading that oil. People will wonder where you got so much and they might come looking."

He adjusted his grip on the gun.

I couldn't stop myself from groaning.

He bent, level with her, showed his teeth.

Xochitl put her head down and watched the pine needles.

He moved the gun, low, all the way to the ground, and put the barrel against the towel wrapped around her hand. He pushed down. Xochitl shouted.

"You live with a bigger group," said Ray. "Tell me where." He pressed the gun harder and she threw her head back and howled. But she said, *"Chinga tu madre."*

"See? This shows how wrong my father is. How can we let you go? You're absolutely right, you're a smart woman, the one thing we can't have is people wondering how we have so much oil. We'll have to be smart about it. And the first thing you'll do is tell people."

"We won't!" I said, and he looked at me like I was a moron.

"Shut up!" Xochitl told me.

He twisted the gun still harder into her broken hand, and what can you say about a person like that, so willing, waiting for a chance to live out a scene from a movie? I won't say he was enjoying it. I won't say he was smiling. He'd have told me he was just being tough—the way Charles liked playacting tough—out of necessity and obligation to his loved ones. But *fuck* him! No more talk about the necessary freak-out, no more talk about unavoidable violence. Another quality of human nature is overcoming human nature!

"Where did the vegetables come from?" said Ray.

Xochitl made terrible noises.

"Where did the metal detector come from? And the gas in your truck?"

"…"

"The longer you hold out, the more sure I am you're militia."

"…"

"Now I know history is a conspiracy of the powerful," Ray said.

"Aaaaaaaaaah!" said Xochitl.

"Words, please," he said. "Words."

"We live on a farm!" I said. They looked at me. "Thirty miles southeast, past Neosho! Maybe a hundred people, more women than men! We're like you, we're out here searching like you do!"

Xochitl's arms collapsed and she rested her face on the forest floor.

"It's not a militia!" I said. "There's barely any defenses!"

Ray pulled the barrel away. Xochitl tucked her broken hand beneath her body and vomited. I was reverse-hugging the trunk behind me.

Ray said, "Convince me."

"Sure," I said. "I'll give you the phone number."

He stood. He wasn't worried at all. He was comfortable. I could see his breath, realized I could see my own. Just a moment before, those clouds hadn't been coming out of us.

I said, "Jesus, do I look like a soldier? I'm the advance party somebody's sending out to intimidate people?"

"Perfect cover," he said.

"Except why would someone with a big army need cover? Why go to the trouble? I've lived it. They'd just come through and take whatever you've got. They wouldn't be skulking around scavenging in somebody's backyard."

He kicked around in the pine needles like a boy, put a hand in one pocket. "We've got guns," he said. "You saw them. There are a lot more. It's a neighborhood of proud gun owners."

"If you think we're coming back," I said.

And he looked down at Xochitl, opened his mouth to say something, thought better of it, sucked air through his teeth. Then he said the stupidest thing. He was a smart person, and I understood his perspective—and in another life I wouldn't have known to hate him—but what he said was damn stupid. He said, "Sorry, all right? It's nothing personal."

He left us. He waded away as though the forest floor was a real challenge to cross.

Xochitl heaved onto her back and tears tracked down her temples, but she was silent. I sat and put her skull in my lap.

We were there a long time. I waited for her to decide whether she could get up again. I tried to figure out how we'd get home. And that led me to think about the Tacoma, and I realized—probably with more horror than it warranted—that the Tacoma was gone for good.

11

So I thought about my travels in that truck. I remembered the time we'd spent around Fayetteville.

It had been seven weeks post-electricity, we were driving around in the mountains picking up work, stealing stuff to trade, gathering gas whenever we could, and near the university in a café that was still serving food Clooney chatted up a waitress named Lynette. She liked him; who didn't like him? She gave him a jumbo portion of field greens and pork, and went out back to reheat our coffee over the communal fire local businesses kept going there. She and Clooney laughed speculating about the fates of their favorite TV stars since everybody in Hollywood was presumably sitting around doing nothing, and then Lynette said we should come home with her, so we did.

She was no bumpkin, and she wanted us to meet her mother.

And we stumbled into the trap, driving behind her to a countryside manor snickering about how long we'd be able to milk Lynette's family for free room and board. On the driveway, she clapped and gave us a *ta-da!* gesture. We got out and while Clooney jibber-jabbered and Majido put on his cataract sunglasses and looked at the sky and sneezed anyway, I thought about the difference between accepting kindness and taking advantage. Oh, but I needn't have worried. Lynette showed us inside and said help ourselves to a glass of afternoon pinot, left us to grin like dummies at our good fortune, and returned with a sixtysomething bent-birch lady in a bathrobe. Her skin was loose, her eyes were crimson and her hair was almost gone. But she smiled and clapped her hands in pantomime of her daughter's gesture. "Oh-ho!" she said. "Look at y'all! Company calling!"

Lynette said, "This is my mother Dorothy."

Clooney got up so Dorothy could sit down.

"Looks like the party got started without me," she said. "We'll have a feast for supper tonight! New friends are one of the best things in this life." She was obviously ill, but spent an hour telling us jokes: "Yesterday I paid $5,000 for a reincarnation symposium. I figured what the heck, you only live once!" and "A skeleton walks into a bar and the bartender asks his order and the skeleton says, 'Give me a beer and a mop!'" and "How do you make a tissue dance? Put a little boogie in it!" and many more. She had us rolling. Only mother and daughter lived here, and they had a gas grill on which they cooked a mountain of chicken and corn on the cob; Lynette presided over the feast, arranged us in a half-circle on a back porch overlooking a glorious green meadow and a Monet-quality pond, and got us drunk. Dorothy looked at the view and said, "Did you ever?" and we had to admit, we'd never.

Darkness fell and we heard a nearby generator fire up, and Lynette fired up hers, and cast some light into the porch. Moths went crazy battering themselves against the screens and I felt pretty crazy, too: these were the first people I'd met in a while for whom life appeared not to have changed.

"Of *course* money's still good around here," Lynette said. "You paid for your lunch, didn't you? I don't know what that even means. You've been places where they don't take money anymore?"

"Most places," said Clooney.

"That's hard to believe, isn't it Mother?"

"I believe it if these gentlemen say it," said Dorothy.

"There's scarcity," Clooney said. "But you've got a wonderful spread here."

"My father did very well," said Lynette.

"Other places," he said, "folks are having a tough time. That's why we've been driving around so much. But what you've got here, this is just about paradise."

"You boys will stay over," Lynette said. "You'll see in the morning, food delivery comes around the neighborhood, they keep it cold enough to travel and we keep it cold enough to cook without getting sick. The farms are up north and east. It's not so bad. Mother did like to come with me to the market. Someday soon again, hopefully."

"Oh, the sacrifices I have to make," said Dorothy and she touched my knee and winked.

What would it have been like to sit there a year before? Would it have felt similarly abandoned? I was sleepy, the same way I got in museums that depicted how people in past civilizations used to live. Maybe it was the weightlessness of escape—my own continued existence—or maybe it was too much freedom or not enough.

The strength in Dorothy's voice faded but she protested when Lynette said it was bedtime. We promised we'd still be around when she woke and she shuffled into the main house. I looked at my glass and drank the dregs.

Lynette returned. "Of course I know the food will run out," she said. "Of course I can see what's going to happen. I'm not stupid. The truck that comes around selling food, it's driven by men with rifles and they don't smile at us, and every day there's less and I pay more. But you can understand why I don't want Dorothy to know."

"We understand," said Clooney.

"There's security in this neighborhood. You'll hear gunshots tonight. Dorothy and I both pretend she doesn't hear them, or we pretend our friends have cars that backfire a million times. Every week the guards ask for more money and we have to pay, and I know at some point it won't be about money anymore. At some point they'll just turn around and come for all this. But I can only fight the fire that's right in front of me."

The three of us looked at each other.

I said, "What's the fire right in front of you?"

"Well. Dorothy's supposed to start up her chemo again. We're already late. But the clinic she went to up in Springdale. They're out. Actually, now they're gone."

"…"

"I don't work at the restaurant," she said. "They were doing me a favor. I was there looking for my knight in shining armor."

I knew what our reactions would be. Clooney would want to help. Majido would want to leave. And I'd go along with whatever verdict they negotiated.

"I have to admit," said Clooney. "I don't know the first thing."

"Oh, that's all right," said Lynette. "I sure am feeling this wine. Let's all snooze and talk about it in the morning."

I took a downstairs couch and slept easily. I dreamed about my apartment in Tulsa: the expensive office chair that felt like heaven, the chimes outside my window whose notes came so slow, my mattress, my remodeled kitchen with the icemaker in the refrigerator door, even the "problems": the overloud central air and the impossible-to-light cathedral ceilings and the spiders assembling jigsaw pieces in dark corners. I dreamed about Band-Aids and the Discovery Channel and Wi-Fi passwords. And then it all morphed into one thing: contact lenses, from before I had LASIK. The scratchy airless feeling of disposable plastic over my corneas.

In the dream, I had a sense Clooney was there,

somewhere in my old apartment.

I woke once in the night, reached over and flicked a light switch up and down, up and down.

Lynnette knew people who had the drugs her mother needed. Ridiculously, they were holed up in an unincorporated township called Accident.

They were three forward-thinking nurses. Early on they'd commandeered medicine from their respective hospitals and clinics. Lynette heard they'd done it at gunpoint. They, too, had a squadron of armed protectors. Acquiring anything from them would require finesse.

Over breakfast, destroying his powdered eggs with a fork, Majido said, "Do they have corticosteroids, too?"

"I'm not sure," said Lynette. "They do have a lot."

Well, what was in it for us? Certainly that was on Clooney's mind: it would take more plunder than pharmaceuticals for Majido. But that was one of the glories in our little band: I wasn't in charge. In late-stage America being a happy pack animal was supposed to be some kind of character flaw, and I understand it—our national foundation myths revolve around self-determination and personal bootstrapping, blah blah blah—but could I condemn my own internal wiring? How fine it was to come upon some thorny problem and know someone else would resolve it. Okay, yes, this was old thinking: the sort activists decried as untenable luxury well before the electric crisis. But is it such an unpardonable crime to be in the abnegating majority?

While they talked, I went for a walk.

It was beautiful out. I dawdled down a two-lane road unable to locate myself. Was this Arkansas? The houses were nice; the trees were fine imitations of ones everywhere else. A hand-painted sign advertised homegrown spinach and dental work. There was a blue sculpture of a flying pig in front of a Baptist church. I turned down an optimistic little lane with a wood-post fence on one side and a chain-link fence on the other and came upon a transformer box.

I placed my hands on it, in the manner of a faith healer.

Elsewhere I saw a group of women selecting items from a six-foot-tall laundry pile to scrub against some rocks, and an old man eating a fistful of chickweed. Then a security guard leveled his rifle at me and I stammered until he agreed to march me back to Lynette's mansion.

There they shaved my head.

We drove to Accident. Clooney told me my name was Philip Kaiser and I was the son of a billionaire. My family owned the Bank of Oklahoma and an NBA team, and I had cancer.

"Elaborate story," said Majido. "You think they'll check on the Internet?"

A dirt road stretched past ranches and poultry farms, then was blocked by a school bus occupied by more guards with guns. They searched us thoroughly, routinely. We all stomped up to a boondocks compound surrounding a yellow split-level cottage, where even more guards searched us while the first guards watched. Clooney prided himself on no firearms; in this case, Majido grudgingly agreed. I could see an open garage that contained cardboard boxes stacked floor to ceiling.

One of the ex-nurses who ran this business was on site. Bailey. She smoked a cigarette and didn't get up from her chair. She was young and bored and splay-legged in a flower-print sundress. On a table beside her: a half-empty tuna can with a fork in it. A status symbol.

Clooney explained we needed chemo drugs.

"Must be a shock," said Bailey. "Knowing your money can't buy whatever you want at the drop of a hat. Knowing your money is hiding from you somewhere in a dead computer."

I looked at Clooney, and said, "Yes it is."

"Well," she said, "we're pretty set."

Clooney said, "You're…?"

"You don't have anything we need. He looks pretty

healthy. I'm sure it'll work out all right for him."

Everyone examined me and I felt undone.

"This is a powerful family we're talking about," said Clooney. "Very good people to be friends with, no matter what's happening in the world. And bad people not to be friends with."

Bailey sat forward and squirmed with the pleasure of saying, "Perfect, too perfect. Come in here and threaten us like nothing's changed. Be the *most* tone-deaf motherfucker in the world. Just keep assuming everybody will line up to kiss your ass. I fucking *love* it."

Majido inflated, these security men uncoiled—maybe they did or maybe I was inventing it, maybe everyone had already been grumbling…maybe a wild-west gunfight was always half-rumor. I felt pressure to say something. I tipped up my chin in what I imagined was a patrician style.

Clooney said, "You're right. That came out completely wrong. The last thing I want to do is come into your house and show disrespect. I've been Mr. Kaiser's assistant for nearly a decade and that means it's fallen to me to keep his son alive."

"Right," said Bailey, "because we're both just working stiffs."

"Actually," Clooney said, "my relationship with Mr. Kaiser the younger has changed quite a bit over the past couple months. Philip?"

I said, "Yes."

"I'll find him medicine his family can't get in Tulsa and I'll keep him alive. But we have no questions about who gives the orders on our expedition, do we?"

I took advantage of my natural slack jaw. Everyone untensed. Whatever bad weather I'd sniffed in this room vanished.

Clooney said, "No matter your thoughts on the future, if things *do* ever go back to normal…. The family's gratitude would be, ah, disproportionate? And for now, we do have something that might be of use to you. We've got gas to trade."

That was news to me.

A less sarcastic look came to Bailey's face. She said, "You're coming from Tulsa?"

They talked a while longer. Bailey was ill-tempered and suspicious, enjoyed the minor-key thrill of sitting while we stood. But she came around.

"I'll have to send for the chemo," she said. "We don't keep the valuable stuff here. Plus I wouldn't want to sell you something that doesn't work. So here's the deal. Bring back your little prince tomorrow, leave him overnight, and we'll give him his first treatment."

Everybody shook hands and I didn't have to fake doomed bafflement.

"Relax," Clooney told me back in the Tacoma, but didn't say why or how.

That evening I played Boggle with Dorothy. She let me win the first game and I put my mind to letting her win the second, but failed. Our quintet ate steak the texture of silk. Majido caught a faceful of sun and sneezed a dozen times, and Lynette said, "I hope it isn't the food?"

Majido left the porch and Clooney said, "Sun allergy. He gets rashes and can't breathe."

"Because of the sun?" said Dorothy. "The poor dear. A thing that hangs over everything."

"Is that real?" Lynette said.

"It is," said Clooney. He nudged my chair. "Sometimes we're out there traveling around like bats, sleeping during the day."

I pawed my bald head and felt little sympathy for Majido. I was imagining poison in my veins. Did I believe they'd let it happen to me?

After dinner, Dorothy and I walked the grounds, sticking to the less-overgrown perimeter and pointing at frogs and goldfish in the back pond. She told me the main challenge back there was keeping the turtles away. I looked at the house and saw Lynette laughing between Clooney and Majido. Dorothy smiled with love and said, "I like your hair short."

"…"

"Well, I'm sorry, I do," she said, holding my arm. "It's a fact."

I couldn't sleep. I didn't ask their plan and I don't know why. I just stressed out in the dark and put my face against a battery-operated clock but couldn't see what time it was. It was no time special.

Then I heard sex sounds. I stormed upstairs, but they weren't up there: they were out back. Lynette's voice quavered in the stereotypical way, acting up a storm, trying to seal this particular deal. *Oooooooh yes yes yes yes yes!* Overselling. I tripped finding the stairs; something smashed. I went banging down with *interruptus* on my mind, and her breathing was like crying. Some piece of furniture out there repeatedly squeaked. I found the generator. I pulled the cord, planning to tell them I was worried vermin were going through garbage. I looked out. The lights were on. And bodies: squinting Lynette all dewy and athletic and riding—for some reason what I mostly noticed were empty piercings up and down her ear, just the height of self-indulgence—and the man beneath thrusting up. But it was Majido!

I laughed at the window and waved my apologies.

In the morning, they drove me back to Accident.

I finally said, "They're not sticking me with any needles."

"It's the only way," said Clooney. "One treatment won't hurt you."

"…"

He brandished a thousand white teeth. "It's her way of knowing we're not full of shit. You get that right?"

"Remember," Majido said from behind the wheel. "Corticosteroids, too."

It felt like walking to the electric chair. All those hulking guards had been told what was going on, and looked away.

"Come on, no," I said, too softly.

And they really did leave me.

All three former nurses were here, managing the day-to-day of their empire. A granite-jawed steward in tight pants served them a late lunch: sea bass and risotto.

"You'll be happier later if you don't eat," Bailey said.

I watched them with my arms folded, as if that would protect my veins.

"Were you surprised, rich boy?" one of them said. "Did the power going out surprise you?"

"I was ready," Bailey told me. "Maybe I didn't expect it so soon. But this is what happens when you put people in charge who aren't curious. When anti-intellectuals are running the government, when they just start shutting down scientific programs left and right."

"Bailey, we were lucky you were as ready as you were," the third one said through a mouthful of fish.

"What do you think happens? Take away funding from the people who keep technology going, the people who crack down on cybercriminals, the people who know how to fix things, what do you think happens? Are you then allowed to be shocked that everything breaks?"

"…"

"You don't like having women in charge," said the one on my left.

"I'm fine," I said.

"I'll tell you what happens," said Bailey. "What happens is faith in our institutions…our *iron*clad institutions…. I mean, smart people just throw up their hands."

"Will you go back and tell your friends what bitches we are? Gee, I wonder what you ever did in your life and what system you were ever a part of to make us be so mean to you."

But they weren't mean. They gave me a plush chair and a nice comforter, they played me classical music, Bailey saw my terror and held my hand. They put in the needle and I didn't feel it. A bag of gold liquid dripped above me. They took turns checking the apparatus and sitting with me. I discovered I was crying and Bailey gave me hugs. Not maternal, just decent. One of them told me her father died from leukemia the day before the electricity went out, how he was so handy that by now he'd probably have solved the whole crisis. When the bag had drained into me and my bones felt ceramic, they eased me into a twin bed. I studied initials carved in a wood beam—"A.L. - 2003"—and a few hours later when I felt so sick I thought I was dying, Bailey dandled the back of my neck as I puked in the toilet.

In the morning they put me in a car flanked by two trucks. One of the former nurses said, "They better not try anything," and Bailey said, "Don't worry, they'll underestimate us for sure," but to me they gave soothing looks, and let me put my feet up across the back seat. I tried to keep track of where we were driving.

One of them said, "The protestors here blew up the post office on Dickson and the army recruiting office by the Dollar Tree. Did they do that where you're from?"

"…"

"Fat lot of good it did anyone," she said.

Our caravan crisscrossed through trees, away from civilization. I was paralyzingly sick. We turned onto a two-lane highway: fields on one side, mounds of clay on the other. It went on. I listened to our thumping tires and they sounded like a dishwasher spin cycle. We turned left and I could see electrical wires and railroad cars and huge mountains of gravel. A quarry. And ahead was the white Tacoma, parked beside a pit.

The guards inspected our surroundings and I signaled to Clooney. The sky was titanic. Majido wore his long sleeves and his fishing hat. Nobody else was with them.

Bailey told me, "Stay in the car."

They talked for a while and it seemed pleasant enough, but now I saw I was being treated like a hostage, and that my release was a final point of negotiation. I thought somebody should tell Bailey I didn't represent much additional leverage. I could see our fifty-gallon tank in the Tacoma's bed, alongside a new barrel that was twice as big.

Tough guys in sunglasses came over and lifted me out of the car. Other tough guys retrieved an empty blue container from one of their trucks and rolled it toward the Tacoma.

Clooney said, "Doing all right, Mr. Kaiser?" I threw up again and the guards backed away from me. Majido stood between the Tacoma and the gravel pit.

They positioned their blue container beside our truck and began siphoning from the smaller tank. Bailey balanced a medical-supply box on the fender. I wobbled toward everyone, staring daggers.

"You'll let your boss know we cooperated," Bailey said.

"I will," said Clooney.

"But don't get any ideas."

"Of course not."

She pretended to examine her fingernails. "The fields around our house have mortar shells. The gates and doors are booby-trapped. It would take an army, half of whom don't mind getting blown up."

"I admire your professionalism."

"Plus only the three of us know where the good stuff is hidden."

"Message received," Clooney said.

Bailey shook his hand, looking at me. "He did well." The other ex-nurses also shook hands with Clooney and then with me, but Majido wouldn't come around to this side. His legs remained out of view.

"No respect," said one of the nurses. I saw Clooney look at the box of drugs.

"Buzz off," Majido said.

"Should I be surprised?" the nurse said. "Fucking trash."

"Relax, bitch," said Majido. "Are you on your period?"

Everything stopped for a moment, they all looked at

each other, then someone nodded and a goon with a gun goose-stepped around the Tacoma and drove a knee into Majido's stomach. The nurses whooped and even I felt a little better. Clooney put up his hands, made pacifying syllables, but something had been unleashed: Majido moaned and the guy kicked him, more bodies were over there as the air grew dusty, it was a schoolyard without supervision. Clooney stared long-sufferingly at the sky.

"Hey, come take a look," someone said.

We did.

Clooney and Majido had fashioned a second siphon at the base of our fifty-gallon tank, removing gas from the bottom as the nurses took it from the top. They'd parked an empty plastic drum down in the pit, and Majido had started draining while everyone shook hands. It was a terrible plan. It relied on the nurses somehow not noticing being shortchanged.

Guns came out. They pointed one at my face, too, and I wanted to complain about the unfairness.

"Geniuses," said Bailey.

"Can't blame a guy for trying," Clooney said. Majido was on hands-and-knees. One more kick and he'd fall a hundred feet into the pit.

Bailey said, "Do you know what I thought when this happened, when the electricity went out? *Good.* The way men look at you and being paid less and having to pluck and shave and understanding no matter what you do…. I mean, burn the fucking world *down*." She was the main character in her own story because we all are. She strode to Majido and said, "Look at me." She seized a gun from one of her guards and put it against Majido's skull. "Look at me!"

He did, he looked up at her, without anything resembling dominion. His features warped out of fear, despite his efforts to be tough. She put the muzzle against his cheek.

Another nurse said, "Do it."

"No," said Bailey. "No, I want to remember his face just

like that."

A guard climbed into the Tacoma's bed and took the cap off the larger fuel barrel. He put his nose against the opening and reported it was filled with gas.

So several men strained and gasped wrestling it down out of our truck. Enough fuel to last for months, except I had no idea where it came from. Clooney protested. He absently picked up the box of chemo bags, tried to get in everybody's way, until someone put a rifle in *his* face whereupon he backed off. Majido was still on the ground over there, maybe was sobbing a little.

"It's too much," said Clooney. "That fuel is supposed to last us another—"

"Take the chemo for your little prince," Bailey said. "But shut the fuck up. And drive the fuck directly out of this town."

Clooney said, "That's not fair!" but the giant barrel was gone, everyone piled in, they peeled out. The world in this quarry—all horizon—became clotted and quiet. I watched Clooney watch them depart and heard Majido snuffling.

Then Clooney handed me the chemo box and hopped in the bed to check our original tank. Then I realized Majido was actually sneezing. Then I realized he was actually sneezing and laughing.

"A lot of it's still in here," Clooney said. Majido lowered himself into the pit, onto a ledge, and hoisted the plastic drum. Clooney jumped down and took it, heaved it into the Tacoma. Majido put on his hat and checked the blue container the guards brought.

"Siphon it back?" he said.

"Never mind," said Clooney, "just throw it in there, too. We'll combine it all later, let's blow."

I said, "Wait."

They pulled in the hoses, gathered everything up, opened the truck doors.

I said, "Wait!"

Clooney did his usual number on me. He slid up the sleeves of his safari jacket and took a breath, half-smiled and made me feel I was the only person around. "We don't want to be here if they come back."

I was woozy. I said, "What was in that other barrel?"

Clooney made a small space between his thumb and forefinger. "Gas." He made a much bigger space between thumb and forefinger. "Water."

"..."

"Two compartments," he said, "Built it special last night. Can we go?"

I felt my scalp. Clooney grabbed the chemo box and tossed it to Majido, who said, "There better be corticosteroids."

We drove. I was in the middle. I couldn't keep my head upright.

"Now we go back to Lynette and Dorothy," Clooney said.

"Fuck we do," said Majido, who was driving. "You know what that box is worth?"

"..."

"No way. This was too much work."

"Turn here," said Clooney.

We didn't.

Clooney said, "Turn around."

But Majido kept driving. And Clooney didn't put up a fight.

It turned out only a few of the bags actually had chemo drugs in them. The rest were urine.

We were down to Fort Smith when my nausea became too much again and I retched cream-colored bile with my hands clutching the Tacoma's gate. Clooney stood aside, smirking, shaking his head.

A woman passed with her small child. She asked if I was all right and said sharply to Clooney, "What's so funny? *This is real!*" and Clooney said, "That's what they tell me."

12

Now the Tacoma was gone forever, and Xochitl and I walked map-less and cold out of the forest, south and east, passing abandoned farmhouses and meadows inhabited by coyotes or wild dogs but no livestock. We had nothing. Our feet were wet and we were thirty miles from home. I thought: *No way I'll be able to meet Majido on the 10th now!* but it wasn't true, it wasn't even November yet, there was still a good chance if I wanted it.

Xochitl chewed me out. She was angry I told Ray about the farm. She said, "Now you know why we can't send out more people to trade. Nobody can keep a secret." Her hand was in that towel, which was spotting with blood.

We stopped to dry our shoes in the sun. I didn't remember the way we'd come and we hadn't eaten in a day.

"Even if we get back," she said, "they know where to look for us."

"…"

"They know where to find the farm."

"…"

"It's the one secret we had to protect."

"I heard you the first ten times," I said. "Stop telling me

the same thing over and over."

She cleaned mud from the top of her blocky brown foot. She said, "I do appreciate that you care," and then we didn't talk for a while.

We walked south and found a family walking north: husband, wife and child. They crossed the road to meet us.

The man said, "You look as bad as I feel."

"Are you coming from anyplace there's water?" said Xochitl. The woman had a half-filled plastic bottle that crinkled when she offered it. We each took a sip and gave it back.

"Can't believe this is still happening," said the man.

"Don't go down that way," the woman said. "The camps are real bad."

Xochitl said, "A few miles up the road are some families with extra houses and some food. We weren't welcome, but you could try. Be a little careful."

"Sometimes I think I'm doing reality TV," said the man.

"Do you know where the highway is?" Xochitl said. And we had our first sliver of good news: it was just behind the tree line.

"And don't get in any cars," said the woman. One of her eyes was cloudy.

"It can't be much longer," the man said, touching his boy's shoulder. "One way or the other."

We said goodbye and soon there was an elevated section of I-49 in the distance like a flying buttress supporting nothing. Xochitl said, "We just can't ask everybody to join us," but she wasn't talking to me. We crossed beneath the interstate and I read graffiti: "Brooke Francis Is A Snitch" and "Fuck You Beau" and "Big Time Zero" and "4 Stacks Syndicate," and over this last mark someone had crossed out the words "Stacks" and "Syndicate" and sprayed "Horsemen Of The Apocalypse."

We walked for hours. We never saw camps or moving cars. We found an old flea market that seemed familiar, then there was a trailer park with some activity inside but we'd grown paranoid, and agreed not to throw ourselves on anyone's mercy until we could no longer move. Now the silence between us was deeper and even gracious. And all that driving had prepared us: this new world was nothing but the ellipses of empty time. The only other thing Xochitl said was she missed her cowboy hat, which she'd left in the truck. I said nothing.

The street was downhill and the houses were far away, at the ends of long driveways. Some generators also puttered, plus there were a couple houses with solar panels. We'd seen these on the road occasionally, these places with self-sustaining electricity, and at first they were beacons of hope—Clooney had finagled a free meal and a night of drinking and dancing at one such place, down in De Queen—but they were such obvious targets that by now anyplace with those telltale photovoltaic arrays was compromised: either taken by force or smashed to pieces. We trudged on. We found a hand-painted sign that read "Riverbend." Then the sweetest sound—running water, a little creek—and the sun was dropping and it was damn cold but we toppled down the bank and kissed the creek like hummingbirds, drank ourselves nearly sick, Xochitl washed her hand, I dunked my head. We slept shivering in a gully with our faces together.

Voices woke me: someone coming down the road. It was day again. Xochitl was awake in my arms, staring at me. She put a finger to her lips.

Footsteps. Many people. I tilted my neck a few inches and could see only a small section of pavement before the road bent. Boots. Boot after boot. They weren't marching in time; they just walked. A few men muttered. Someone inhaled and spat phlegm. We knew not to move: we had the mutual instinct that being discovered would be bad.

So we waited, and I wasn't cold anymore.

One of them laughingly said, "Fuck you, she did *not!*" and then his voice blended with others.

They passed but we stayed still. I saw an image of myself from above, cowering like this in the dirt, and I wasn't offended by vague notions of courage—I had few illusions on that count—but rather by knowing what Clooney would've said. *Jesus, just get up and talk to them, see if they have any grub.*

Finally we cleaned ourselves in the creek, Xochitl rewrapped her hand, and we walked south, following those men, hoping enough time had passed. We didn't talk about them. We passed empty paddocks and scorched grassland, little houses with propane tanks, a massive wheat field turned to dirt, and by afternoon we reached the familiar outskirts of Neosho. We'd traded here. A lawn sign asked us to vote for Jim Jackson in some bygone election. Kids in oversize NRA baseball caps were on a swing set and playing on the railroad tracks and there was a picnic shelter labeled "Pet Milk Co." and we rested.

"Wish we could hitch a ride," said Xochitl.

We were halfway. I was weak.

"What about just asking someone for a little food?" I said.

She tapped my knee, kindly, conspiratorially. She said, "No more publicity right now."

We kept going, passing the Church of Hope, from which emanated the sound of children singing.

"It's weird they don't let kids on the farm," I said.

"It's not weird," Xochitl said. "Kids can't work."

"So they turn away pilgrims with children?"

"I don't know what they do."

Now there were more people: walking, laughing, trading. A few homeless folks asked us for food. This town had natural springs and we drank. A worried lady stood at a forest gap shouting, "Tory! Tory!" and a squirrel ran by carrying something flesh-colored that could've been—but probably wasn't—a human finger. A soccer field was covered in huge white tents and lots of people were milling around. There was no sign that the men we'd seen had come this way.

The day was so long. I emptied my head. It was the hardest thing I'd experienced, maybe still physically harder than anything I've ever done. We left the town and my eyes felt hollowed out by hunger. Trees were dead and scratching at the sky. On Highway D we heard a car coming and jumped off the road. Now we weren't far, but we couldn't beat the sunset, and the night became cold and the soles of my shoes wore through. But we were going to make it. A little house on Highway A was lit up and someone was playing guitar and violin and I could see Xochitl's face well enough to read disgust at the frivolousness. *Don't they know those men could be coming?*

Then it was completely dark but we were a half-mile from the farm; it was a matter of staying on the road and not falling into some random ditch. We went slow, kicking the ground to make sure we were still on pavement. I smacked my forehead against what was probably a speed-limit sign. One more right turn and we'd be home but there was no light, we'd never find it, we could easily walk right past. I thought maybe we'd have to sleep out here.

But we passed some trees and saw it to the south, below our feet and shining like an arc lamp: the farmhouse. It was completely lit up like the grand opening of a furniture store.

They were splurging on electricity to have a party, and Xochitl sighed.

13

Long around seven months after darkness, people began talking more openly about the past.

I overheard how couples met. I heard about distant undergraduate hijinks and romantic trips to the Mediterranean. Several women discovered they'd independently flown to the same march in Washington, D.C. Several men reminisced over an improbable Royals baseball championship. I heard about car crashes, ski adventures, terrible bosses, house remodels, favorite restaurants and TV shows, romantic entanglements, lucky breaks, tragic coincidences, lifelong regrets and professional triumphs. Nostalgia was a pathogen. They didn't realize they were doing it until everyone was doing it. I heard the same stories over and over, as they were repeated to different farm residents.

And who wouldn't understand the impulse? There was an accelerating sense that the record of these things now began and ended with our own minds. I was tempted to recount stories, too. I had "Painting Garth Brooks's House" (he gave me a beer and talked about French fries) and "Insane Freshman Year Roommate" (he serially threatened his department chair and the police found seven firearms in his closet), to say nothing of being forced from my apartment and my home city, meeting Clooney, looking for the boy while robbing houses, stealing chemotherapy drugs, *taking* chemotherapy drugs, invading Shreveport…but for the time being I kept my powder dry. I'd nod off in Maribel's cubicle or by the fireplace or the back woodstove narrating the details to myself. Winter was coming but who knew when?

It came. I woke one mid-December morning and padded around the house, nodding at other predawn risers who quietly ballyhooed about two fresh feet of snow. Ben was in his kitchen putting on boots.

"I'm shoveling out the generator and cars," he said.

I said, "Let me do it. You cook."

"Not a one-person job," he said.

"Cook."

It was still snowing. I shoveled until my pulse rattled my teeth.

It was bad. If any more accumulated, we might not be able to drive. Whatever we had now might be all we'd have until spring.

I only went to one of their community forums. A week after Xochitl and I swung down out of the north bearing news of our capture, Elizabeth insisted I attend. But the forum was too chaotic. What day-to-day seemed like smooth operation on the farm was exposed as raucous underneath: people waited their turn then shouted about unfairness and poor planning and perceived slights, and Elizabeth and Sonya explained their decisions while Charles reprimanded everyone without saying a word. People were angry about the lack of meat in their meals, the lack of privacy, what they perceived as loafing by some of the farmhands now that there was little harvesting left to do, the lack of respect for the veiled, the bending-over-backward required by the unveiled…and other things, stupid things, the color and quality of the farm's remaining toilet paper, women who still wore lipstick and left marks on glassware, people leaving farm implements with handles crisscrossed which was supposedly bad luck. Basically: the weather was changing and they felt cooped-up and the indignity of loss followed by communal living and helplessness…for an hour, they allowed it to drive them crazy. I hated hearing it, but then most days I was still driving away from that place—and seeing proof of true misery and deprivation everywhere else—so probably I shouldn't have judged them, but I did. It was noisy and horrible and I wondered how these people could go back to close-quarters survival without spitting venom on each other.

When our time came, Elizabeth asked Xochitl and me to describe our ordeal with Ray and Rudy, and also the marching men we'd seen headed in the farm's direction. We did, and instead of quieting these two dozen squawkers, it resulted in more unsolicited wisdom: we should send out a delegation to minimize the shock of eventually being discovered, we should stop trading altogether to prevent being discovered, we should devote ourselves to finding firearms, we should travel north and take revenge on Ray while reclaiming the oil we'd unearthed. None of it was helpful, nobody could understand how simultaneously tedious and terrifying the places around us had become, but I understood why Elizabeth wanted everything public. She needed an excuse to make rules. Or, to put it more charitably, she was trying to found a democracy.

They asked Charles what he thought and he made a funny face that tried to say *I thought I'd escape without commenting*, but which really said, *finally you're asking the right person.*

"You know what I think," he said. "I think: defenses. I think: a wall. I want to be able to tell anybody who wants to steal a piece of what we've got to go to hell."

"There are a lot of people," Xochitl told him. "Eventually they'll come."

"But maybe not?" someone said. "It's colder now. When was the last time we had new pilgrims? Have they stopped coming for the winter?"

Someone else said, "There are houses and spreads up

and down these roads. They just randomly go for a walk, they see us, they start talking. This is inevitable."

"We need outreach. We need to make allies."

"Don't be dramatic. This isn't TV. What do we do on this farm that's so visible? How would anyone know what we have?"

"Maybe it isn't about security, maybe it's about moral decency."

"It wasn't so long ago we took in most of the pilgrims who came our way, and we didn't worry because it was the right thing to do."

"But that was always going to change because there's only so much we can give."

"But have we reached that point?"

"I think it's adorable you think it matters that we're kind to a few strangers, like that earns us credit when the military or the government or whoever the guys with guns are, whenever they decide they want what we have."

"But that's the point: we're supposed to be better than they are."

"If there are so many soldiers around, close by enough to walk, how have they kept missing us? All due respect, it just seems exaggerated."

Around and around.

Eventually everyone waited for Charles to respond, and he said, "Everything is risk, and every time we make exceptions there are consequences," and he looked at me.

So nothing was resolved.

The other thing I could've done in that forum was make a plea for the men who were still living down in the shacks around the property, including Kimo, and I didn't do it. I planned to. What determined who got to be warm at night? Seniority? Gender? I told myself I'd be strong, but then Charles unnerved me.

And so for weeks more Kimo and Morales and others still slept down the hill and didn't eat with us in the farmhouse, but then came that first morning whiteout.

I excavated part of the circular driveway then waded out into our dirt pass. Anyone watching would've seen me taking stock of the snow trouble, assessing navigability, trudging toward the highway. Ahead in the gray I could see the beginnings of Charles's new wall and thought construction would be delayed. I detoured into the side field, as though for closer inspection of his pilings: train rails he'd scrounged from inactive tracks that abutted the property. He touted the wall as an emergency barricade; it would cover a fraction of the farm—the house and rear growing areas, the nearest barn, the livestock pens and coops, two of the barracks, one of the main fields—while leaving the rest of the fields unprotected. The project had skeptics: nobody knew where Charles thought he'd find enough materials, plus once food was growing again next spring most of the stuff worth protecting would be outside the wall, once again only guarded by barbed wire. But ultimately Elizabeth had given the go-ahead because she had idle labor, and because she wanted to placate Charles, and because one evening she called me aside at dinner and asked what I thought, and I said it was a good idea.

I tramped past a log pile. The ground was frozen. I folded my arms and shook my head, an acting job for nobody.

At the wall's proposed back corner, Ben had started his greenhouse. Xochitl and I had found a big castaway fiberglass fuel tank—formerly buried, long empty, cracked from exposure—and brought it back. Ben planted it sideways, so you could walk in; he had visions of harvesting tomatoes, carrots and beets in winter. It wouldn't happen this year, but maybe people were allowing themselves to think of the future. Again I paused, pretending to assess the weather's consequences.

Fifteen paces beyond the would-be greenhouse, I stared down the panorama: its welter of gray shapes. My heart rate was up again.

But then I kicked aside a square of snow and thank goodness: it was all right. The sand was still here, and it hadn't frozen. I kneeled and dug like a boy by the sea, until a couple feet down I reached the nozzle of the plastic drum that held my stolen gas repository.

I still had options.

But I felt something. I felt someone watching me and my telltale gasoline. Was that a distant person standing in the snow? Someone with binoculars up to his or her face? I filled the sand back in, fast as I could. I scooped snow over my hiding spot. Then I spent an absurdly long time untying and retying my boots, flailing my arms, putting on an act, playing to the back of the room. But it was stupid, of course nobody was watching.

How much had I skimmed from what we'd found and traded for over the past month-plus? How much did I have? Probably eighty gallons. A lot.

It was treasonous. Even before this storm we were on austerity measures with the farmhouse generator, and the group's total reserves were probably less than a hundred gallons. I'd justified my treachery by promising myself that if we couldn't find more fuel for everyone, I'd sneak mine into the mix or cop to what I'd done. But now came the real possibility that we wouldn't be able to leave the farm for weeks or months because of the snow. And still all I could think was: *mine mine mine.*

Would Majido show up at that highway spot two months after we made our pact? Had he shown up after one month? I knew it didn't matter, he wasn't a trustworthy person, if I was making a move back to Tulsa it would have to be on my own…but in my messy mind it was all part of the same jumble. I couldn't tell what I believed anymore. Hadn't I endorsed Charles's wall and Ben's greenhouse because digging projects would make hiding my gas easier? Or did I actually believe it was possible to live here forever? Was invasion imminent? Or was it an easy fear in others I could take advantage of? Even near the winter solstice, the days contained enough hours for me to convince myself of everything. I partook. I ate their food and followed instructions and fixed things and drove around trading, but I always eventually scrambled back to my double life behind the greenhouse.

Could a big city like Tulsa really have an admissions policy like that? The truth mattered less than what I believed, and was willing to plan for.

I returned shivering to the house and made myself seem extra breathless. I helped Ben finish making wheatcakes. Several people had decorated a Christmas tree by the stone fireplace; its lack of lights was a familiar taunt renewed.

"Ah, Tulsa," said Ben.

"…"

He laughed. "I scare you?"

"No," I said. "Sorry."

"That's your hometown, right?"

"…"

"My father grew up in Greenwood," he said. "His father died in the riots. But before that he owned a pharmacy, a black man in the 1920s, imagine that. And they rebuilt that part of town and the whole time my grandmother stayed. She said during Jim Crow it was about the best place to live. And my father liked it there. Only two places he ever felt at home: Tulsa and Vietnam."

My ears burned. I searched his face and said, "We need a plow for the front of one of those pickups."

Ben rang the bell that meant food was coming out. "It was called 'Black Wall Street.'"

"They…still do teach it in school," I said.

He thought about this. "We'll figure something to make a plow. Or a cowcatcher."

Everyone ate: cakes and individual cups of applesauce. (Xochitl and I had traded with a consortium of families who held a Price Cutter in Cassville. We had a crate of snap beans and they'd had their fill of applesauce.) It was cold in the house, unless you were ten feet from the main fireplace or five feet from one of the back woodstoves. We crowded together in those rooms, maybe fifty of us.

The punter, Scoggins, was here, somehow still tanned in December. He hugged a veiled woman hello, shook hands like the mayor. Fein dawdled alongside him. They were Charles's crew. They slept in the back of the farmhouse and I didn't know exactly what they did all day: presumably they planned the wall, and I wasn't sure if that left them time to playact for more pilgrims. Most evenings they were out in that backyard barn where our winter food was stored; it was impossible to keep track of every individual's private plans and contingencies. I imagined the three of them months from now, standing high atop a turret peering down on passersby. Elizabeth asked Xochitl how likely finding mounted machine guns might be, and we knew the request was coming from Charles.

This first snow day brought its own kind of ill-fated cheer, people buzzed as they ate, nobody knew what a day without outside work would even look like. I remembered my beautiful stainless steel refrigerator in Tulsa, the light that fluttered on a half-second after it opened. Then someone knocked on the front door. Everyone looked at everyone like mice caught in a pantry.

It was Kimo. His face was gray. He'd had to force the shack's door off its hinges. Morales and several other men were behind him.

It was, finally, the revolution.

Except it wasn't: everyone yanked the men indoors and dried them and gave them food and suddenly it was as though there had never been any separation at all. With tears in his eyes, Kimo accepted backslaps and towels and food. The only ones who didn't comfort him were Scoggins and Fein, who stayed back. I gave him my wheatcakes, and Maribel in her veil pretend-punched my shoulder, indicating a running concern that I was somehow too generous a person. I looked at them all and it seemed so clear: they were a mosaic of hope and selfishness and good intentions and selective blindness and ruin. Ben came out of the kitchen balling up his apron.

"How cold is it going to get out there?" he asked me.

"I'm not sure," I said.

"But it's already below freezing," said Ben, "which is bad for the chickens."

Maribel gathered empty plates from the folks standing around us. I'd found her some satin opera gloves and she loved showing them off. "I switched on the coop heater," she said. "It's on the schedule. Everybody in there still looked alive."

Ben nodded.

I said, "Ben was telling me about Black Wall Street."

"It's always educational in that kitchen," said Maribel. "Oh, I just love us so much."

Ben looked up at chewing Kimo. "When the snowball fight happens, big man, I'm on your team."

"I didn't mean to seem uninterested before," I said to Ben. "I was lightheaded from shoveling."

"It's fine," he said. "Black folks made money off other black folks, because they weren't allowed to go shopping anywhere else. It was also called 'Little Africa,' and the whites burned it down in 1921. If it gets below 20 degrees out there, the cows will start dropping."

Maribel said, "It's on the schedule. I'll make sure."

I made chess eyes at Ben. We'd had games going for a few weeks, but mostly we played a few moves at a time, by candlelight. Now we were snowed in and I thought we should play a whole-day game, beginning to end. He said, "How much longer do you think we can run the well and the kitchen on the gas we've got?"

Tiny Maribel—suddenly the most important person we had! She knew the formulas, how much each appliance drew down from the generator, and now she seemed to be thinking under there, and sure enough, a few people standing around us got quiet. With little farm work left to do, with chores maybe about to be limited to indoor work, only scorekeeping remained: had we harvested enough, had we stored enough, did we have fuel enough. And that final bit was secret. Maribel didn't publicize the latest measurements, so as to avoid panic and helpful suggestions about which electric needs could be eschewed. Even Xochitl didn't know the daily totals for sure, though she knew when things were becoming problematic. Of course I knew everything.

Maribel said to Ben, "I'll have to check. Can I get back to you?" and the people around us exhaled.

"That's all right," Ben said. "We've got some good cold recipes, too."

The rest of the morning was charged: women who were still sleeping would come from the back rooms rubbing their eyes and delight at the beauty outside, everyone seemed optimistic and restless, someone started caroling and many joined. It was so crowded: now we were an extended frontier family making the best of things. Having that many bodies around me was strange, but hadn't I been squeezed between two large men in that front seat week after week? Some of the more religious farm residents would say to each other, "Strength in numbers!" and then hold hands to pray. Was that true? I'd lived alone for so long, plus to most of these people I was a dangerous man. Having Maribel in the crook of my arm only washed away so much infamy.

I saw Xochitl slouching beside the main fire, chewing, listening to a veiled woman and an unveiled woman speak. Her hand was still in a homemade cast, which she'd painted black. Were these people all so innately kind? In pairs they gossiped and argued and cursed each other. There hadn't been violence or theft, at least that I'd heard, but claustrophobia was coming. The smell of these rooms was often aggressively good—one of the many people whose names I'd never learned made it her project to disperse dried flowers, light scented candles, hang cloves—but every so often I caught a whiff of bad: dried sweat, unwashed fungus, flatulence.

The kitchen was really cold, but I set up the chessboard in there, lit the candle fixtures above the side table, and poured two mini-glasses of wine. (There was contraband, even if we didn't call it that.) I wanted to surprise Ben, but he was off doing something else. I found him standing outside the front door regarding the roof.

"I was up in the attic last night," he told me, "and I'm not sure about the insulation. Will you help me keep an eye on how much snow collects up there? It won't give way or anything, but it could make ice dams."

"Yes," I said. "Even though I don't know what an ice dam is."

We kept on our heavy coats and played chess. As a kid, I went down that rabbit hole: park tables and tournaments and lessons from a Serbian man who complained about the politics of chess ratings and who flipped out whenever someone touched his hands. I was better than Ben. But that made it relaxing for me, because I could take circuitous routes and make delaying actions, extending games to hear him speak or just enjoy knowing we could play quietly. Most everyone else in that place loved speculating about the big picture, every day.

Today we'd been silent a while and I watched him eat carrot sticks. He was stuck on a piece of tactical ephemera, gazing at the board, and I watched his mouth. I wasn't thinking anything. But then I realized he wasn't chewing any longer and was actually smiling a befuddled smile and I met his eyes.

I said, "Sorry, I was just thinking you've got really straight teeth. Did you wear braces? I kind of wish I did."

"All natural," he said, and I squinched my mouth to one side and nodded.

"So," I said. "Ice dams."

"I was thinking about the cows, actually. Cold like this, getting milk when the air's so dry. They can probably get rashes. I should see if I can figure out some udder balm. Cooking oil and something. Beeswax maybe, if we had any."

"I used to know someone who gets rashes," I said.

"And what do they do?"

I shrugged.

His milk-skimming contraption was on a shelf near my feet: a tube slowly drawing out milk to a mason jar on the floor, leaving behind cream. I said, "How do you know all these tricks if you grew up in a city?"

"Well, I think I've long since been classified—and you've got some of this, too—as being pretty good at lateral thinking. You've got your problem, what are some things that are known to help fix that problem, and what other things might be good substitutes for those first things. People get frustrated too easy and give up."

"You give me too much credit," I said. "I've spent my life knowing five or six facts and making everything else up."

"My friend, I think you may have just given the definition of civilization."

He'd never married, had been living alone near the state university, and took the outage seriously right away. He predated nearly everyone here, including Charles by a day or two. (I was hazy on Elizabeth's timeline.) The one thing he wouldn't talk about was what his job had been. He called himself a former technical underling, which I found difficult to believe. He got up and took a cigarette from his stash, and we passed it back and forth.

I said, "People will be on top of each other if they can't go outside. If you don't watch out, they'll be escaping in here to bug you."

"Then we'll bar the door," said Ben, and he raised his plastic cup, and we toasted and each said the word *clink*.

Later Maribel came by and said Elizabeth wanted to see

me.

"That's all right," Ben said. "You've let me stay alive long enough," and he pushed over his king.

Elizabeth had an entire bedroom to herself, close to one of the woodstoves. Charles was walking out. He saw me coming and probably knew Elizabeth had called for me, but he shut her door anyway. And he was wearing his holster. He nodded at me as a general nods at a private.

She was at her desk, writing in a journal. I sat in a wing chair. As ever, her veil was in place. I'd heard other people ask about it, too, and her standard line was that the veil was a reminder—for herself and everyone else—of the ways she never wanted to be treated again.

"So!" she said. "Serious snow. Good news and bad news, I guess."

"I know the bad part," I said.

"Well, the good: if those militias haven't found us yet, they're not finding us in a blizzard."

"Ah."

"I choose optimism." She was smiling under there. "And I've been thinking that every day people aren't stealing from us is a gift, but in fact maybe things have reached an equilibrium out there. You don't think so?" We'd had this conversation several times: the queen asking one of her putative enforcers permission to view the world as less threatening. It didn't matter what I said. "But now we'll be leaving tire tracks on the highway," she said. "If we're still hiding, that's a problem."

"Or I guess a chance to really know if someone else is driving around, suspicious we're in here."

"Well, who's the optimist now?" said Elizabeth. "But actually that's one of the reasons I wanted to talk. Assuming you get out there and you do see tracks, it isn't necessarily someone else. There's a pretty good chance it's us."

"..."

"Charles just told me: he's been sending out a couple of

his guys. It's the first I've heard of it."

"I should get Xochitl."

"She'll be here in a few minutes. I wanted to talk to you first. It doesn't take a wizard of human psychology to see how much you resent Charles and I wanted you to be the first to know. I'm not happy with Charles and I just told him so. Secret initiatives. Not consistent with what we're building here."

I bit my lip to prevent a scowl. "When we're out there and we see other vehicles, I mean, sometimes we're flipping over into a ditch so they don't see us."

"I told him. He apologized."

"…"

"He said it was for scouting, for independent confirmation of what's happening out there. They don't trade, and they're careful."

Of course it was Charles. Of course he doubted what Xochitl and I told him, of course he assumed we were withholding the true lay of the land.

It was 120 miles to Tulsa. I could just go. And if I didn't have enough gas with me to get in, at least I could get the straight scoop on what entry required. But maybe Tulsa was a pile of ash! Or maybe I'd be stopped and robbed before I arrived. A part of me stood aside and laughed at myself: I would never leave, I would work myself into a daily self-loathing uproar but never be able to decide.

Elizabeth leaned back, put her hands behind her head. I wondered if she offered Charles these casual flourishes. I did respect her. She was probably about my age and we never talked about our lives before the past six months; instead she told me about Hannah Arendt, and G.A. Cohen skewering Robert Nozick responding to John Rawls. It was all news to me. She was high-minded and fair but couldn't stop talking. If she was very kind to everyone on the farm, sometimes that kindness could seem like an academic exercise. Once we (mostly she) talked about the morality of animal circuses for an hour. At night she slept with a woman named Paola, and she reserved a range of irritable sighs for Maribel.

"Believe me," she said, "I did read him the riot act. I understand: the whole point of one car going out is using one car's worth of gas and controlling how many people see us."

I said, "What did he tell you about what's out there? Did he say we've been exaggerating? Did he call us liars?" It was laughable these people considered me more dangerous than Charles.

Elizabeth spread her fingers. "Actually, no. Just the opposite. He just told me he has newfound respect for you and Xochitl."

"…"

"'The threats are real.' That's what he said. 'Serious as a heart attack.' 'If anything we're not doing enough.'"

"Okay…."

"If your point has ever been that the people living on this farm don't have enough appreciation for how tenuous their relative comfort is, Charles agrees with you. But I think you always knew this, right? It's part of why…. It's why he initiated you that way. If anyone takes what you've told us seriously…."

"…"

"I'm going to tell you something not many people know. Certainly not Charles. I've been informed we have our first pregnancy."

I coughed. Maybe surprise forced saliva down the wrong pipe; I gagged and hacked. It was so theatrical that Elizabeth came around the desk and slapped my back.

She said, "I know I'm supposed to worry about a worker who might not be able to pull her weight and then a child taking resources, but personally I'm delighted. A bundle of joy."

"But there are no kids here," I said, "and now this is a secret…?"

"Well. I'm not stupid. Families are currency people

understand. They think about what they work so hard for, they think about *why* survival matters so much, and the way they've learned to understand it is: I do this for my children. Not everyone. I don't think I ever wanted kids. But Maribel does. I hope you've had that conversation with her. This will be an adjustment. But our women are strong. Our women don't put up with bullshit. We outnumber you by design. You know this."

"I'm not sure why you're telling me," I said.

"I'm glad you're here," said Elizabeth, "and I finally want to earn your trust. Also, I need you and Xochitl to try and find some prenatal stuff." She handed me a scrap of paper, as if the world was a supermarket.

"Ah."

"You may be right," she said. "This news may not be received well. The mother thinks she'll start showing soon, and she's coming up with ways to hide it. Those early days, we turned away families with children and people saw it happen, and it was hard. Maybe I'm proceeding under the assumption that homegrown is better than imported. That's a terrible way of putting it." She scratched a spot on her face beneath the veil, a spot I'd never seen. "What did I imagine for this place? It's impossible for me to remember. I go back through my journals and I don't recognize the person who wrote them. And then at the same time it doesn't seem so long ago there was power and I was checking my phone every thirty seconds. At first I thought it should be all women here. If there's a chance for a do-over, why shouldn't we have a place? And that was impractical, you have to choose from what's available. But no alpha males and no kids. Why did I feel that way? I was very strident."

"…"

"Well. Now we'll have them both: kids and alpha males," and she pointed at me.

I ate that. I took it and swallowed it and I remembered the feeling of starving with that pry-bar in my hands. What they did to me was: every time I felt outside, they brought me in, and every time I felt inside they kicked me out.

"I love babies," Elizabeth said. "I always forget how easy it is to fall in love with something so small and helpless." She stooped in her chair, reaching down for something on the floor behind the desk.

I said, "One fact of order over chaos is people need stories."

She returned to view with a little black box I thought was emblazoned with the word *Yahweh*. It actually said *Yaesu*.

"What is it?" I said.

"Charles just gave it to me, those men of his found it. It's a transceiver. There's no battery, but we remember what you said: the mountain man with a ham radio in his shelter."

A little handheld mic dangled from a wire, *breaker-breaker-one-nine*, as in some amalgam of trucker movies recycled on the cable TV of my childhood. Its metal was ice-cold, and it had a spot of rust or dried blood on its underside. I said, "Great, I'll just plug it in."

"Talk to Ben," she said. "Work with Ben."

"…"

"I know my sister updates you about the generator, so I know you don't need a pep talk. If you can get back out there on the road, take whatever food, take anything, whatever you need to trade for fuel. Anything that's not bolted down."

"Yes," I said.

"Otherwise everything shuts off and I don't want to think about it."

"Yes."

"And do a dance. Get this fucking snow to stop."

14

The snow didn't care what we said about it.

The air was half particulate. The whiteness came as though in waves of rippling sheer linen. People went outside and came back marking higher and higher stations on their bodies. The humped car shapes were from an elephant's graveyard. I shoveled Maribel's path to the pink enclosure, again and again. Whenever she turned it on, the generator still buzzed away gamely. Everyone nibbled a small dinner and went to sleep, and I felt Maribel's cold feet against me and her snoring began, and I spent most of the night pacing, stoking the woodstoves, waiting for morning's tamperproof truth.

And the truth was bad. Four-and-a-half feet.

It was the kind of event that doomed pioneers.

What if we brought the walk-in freezer's contents outside, reconciled ourselves only to cooking over open flames, melted snow for water?

Hell, I couldn't get to my buried gas if I wanted to. Could I?

I recalled the momentous January storm of my childhood—a mere two feet—and the clattering rescue of the snowplows. It had been fun: the thrill of being cut off from civilization. What if the newspaper didn't come for two or three days!

I showed Ben the radio. He blinked; he stared through it. People were doing something in the next room. He found a pencil and pad, stood near the main kitchen sink where windowlight was brightest, and turned the radio over and over in his hands, looking for markings, digits, instructions, and he wrote in tiny hieroglyphics on the pad. Xochitl came in.

She said, "Let's dig out a truck," but then she stood with me for several minutes, watching Ben.

"Takes eight AA batteries," he said.

We had three that worked: one powering a big old-fashioned clock on the hearthside wall, one in an LED emergency flashlight, one in someone's antediluvian hearing aid. And then we had a drawer half-filled with expired batteries Xochitl had insisted we collect as part of her weird gratuities in trades: dead batteries, empty soda bottles, fishing lures, rubber bands, broken mirrors. Ben began drawing on his pad and I watched him and Xochitl watched me. He diagrammed grids and rectangles and voltage requirements, stared out the window for a minute, tore up his drawing and started again. A late riser shuffled into the kitchen and asked for leftover muesli and I wondered if she was the expectant mother. Someone came in and complained to Ben about the method they'd used to freeze fruit, its implications for edibility, and someone else wanted to talk about the firewood-rationing schedule. Ben listened and nodded and I was impatient for him. Here came Maribel to check on the kitchen appliances. She had her veil tucked into a hooded sweatshirt like a surgical mask, to keep her face warm.

More bodies came in, Xochitl and I withdrew and put on more clothing and lurched outside like arctic explorers. The sky was neon. We waded at first, then were hands-and-knees in the snow and sun. I threw my shovel in our truck's direction. I attacked the front wheels and Xochitl did her best on the back, with her cast wrapped in a plastic bag. At first it was a little bit fun, but then it was very cold and the going was slow: we burrowed into the shape, bodied and kicked aside as much snow as we could, and every square foot of black quarter-panel we uncovered was a victory. My back ached. Finally Xochitl squeezed into the cabin and I shoveled down to the exhaust pipe and she started it up. I climbed in, too. She made it warm. We dripped on the upholstery and gazed at the drifts against our windows and it felt like being inside an ant farm. And I really, truly felt it: the isolation. We were nowhere.

"If I stay here," she said, and didn't complete the thought.

I heard shouting outside the truck: it was three men horsing around in the snow, winging handfuls at one another, climbing atop the pink enclosure and diving face-first into the drifts, pulling off backflips and belly-flops. It was Charles, Fein and Scoggins. Usually their severity arguing about components of the wall or convening in that back barn seemed a rebuke of others' lightheartedness. Why was this the moment their inner children revealed themselves?

Back inside, drenched and chattering, Xochitl and I found the kitchen as overrun as everyplace else in the front of the house. Ben listened to plans for a firewood expedition, people laughed at a story about the President, someone was sitting on the counter trying to open a jar of preserved rhubarb. Xochitl slipped into an empty space and promptly was part of the scene. I looked at them all and knew I could pick off someone who chose the wrong moment to make eye contact with me, knew they'd be polite and ask how I was bucking up and I could ask the same and it could be an approximation of pleasant and human, but then that person would feel they'd done their duty and make an excuse and walk out of the kitchen, and the artificiality would be laid bare—*this is how we've learned to behave so as to avoid the few immutable truths involving selfishness and superficiality and death—* and so I didn't, I didn't talk with anyone because I knew deep down they feared me and hated me: I left the kitchen and changed clothes and looked around Maribel's cubicle and it was absolutely silent back here and I wanted my apartment back. (Sometimes I wouldn't step out of that apartment for days—emailed articles, food delivery, streaming TV, treadmill—and it had been both wonderful and horrible.) I looked down at my own bare waist and my ribcage in harsh bony relief. What would rescue be, exactly?

I found a cardboard box and gathered the radio and Ben's notes and a toolbox, and Kimo and I waded down the hill toward the shack we'd once slept in, him more recently than I. Kimo held the box above his head and powered through the snow, and I walked more easily in his wake.

Kimo said, "They don't need a wall now. The snow is the wall."

So we set up a battery lab for Ben. The days and nights of elaborate meals were finished for now; anyone could thaw and cut up frozen fruit and blanched vegetables and bread. Whatever meat we'd traded for was gone, our milk supplies were day-to-day, and sticking foil-wrapped items into fire wasn't rocket science. People still wanted to work but there wasn't much to do. They passed around the same Stephen King and Agatha Christie novels, they fashioned dice out of a broken chair arm, they put on elaborate stage productions for each other. And they shoveled. Within days there was a new *al fresco* outhouse and there were paths everywhere, including the half-mile down to that tarpaper shack, the place of my second incarceration. Kimo and I fixed the door and stacked the cots and improvised a table, spread out the radio and all those dead batteries and whatever screwdrivers and pliers and metal shears we could find. The woodstove in there was as feckless as ever.

"I'm hungry," said Kimo, and it struck me as the perfect tone, an encapsulation of the misery we all now knew lay

ahead. They'd worked hard, they'd produced an unlikely
amount of food, but surely they'd done it partly as an
experiment, with humor in their hearts, assuming it would
never come to this. Surely those little electric holes in the wall
would flicker again.

I also worked with Xochitl and one of the veiled women
to make a cowcatcher, per Ben's instructions. We stole a
couple sheets of corrugated aluminum from the chickens,
nailed the sheets across two-by-fours, fixed them against one
another at an angle, and strapped the whole mess to the black
truck's front bumper. And while we worked, while the farm
frittered around us, Xochitl and this woman talked:

"I did nothing but go to church," said the woman. "It
seemed like that was our whole lives. And when I got to
college, I felt so lonely. They don't really prepare you for
what happens when everyone isn't like you."

"What happened after you left?" Xochitl said.

"I wasn't strong enough to keep all those other voices
out of my head. Oh, yeah, after that I worked at Montana
Mickey's. The line cooks did coke off the same tables where
they did food prep, and customers squeezed my butt every
night."

"If I was cleaning alone and if it was dark," said Xochitl,
"I always wished for a gun."

"'Meat at the steakhouse,'" the veiled woman said. "They
called the waitresses that. I went home and just stayed there.
It was so nice: I had a fish tank and a little garden."

"And now you have a big garden."

"Of course I'd like to go back there. The price of all the
good things we had is some of the bad things. But if it's
God's will, I'm lucky to have found this place."

"I like it here sometimes," Xochitl said.

"Yes, so do I," said the woman. "I'm glad I can talk to
you. I usually don't feel so comfortable talking to the ones
who don't have a veil."

"…"

"The nicest thing of all," she said, "is it doesn't really matter what you wear or what you say. I can look at everybody here and know for a fact everybody has the same goal."

"It's pretty good," said Xochitl.

"But this could be Armageddon. Would we know it if it already happened? There was a city in the Bible, I can't remember what it's called. That was the place where the battle for end times would happen."

Xochitl wrenched one of the bumper straps tight with her good hand and laughed at me, because she knew I was listening, and maybe she figured I thought about Armageddon a lot myself.

We'd pumped fuel out of all the other cars but left a little in this truck, and I pulled out where the circular driveway became the dirt pass and gunned it. The snow was light, and slowly piled out of the way. The cowcatcher worked. I had to back up and move forward, over and over, but it worked. But I couldn't tell where the pass was, couldn't tell which way to steer, and out on the highway it would be impossible: within a hundred feet I'd drive into a ditch. I killed the engine and sat there looking at the empty sky.

While all this happened, Ben sat a few days in the tarpaper shack fashioning a miracle. Kimo had volunteered the AM/FM radio I'd given him, and Ben cannibalized wires from its innards. He also cracked open a hot chocolate dispenser that had been lying around the kitchen, for its motor, and removed the crank from a pencil sharpener. He fastened the crank to the motor's axle and told us about rectifiers. Among Xochitl's battery inventory were three rechargeable lithium-ion AAs, and to each end of these, Ben attached exposed copper wire. He cranked the motor a while, detached a battery, and tried a flashlight to see if it worked. It didn't. He adjusted the setup, played with wires, tried again. He made notes. Kimo and I sat and watched. It went on for hours and Ben never looked up, never expressed frustration.

Every time he tried the flashlight was an event, and Kimo stood, and when the light didn't go on Kimo groaned but to Ben it was data.

Finally, the light went on. We hollered and he nodded and made more notes.

He still didn't have enough power to run the transceiver. He had six working AAs. I ventured down there one afternoon to find him clipping open a nine-volt and unpacking the smaller skinny batteries therein. He tried leaving those in a bowl of vinegar, lamenting the farm's lack of lemon juice. He told me to run to the store and grab some solar panels, and I told him all this was like *Gilligan's Island*. He fastened alkaline batteries together with electrical tape, ran wires out of the vinegar bowl...I lost track of it all. When he needed a break, he made a long antenna out of a dozen coat hangers strung against old PVC pipe, and nailed it to the shack's roof.

It happened. He got one of his makeshift batteries to work the flashlight, and for the eighth, he crumpled aluminum foil in the shape of a battery to conduct power from the others. He flipped on the transceiver and its front-facing screen lit up blue with black numbers, and the microphone squeaked and hissed, and I grabbed Ben's shoulders and shook him and pulled him out of his chair and we hugged, I made him dance around, though not before he turned the radio back off to save whatever small minutes of use we might have. I was taller than Ben, and younger and stronger. His arms felt thin and spongy as I spun him around that absurd frigid cabin.

"You should be the one," he said, looking at the floor. "Let me go up to the house and get warm and I'll come back down with Kimo. But you should be the one to talk with whoever. You've seen what's out there."

"I don't know how it works," I said.

"I don't either!"

"Something tells me you'll figure it out faster."

"All I know," said Ben, "is we want shorter waves if we're going to hear people who are far away, so when you turn it on, pick the higher-frequency bands."

"…"

"All right. Let's turn it on together."

We did, and he stepped through the high-megahertz numbers, turned the dial slowly through each band's frequencies. I wanted there to be so much chatter. I wanted to hear dozens of people babbling about their days, or at least prerecorded messages giving survival instructions, rallying point coordinates, updates about the government…. But there was only static. What was the feeling? I was frantic, but not—at least not in that moment—for a jailbreak. I wanted to *know*.

"I can't be sure," Ben said. "I don't know if we're generating enough power to actually hear what might be out there."

"Okay."

He smiled at me. "Don't be discouraged."

"…"

"We're not going to die here."

"Yes."

He flicked off the transceiver again and put on his gloves. "I just put two and two together," he said. "What's that they say, when you die? They say, 'His lights went out.'" He laughed and shook my hand.

I said, "You want me to keep trying?"

And he said, "Always, my man," and he left the cabin.

I assumed the radio might work better as the sun went down. That felt right. I had an image of nerds from the past drinking obscure sodas beyond midnight, disguising their sadness in transmissions about fast cars and hot girls. So I walked up the hill and stood outside a while. Around me it felt like a continental deep freeze. I mourned and was excited. After so many years of never experiencing them, it seemed fresh starts were the thing for me. I was cold and worried but also had a guilty few minutes of imagining that in all the misery the electric situation had caused, maybe I'd finally started to become something else. I knew I was supposed to hate this thought, but for that short moment, I didn't.

I saw the three men again—Charles and his minions—no longer frolicking; now they were dragging something on a pallet, up the dirt pass in the snow tracks I'd made with the truck. Probably more wall materials, but that seemed ridiculous: their pilings and foundation were entombed. To me, their little secret society was inevitable and hyper-masculine and foolish, based on a need for secrets, no matter how small.

After a cold dinner, I tried the radio again and in fact after dark the static was softer and more hopeless and I worried the batteries were already giving out. But it would be better if it were the batteries! Eventually we'd come by more of those; I didn't want to admit the possibility that nobody was broadcasting because by now the entire world was dark.

Back up in the house, the fires were low and many people had gone to bed. Some of the women were dejected. A cow had gotten out of its hutch and died. I wondered where I'd be at this moment if Xochitl hadn't stopped me out on that highway. It had been policy: stay out of unwieldy groups. I thought it was too easy to blame the snow. I checked Elizabeth's room but her candles were out.

I looked for Ben in the kitchen but he wasn't there. Instead, I found Fein standing near the walk-in freezer. He said, "Turn around. Kitchen's closed."

"I was about to say the same to you," I said.

"Well, it's all covered. Nobody in here but us chickens." His punchable face rose as he stood on tiptoes to block my view. Somebody was in the freezer.

I was no justice warrior. They'd equipped the freezer with a padlock, which was dangling disengaged and candlelight flittered in the freezer doorframe, and if anyone else had stood before me probably I'd have shied away from the hypocrisy of confrontation. But I said, "You must think you're owed a little something extra, all that hard work you put in."

"Move along, riffraff."

"Must be pretty boring for you. No pilgrims to torture?"

"You know what's boring?" Fein said. "People who can't get over other people who are just doing their jobs."

"Ah, torture is your *job*. Got it. Well, that makes it all right."

"'Torture.' Jesus. Soft much?"

"…"

He folded in his lower lip and raised his eyebrows.

Loudly, I said, "If you're all alone, there's nobody here to stop me from doing to you what I did to that boy."

"Not quite nobody," Fein said, and the freezer door did open. His accomplice was the punter, Scoggins: candle in one hand, a half-canister of frozen cinnamon rolls in the other.

"Hey there!" he said, dripping wax. "How's it going?"

I said, "I'm pretty good friends with the guy who's accountable for all that food."

"This? We were just taking this out to our pals by the fire so everyone could have a taste."

"…"

"Hey, how are you enjoying that radio?" said Scoggins. "Get it working yet?"

People knew things I didn't. Again I wanted to be a hundred miles away, far from a big group.

"That was you," I said.

"It was!" Scoggins hip-checked the freezer closed, and Fein held the lock. "Two days ago now? Can't keep the time straight. Have you been up to that one Wal-Mart? I got it in my head to sneak around the back roads around there and do a little dumpster diving. Radio looked broken, but we figured we'd grab it just in case."

I looked at them both, back and forth. "What's it like out there?" I said.

"We don't have to tell you, right?" said Scoggins. "You live it every day, practically."

"..."

"Me with the gas in my basement. Fein with his parents disappearing. Some really bad shit happened. It's scary out there, man. I've got big respect for you and Xochitl."

I said, "I've been through all the Wal-Marts. The one on 60, the one on 37. They were picked clean a long time ago."

Scoggins nodded. "We were lucky."

I didn't care. I didn't care about any of this stuff. I was biding *my* time. What did someone else's dopey gambits matter? Scoggins was tall and smiling and plastic. Behind him Fein seethed. I looked at the raw cinnamon rolls.

"I'll come with you," I said. "Nothing more rewarding than seeing hungry people get a happy surprise."

"Oh, that's all right," said Scoggins. "What do you think, Fein? Getting late, these have been in there a long time, maybe save 'em for tomorrow night?"

Fein twitched a smile. Scoggins reopened the freezer, reached back in, and I could see him hide the rolls in a blue tarp's folds. They clicked the padlock closed. I had an antic moment picturing Elizabeth watching us: all her unease about testosterone-addled dummies. I thought about asking for the freezer key, reminded myself I didn't care.

Fein walked out. Scoggins paused, said, "We don't talk enough, man. Let's do better. It would be cool to know each other. Like, maybe, let's go for a walk sometime out back of the greenhouse."

He left the kitchen.

15

He knew.

I had to relocate my gas.

I watched Maribel's mouth move and pecked her cheek, but my mind was on solutions. There'd be no way to get a truck out there now. What about a hose and a backpack container? Transfer it out a little at a time, so eventually all a snooper would find was a buried drum. But put it where? Wouldn't Fein and Scoggins just spy on me wherever I went? Probably it would be better to store it away from the farm. I tried to relax. It seemed likely they didn't know what they'd seen me doing, only that I'd acted fishily. Maybe.

In the morning, Elizabeth joined me in the tarpaper shack to try the radio. Ben said we should go without him. "Scan the higher bands. You don't need me, and the complicated part's over. I'll stay up here and think about how else to charge those batteries." He didn't seem annoyed or beleaguered. He cut potatoes into the tiny pieces that would have to sustain us.

Down the hill, I lit the stove and Elizabeth said, "Even if we don't have enough power to talk, I'd love to hear someone far away acting like it's just another day."

I turned on the transceiver. The blue square and black numbers came on.

I pressed the buttons, turned the dials. There was only static.

It took a while to get through all the higher bands, but we got nothing.

"Let's turn it off and think," she said.

I did. "Ben says the atmosphere has a lot to do with it. We need solar flares, apparently they help."

Elizabeth put her fingers to her temples as though she were really concentrating. Then she said, "There, I believe that oughtta do it." Her veil puffed with a laugh. "I was thinking about Ben last night. You know what a cephalophore is?"

"…"

"A saint carrying around his own head."

"I don't get it."

She sat back and stared at the radio. "Oh," she said, "I don't mean anything."

"He's a really good person, if that's what you mean."

She was in charge, but there really was no *in charge*. She was admirable, too. She wasn't trying to remake the world in her image, or rectify all injustices. Ultimately what Elizabeth propagated was a tone: recognize the extent to which others' well being determines your own. I don't blame my not understanding her inner workings on her being a woman. With me, I guess, everyone was a puzzle.

She said, "What would this place be if we just opened the doors to anyone? I'm really asking."

"It would be one of those camps," I said. "People are hanging on. If the word got around, we'd be overrun."

"I keep wanting to think of it as society in miniature, there should be a way to take care of everyone. We have a lot of land, we could probably produce more food with more people. But there's a limit, right? There's a spot on the curve where production-per-person drops."

"…"

"I don't know what the spring looks like, if everyone's still wandering around in the dark. I don't want it to be them versus us, but show me a way around it. It's not civics class. I would love to just give everything away, but it wouldn't last. Any New Jerusalem is a closed circuit." I did occasionally hear people reminisce about their first day on the farm, what they went through: mostly a few hours of stern conversation, nothing like my…*initiation*. As far as I knew, we hadn't admitted anyone in weeks. Elizabeth said, "I know you can handle yourself no matter what happens. The rest of us, I'm not so sure."

We sat feeling the floorboards bend beneath us. We reclined. Elizabeth's hands were behind her head. Mine were crossed over my chest. Everything smelled like the smoke leaking from the stovepipe. We just sat there, and that was uncommon for Elizabeth. Maybe she was lost in thought, but I was blank. It was pretty nice.

We tried the radio again. It still turned on. I sifted through those higher bands and heard nothing but sizzle. So I took a shot on some of the smaller MHz numbers, pressing and re-pressing the talk button to make a little static on each. After a few minutes of trying, the radio said:

"Hello?"

It was a woman's voice. I offered Elizabeth the mic, and she said, "Talk. You do it."

I said, "We're here."

"Who's this?" said the voice. "Where are you?"

Elizabeth nodded at me.

"We're farmers," I said. "We're in Missouri. Where are you?"

"Well, I'm in Arkansas."

"You're the first person we've gotten on this thing. I don't think we have much battery left. Have you talked to a lot of other people? Do you know what's going on other places in the world?"

"You broke up there a little bit," she said.

"I want to know if the electricity is out everywhere in the United States."

"Oh. I don't think so."

Elizabeth put her hands under her veil and blew hard. We both stooped in our seats, leaned forward to the transceiver as if it discharged warmth.

I said, "What do you mean? What do you know? Do you talk to people all over?"

"Where are you again?"

"Please. We don't know anything."

She said, "Grids are back up in some places, we're pretty sure. I used to talk with a guy in Florida, he lived somewhere where it was coming back. And in San Francisco I'm not sure it ever went out."

Elizabeth nodded and I pushed the mic toward her. She said, "Why haven't they sent help?"

"Wish I had a better answer for you. Listen, you have gasoline there?"

"Very little," said Elizabeth.

"It got cold," the woman said. "Little bit of snow. I used to go to PrepperCon with my husband and my kids, people joked the government had a way to control the weather."

Elizabeth said, "We're buried in snow here," and I said, "Have you talked to anyone outside the country?"

"I didn't get that," said the woman.

"Do people have power in other countries?"

"My guy in Florida used to talk Spanish with some people, he swore up and down they had electricity, and they talked about the U.S. like it was going crazy. But who knows, right? Wouldn't put anything past anybody. And my Florida guy is gone."

"Are there a lot of people talking?" said Elizabeth.

"Oh, a hell of a lot of talk," the woman said. "A hell of a lot."

"Does anybody know what to do?"

"Stay away from the army guys. Whereabouts in Missouri did you say you are?"

I took the mic. "Do you know anything about Tulsa?"

"..."

"We can help," Elizabeth said. "We can help with finding gas. Will you let us talk amongst ourselves, and meet us back on here again?"

The woman seemed to hesitate, then she said, "Nobody's on the same time anymore. Everybody's a few minutes off. Why don't I call you on this channel at dawn." She was gone, and I turned off the radio.

Elizabeth said, "This is officially a whole other thing."

We walked up the hill to conference. Elizabeth summoned Charles and Sonya, and I fetched Xochitl and Maribel. I asked Ben to come, but he said he trusted whatever we wanted to do. We gathered in Elizabeth's room and talked for hours. But it was sound and fury; what choices were there? A couple days out from the storm, the weather was a little warmer but until we were melted and mobile, it was no cooking, and half-rations, and the specter of no well water. And once we could drive again? There wasn't any gas to trade for in the area anymore. It was fine hearing about San Francisco's possible good fortune, but something was still wrong, someone still hadn't regained control or reinstituted modernity. If this was the revolution, fine, what of it? All it looked like from here was another hungry Wednesday or Saturday, with no end in sight. Xochitl and I hammered this point: it was awful out there, but the line between "there" and "here" was thin. We needed allies. Charles looked at Elizabeth, and he said, "You know my preference: devote everything we have to protect what we have. Do whatever we have to do. *Sua sponte*, which is something they say at Fort Benning. It means, 'of their own accord.' Do it without anyone telling you to do it."

"But Charles," said Xochtil.

"I understand," he said. "I've been listening. I agree we

need help. We just can't attract anybody here."

"Yes," said Elizabeth. "Anything else is okay, but we can't tell these people where we are."

"We're not ready," Charles said. "Nobody understands how bad it would be."

"We understand," said Xochitl. "I've told you these stories many times. Who understands but us?"

"Sometimes people don't know when they're giving something away," he said. "That's my only point. Meet them. Fine. Find out what they know. Yes. Trade with them, steal from them, kill them. The homestead is prime. It can't be compromised more than it already is." When he said this, it looked as though something had grasped him around the skull and was pulling hard, so that the skin around his eyes was tighter, like a worried animal.

"You'll be on the radio with us," said Elizabeth. "You'll make sure we don't say anything wrong."

"Guns are what we need," Charles said. "Anything short of guns, I don't know how much help it is."

"Charles," said Elizabeth. "Don't be melodramatic. Gas would be lovely, too."

"She's so bossy," Maribel said to me later. "She was always like this. I wanted to be a musician, and there was a café in our town where they let people play with their guitars sometimes. And Elizabeth was friends with the owner's daughter, and it was pathetic how many times I asked her to ask the friend to ask her dad. And it was like, 'Maribel, you have to practice more, you have to get better on the guitar,' but I was pretty good and what does it hurt to ask? It was like she was my manager or something, but without being nice to me or telling me I was good. I practiced *so* much. I would've done it anyway, but she had to boss me around, then she says her friend says that her dad says, 'You have to be sixteen,' but I heard about another girl who played there when she was fourteen! Elizabeth was just like, 'No no, you must be mistaken, little girl, I know everything.' Then I turned sixteen, and then…" and she held out her afflicted hands, those molten fingers mottled brown.

At dawn, Elizabeth, Charles and I were back in the tarpaper shack. It wasn't as cold. Even before sunrise, the dripping sound of melted snow surrounded us, but it still seemed we were at least days from being able to drive. Overnight I'd outfitted a backpack with a siphon and a gallon jug, still unsure whether Scoggins and Fein really knew anything. Elizabeth and Charles reminisced about the schoolyard game Telephone—where a message was whispered from one child's ear to another's to another's, until the message became a garbled rendition of itself—and how pretty much everything was like that now.

I pressed the transceiver's power button and the blue panel flickered like a fluorescent light, but it stayed on. I toggled the mic.

"I'm here," the woman said. "You there?"

Charles gestured, *give it to me*, so I did. He said, "You can understand why we're reluctant to share our exact location. I assume you feel the same way."

"I know you're not that far," she said. "We're on 1.8 MHz, sun's up…you're inside a hundred miles, probably closer."

"Tell me about who you have there with you," said Charles. "We're a peaceful group. You talked with Elizabeth yesterday, she makes the decisions here."

"Well, good. Go Elizabeth."

"Do you talk to many people on the radio?"

"…"

"Hello?"

"…llo?"

"I'd like to know who else you talk to." Elizabeth reached for the mic, but Charles didn't hand it over. He said, "Do you know what happened to the electricity?"

The woman said, "Couple solar farms in our area. Sometimes we see lights at night, but we're not stupid enough to get near 'em. If we both need gas, and you want to help, why don't we meet someplace in the middle?"

"We can't assume this channel is secure."

"Well, that's true, you never know who might be listening in. But at some point you have to trust somebody."

Charles shook his head, Elizabeth scratched her knees. He said, "We have maybe eighty people. I don't know what you have in mind, but we're mostly not fighters."

The woman's voice became mostly static.

"I didn't get that," Charles said.

"I said, 'Eighty people!' That's a lot. You better say yes. That's a lot of people to feed and keep warm."

"Have you fought?" he said. "Do you have militias where you are? Have they come for what you have?"

"There are. The world is crazy."

"And you're fighting back? How are you fighting back?"

"Fighting back, hell, son, we're hiding."

Elizabeth leaned in, cupping Charles's hands, and she said, "Where and when do you want to meet?"

But we were losing power. The static grew softer.

"…didn't get…"

"Where and when should we meet?"

"…"

"Oh, fuck," Elizabeth said. "Hello?"

The woman was saying something, maybe giving directions or coordinates, but her voice was beyond language and beyond reach. Then there was nothing. The blue panel was still on, but the static was down to nothing. I clicked the radio off.

"We need friends who can fight," said Charles. "We can't waste time on some granny hiding in the bottom of an apple barrel."

Elizabeth looked at me, and I said to Charles, "Are you sure that's what you want?" I pressed the power button again and now it wouldn't turn on.

"Yes," he said. "Otherwise they'll just want to come here

and be more mouths to feed."

"I don't understand," I said. "You want to find people with guns because you're worried about people with guns."

"I could tell she won't be useful. She's barely hanging on, with however many people she's got. We won't get many cracks at making expeditions, so let's not lose our heads because we had a little snow. We'll get through the next however many days and we'll find some batteries and then we'll use the radio to find people who can actually help." He stood to leave. Elizabeth still held the dead mic.

"Wait," I said. "Ben can probably charge them again."

But he banged out the door, in the manner of someone who can't believe how much stupidity surrounds him.

Elizabeth said, "It's all right. Charge the batteries, get a meeting."

"I don't understand what he wants. What's the point of the radio if not to find real people who can tell us real things?"

She gently touched the back of my neck—it couldn't have surprised me more if she'd held a sparking wire to my skin—and she said, "Yeah, well." And she also left, and that unnecessary contact, unrehearsed and sweet, had the effect of making me consider that maybe everyone's motives, even Charles's, were basically good when viewed from a certain perspective. It made me ashamed for my selfishness. I stuck my head out the cabin door and watched her stride up the hill.

I brought Ben the radio. He connected his wires again and cranked. I watched him. He said, "Some friends I knew from grad school worked up the ranks in cyber-terrorism at Homeland Security. A few years ago I visited them in D.C. and we went to a party and got drunk in somebody's brownstone, they talked about work, how they were starting to see a new kind of malware. It hit Kiev first, shut down electricity in a big part of the city. None of my friends are programmers, they didn't read code, but they were told it was this super-malleable thing that could be modified slightly, and attack gas providers, water providers. Basically sabotage any grid. The malware would send messages to switch breakers, overload any substations it could find. But there were limitations, they said. It would only work for a few days."

I didn't normally hear him speculate like this. Things were weird. I said, "So you think that's what all this is?"

"You're right," he said, "I guess it doesn't really matter."

While he was talking in the kitchen, I ate a falling-apart piece of bread and some fruit preserves. We were silent for a while, and he kept working, so I stepped into the freezer, found the half-can of cinnamon rolls still hidden in a folded-up blue plastic tarp, opened it, urinated a few drops onto the topmost roll, and replaced the can exactly where I'd found it.

"Need something else to eat?" Ben said.

"No that's okay."

It took until near sunset to get the Arkansas woman again. I went through the bands twice and heard: some voices speaking in a Slavic language, what sounded like a recording of a political speech (with a crowd applauding) in a language I didn't know, and a half-dozen Spanish AM radio stations playing over each other on a single channel. The only English I picked up was a series of men speaking in whispers. One of them would say, "Level one audio check," and someone else said, "Confirm," and then "Level one visual check," and then, "Confirm," and then, "Level two audio check," and I realized this was some kind of surveillance team, and I didn't transmit anything to them. I convinced myself they were right nearby, spying on me. The jig was up. Then one of them said, "Level five, can you see down into the street? I think that should be East 5th?" and it was clear they weren't at the farm, and I expected to feel conflicted about this but instead discovered myself relieved.

After that, every fifteen minutes for several hours, I turned on the transceiver in the 1.8 MHz band, said, "Missouri farmer seeks employment opportunity," waited, then turned it off. I didn't know the protocols.

Finally she said, "You're pretty funny."

"Hello," I said. "Sorry, our battery situation is bad."

"Are you the paranoid one or the other one?"

"Oh, I'm pretty paranoid."

"Our first place was close enough to Camp Asa that I saw a thousand dead bodies," she said. "You don't have to tell me."

"We want to meet," I said. "We want to help. But right now there's too much snow. We can barely get out of our driveway, and we don't have gas enough to make it very far."

"We're close to the Missouri border. If you can meet us on the way, we'll drive you down to where the gas is. Can you make it to Bella Vista?"

I'd been through there with Clooney and Majido, down then up I-49. It was twenty-five miles from here, over a country turnpike that coursed through bleak and picked-over territory. "In theory, yes. It's not far."

"It's a resort town. There's a golf course that's gone to hell on the side of the highway, and after that there's some shops and a dead cherry picker, been there for months. We'll meet you there."

I said, "We still have multiple feet of snow. It might be a while."

"We need to move soon: tomorrow or the next night. The window's closing. It's nine of us now and if you have any food you could bring…."

"How much gas is there? How much could we get?"

"A lot. We'll tell you all about it tomorrow."

A thousand dead bodies. Was it likely? And the added request for food…either desperation or clever improvisation. I told myself it didn't matter, why seek gradations of trust, I didn't trust anyone. But I did, of course I did. And one of them, badass Xochitl, would insist on coming along. "Sundown tomorrow," I said. "We'll do our best."

"If you have guns, bring 'em."

16

Xochitl and Kimo were in. Charles insisted on coming but Elizabeth wouldn't let him. So Scoggins would be his proxy. They debated squeezing in more people, but I argued against it: I cited payload weight and fuel economy and protecting the homestead and not putting too many eggs in one basket—I had acquired Clooney's way of talking myself into motives—but really I wanted options. If we could score enough gas, maybe I could take my share and be gone; the fewer possible dissenters, the better.

Ben tried to calculate how much fuel we'd need to reach Bella Vista, but we didn't know how far south the snow would be a problem. What fuel mileage would we get while plowing an entire highway? Just getting up the dirt pass had taken nearly half an hour. But Ben did his best: making assumptions, estimating the snow's downforce, basically trying to find a scenario in which we could make it. We needed the snowline to be damn close. While Xochitl and I double-checked that we'd drained every ounce of gas from the four other cars in our driveway, Ben and Maribel deliberated inside the generator enclosure. For as long as the weather stayed as warm as today, the livestock would be safe.

The kitchen was already shut down. As for the well pump? People had marked off "clean snow" areas out back and were melting it in buckets and jars left in the sun, they'd been boiling it over the central fireplace and the woodstoves. Worst of all they trusted us. They all seemed to know we were going, and they all seemed confident we'd return. Maribel came out and said, "We want you to take all of it. We'll empty the whole generator."

It came to a combined four gallons. And I had twenty times that buried out on the property. But Scoggins wouldn't let me out of his sight, and I wouldn't admit my crime.

No question, we wouldn't be carrying enough fuel to make it back.

Ben and I played chess deep into the night. Things seemed heavy between us. One moment, I felt I understood him and believed that beneath his tinkering and thoughtfulness resided the sadness I sometimes felt: that it was easy to disappear inside a routine or problem and wake up much later to discover it was all distraction and life had happened. But then he'd snicker and say, "The human race wants to be immortal but doesn't know what to do with itself on a lazy Sunday afternoon," and he'd be opaque to me again. I was jittery. I blundered into losing my queen and Ben pretended it was a big deal, but he didn't actually want to hurt my feelings. He was the only one I could've told anything real to. No matter what I said, he would've nodded and ruminated. But no, I was wrong: things weren't heavy at all. He laughed coolly and peered out the dark kitchen window, as though we could see anything; I wanted to tell him I was worried I'd never get to hang out with him again, but it was too late. I returned to Maribel's cubicle and she was asleep: rigid on her side but kind enough to leave my half of the mattress accessible. I got in bed, very cold, and she half-consciously wrapped herself against me, her hands in my hair, and she said, "You have to make it back, I'd miss you too much." Then she started snoring, and they also half-snored in the other two cubicles in this room, and I got up and slept in a chair by the woodstove.

Our foursome left at dawn. Many of the farm's inhabitants got up to wish us luck. I'd thought about handing Ben instructions about how to find my gas if I didn't return, but I worried he'd read them right away. So I filled a small duffel with spare clothes and a folded-up note addressed to Maribel—whatever personal effects I might've mustered were mostly lost with the Tacoma—and arranged it in the cubicle for her to uncover if I left for Tulsa, or died. Some of the women gathered around our new truck were singing, "You Are My Sunshine." Xochitl hugged many of them, while Kimo and Scoggins shook some hands. I stood beside Elizabeth like a lieutenant at a grand auxiliary review. Charles put three pistols and a hunting rifle in the bed. Then Maribel made me lean down and turn away from the crowd, and she lifted her veil and kissed me hard. I heard Elizabeth saying to Xochitl, "Are you sure?" and she was, we all were, it was time. The truck was a four-seater and I drove. It was an easy quarter-mile up the dirt pass, and then a three-foot wall of snow. I put on my blinker.

We got a good head start and sledgehammered into the pile. The truck did well: we'd added a gutter to the cowcatcher to angle snow up and off. My worry was gliding atop the drifts and getting the wheels stuck, four-wheel drive or no. But we dug down and in, snow piled up over the hood where we'd fastened a 'V' of two more metal sheets to keep the windshield clean. Once we were on the highway, I backed off, feathering the gas, letting the truck's momentum slow, putting it in reverse and slamming forward again. The melt hadn't yet made things icy or heavy; it was the powder of Rocky Mountain ski vacations from TV. The truck fishtailed a little but mostly was true, and for the first couple miles there would be trees to demarcate the road. After that, finding the pavement would be harder.

"Just got a great idea," Scoggins said from the back seat.

"I had an uncle who flew messenger pigeons. Went a couple hundred miles. That there would be a growth stock right about now."

Xochitl looked back. "You okay?" she said. "You're looking green."

I saw him in the rearview. He was twisted and sweating.

Kimo said, "We'll come back tomorrow night. They'll all be waiting up for us."

"'I love us so much,'" said Xochitl in an Anglo accent, and it took me a second to realize she was imitating Maribel. I backed up again, feathered ahead.

"The snow will protect them, I think," Kimo said. "Only for two days."

Xochitl said, "I don't think that's what's on his mind."

"What?" I said. "Me? I'm focused on driving."

"Whose name do you know?" she said. "The girl who helped us make the plow. What's her name?"

"…"

"Come on, I'm just teasing you a little. It's Breanne."

"Breanne is cool," said Kimo. "She's a religious lady."

"Who's the third person on the council," Xochitl said. "Elizabeth, Charles and who else?"

I gritted my teeth as the snow gave way easier. "Sonya."

"He got one. And what do you know about Sonya?"

"…"

Kimo said, "She's a professor of something. She retired."

"Professor of English at KU," said Scoggins. "I haven't heard of the authors she studied. When you get to the league they warn you about ruining your eyes from reading too much. Ha. Margaret someone? I do know Sonya's daughter and granddaughter live in California."

"Congratulations," I said. "I'm a little busy here."

"Whose story do you know?" said Xochitl.

"I know *your* story," I said, shifting and re-shifting, and that quieted the chorus. I looked back and could still see the farmhouse atop a toy hill.

Xochitl said, "So what if you do know it? That's what you're supposed to do, you're supposed to let people in. Those are the people we're doing this for."

I'd hurt her feelings. I said, "I know your story and that's enough for me," but I couldn't tell whether it made anything better.

I got some momentum going. I figured advancing without reversing would save gas, if I could do it. The land was white and flat: too flat to see whether the snow ended ahead. Our engine blew loud. Xochitl and I had been this way a dozen times, had seen these sporadic ranch houses that had long since lost evidence of life. After the trees ended, utility fenceposts poked out of the snow frequently enough to keep me on course. Running out of fuel wouldn't doom us: we'd just tramp back to the farm. But subsistence there would be rough with no generator and no transportation. (But by then of course I'd share my stockpile!) We creaked past the abandoned fire station and the abandoned kicker bar and the abandoned gas pumps, and a house bore a bed sheet that read, "Where Are You Davey?"

"This is crazy," said Scoggins. "There's *no*body."

"…"

"I know we're out in the country, but man," he said. "Three hundred million people and where is everyone?"

"But you know this," I said. "You're a veteran of driving around out here, finding radios…."

"Hey!" said Xochitl, and I braked. She had the binocs out: there was smoke in the distance. "Somebody's burning down something."

Kimo leaned forward between us. "You think it's some of them soldiers?"

"I think there's no way to tell," I said, "and this road goes south all the way to Arkansas, so whoever it is, they're not in our way. Xochitl is showing off her eagle-eye skills."

We proceeded, hacking through more and more snow. Scoggins didn't like this much quiet; I peeked back and his fingers were over his lips, and he was rubbernecking the desolation. The truck hiccupped and I tried to ignore it. There was an elementary school on the left, surrounded by endless white nothing, and I searched the signboard for drollery but all the plastic letters but one had fallen off, and the only thing left was a capital "Y."

Scoggins said to Kimo, "Tell me what it's like to beat the shit out of somebody, big man. You'd have made somebody a good linebacker," but Kimo was perched up between the front seats like a spaniel and didn't answer.

Minutes later, he said: "Look!"

Ahead in the expanse a cluster of oaks awaited us, still just a polyp against the horizon. But the trees were black and then they were brown: bare limbs free of snow. The cowcatcher began to drag less. I let up on the accelerator. About five miles in, and we'd found the snowline.

"See?" said Xochitl. "We're lucky."

A few minutes later, the blacktop was bare. The cowcatcher made a godawful grinding; I stopped so we could get it in the bed. Now came the old problems: most anyone we ran across down here probably wouldn't be good news. On our right a river swelled to its bank and rushed south like an amusement ride. Kimo walked down and filled some bottles. We passed shacks set up on outcroppings and propane tanks rusted by disuse, then a white cabin whose sign said "Albert E. Brumley and Sons: Music Publishers."

"Oh, shit," Scoggins said. "I know where we are. That's the little house that invented gospel music. You know that song, 'I'll Fly Away'? 'When I die, Hallelujah by and by, I'll fly away'? The writer did it here. This place we're in is called the Memory Valley." Xochitl looked at him. "I've heard my share, gospel music was my wife's…*is* my wife's—"

"Nobody's in there now," said Xochitl.

The way became hillier as we approached the Ozarks. The truck hesitated going up, and I switched off the engine going down. In front of a chicken farm, a clean green truck was unoccupied. It was something we told ourselves often: people lived for millions of years without electricity; they might have to do without their next-day shoe deliveries and their artisanal kale, but probably they'd mostly be all right.

We didn't stop.

Every creek had a depth marker and the dead grass was tall and we passed dead cattle whose black shapes produced black birds. One highway hill climbed for a mile and only grew steeper and Xochitl said she remembered it, we'd come this far at least once, the incline would end soon. The truck jolted and faltered and there was nothing I could do, I floored it. We passed an electrical substation as abandoned as all the rest, and a sign that said, "Pea Ridge, AR: 10." Finally we reached the top, and I shut the truck off and we opened our doors and pushed with our feet, even little Xochitl who was just the toughest person. We got it going over the crest, and we glided past more farms, past a Church of Nazarene, we had a bad moment where it seemed we'd stop but then the elevation dropped again. At peak speed in neutral we did 75. But it didn't last, more climbs stole momentum, and finally I couldn't get the engine to turn over. We were empty and stopped.

"Two miles to the border?" said Xochitl.

"And six miles more after that," I said.

"Half a day," she said.

"I have to pee," said Kimo.

"We don't waste a precious flush on strangers," she said.

We carried water and Charles's guns. There'd been no sense bringing the radio, which wouldn't work away from Ben's antenna. I thought I knew the way, but on foot a wrong turn might kill us. Single file, we stepped in the bowed shadows of electrical wires.

Kimo said, "You have to spend gas to make it," and then he farted.

Houses up ahead were charred black. The only thing that hadn't been burned was an empty aboveground pool.

"Follow what we do," said Xochitl. "Tell us if you hear something."

"It really is like that movie," Scoggins said. An American flag flapped on its pole; someone had carefully spray-painted a crucifix across the flag's width, with an alpha and omega on either side.

It was warmer than I'd expected. We removed our heavy coats and tied them around our waists. Every time we passed a chicken farm my heart went fast and I scoured for signs of humanity, and was glad to see none. A hybrid liquor and tire store was vacant and looted. There was one final burned-out gas station and a beer sign in the shape of Missouri encouraging the viewer to "Show Me Great Taste." Then we were in Arkansas, if that mattered. A new sign boasted "Quick Cash Loans." The houses stopped and we took a right turn and tramped four abroad.

Scoggins said, "I miss a certain kind of stupid."

"…"

"You know, like, stump-speech stupid, politicians-appealing-to-their-base stupid. Facebook was fun. Who can pretend to be more populist while actually hating people. That bothered a lot of guys I knew, but it made me laugh."

"There's still enough stupid," said Xochitl.

"Naw, not the fun kind. When everything is theoretical, it's easier to watch people hammer themselves into dumb shapes." Everybody thought about this for a while, or anyway I did.

Xochitl said, "You sound like a person who's never had the police look at them funny."

"No no no," said Scoggins, "you don't understand what I mean. I'm on your side. I'm talking about people willing to be fooled. They like it. They prefer it. They're so tired of their lives they'd just rather drive everyone off a cliff dreaming of a golden era that never existed."

"Maybe I don't understand," she said, "but it's pretty easy to say you're on my side when you don't know what my side is."

Scoggins made a few exaggerated, beleaguered steps, then he said, "Well, okay. What's your side?" but Xochitl didn't answer.

"Why does Maribel wear a veil on her face?" Kimo eventually said to me.

I said, "You'd have to ask her."

"You didn't ask her?"

"I guess not directly, no."

"It's solidarity," said Scoggins. "It's not wanting to be objectified." He looked at Xochitl. "Right?"

"Maybe," she said.

"Sure, like: the world has judged our worth based on what we look like forever, so we want to take away that option."

"It isn't religious?" said Kimo.

"In a way," Scoggins said. "In the way that any system of beliefs that causes discipline is a religion. Running can be your religion, or lifting weights, or punting a thousand balls a week. A way of making the world make sense, a way of exerting a little bit of control in the face of chaos."

"Because I've seen some religious people who cover up their face," said Kimo.

"But I have to admit the effect it has on me, it's counterproductive, because I have to admit any time I'm around any of them, all I'm thinking is: 'Wow, I wonder if that one is really, really pretty.' Removing the label doesn't make the contents matter less, it just makes us wonder why they're being withheld, and we suspect that revealing them would reveal some incredibly important truth that probably in reality isn't there at all."

I tried to follow this.

Later there were houses again. Xochitl, Scoggins and I hid guns we didn't know how to shoot in our waistbands, and Kimo carried the rifle over his shoulder like an outlaw. This was an arriviste neighborhood as despoiled as any other—

broken windows and fires and a giant maple smashed diagonally through a living room—but there were people, too, and they ran when they saw us coming. I was on alert, but what could we do? Just puff ourselves up and get out quickly.

We came to civilization: many churches and dead cars left on the road. A fancy marquee announced the Bella Vista town center and some other local attractions. We came down out of the hills and it was banks and realtors and more churches; by town ordinance all were the same precious red brick with brown roofs. There were other people walking these roads, slowly, hoping for a break. Someone shouted, "Merry Fucking Christmas!" No cars were moving. Fire trucks and ambulances peeked out from nearby barns. We crossed over I-49 and then walked right down onto the highway and it was so quiet. Three clean vans were parked near a huge electrical substation, and I kept an eye on them. Who knew what went on?

The golf course was on the right, but it was overgrown and trashed: people had slept here by the hundreds and left behind their detritus. A few bodies hung in trees. I'd driven here about two months ago and it had still seemed a lark.

A street sign pointed to Shakespeare Drive.

Another mile and the sun was low, we were hungry and tired, and we reached a strip of chain restaurants and car dealerships. In front of an investment brokerage was a cherry picker with four flats. Nobody was waiting, but it wasn't quite time yet.

"We're sure there are no zombies?" Kimo said. We all laughed a little.

What did Clooney say to me once? This whole event was society reaping what it sowed, it was about the futility of choice especially when all we *had* was choice. From where I stood I could see ten fast food franchises. But then he also said it was way too easy to attach stories to things that weren't actually stories.

Dusk was underway and we didn't talk about what we'd do if the woman from the radio didn't show up. An elderly couple shambled to our side of the highway and asked if we had any food, and we let them drink the rest of our water.

Then a pickup came up out of a pharmacy parking lot.

The couple disappeared into an insurance building. I felt for my gun, never having fired one. Xochitl waved them in.

"Amazing!" a woman's voice said out a window. "Y'all came down!" The truck U-turned and its headlights revealed us. "We need you. We need partners in all this. Which one's the paranoid one?"

I said, "That's me."

They parked across multiple lanes and I felt stupid for momentarily worrying about traffic. Four people came out of the truck: two women and two men.

"I'm Annie," said one of them.

I didn't say anything. Daylight was still strong enough, and I could see them: all four of them. They all wore uniforms. Blueback uniforms, replicas of the Union Army, exactly the same as the boy I killed.

17

Xochitl recognized the uniforms, too. We both concealed the recognition within smiles.

They gave us some kind of jerky and we devoured it. Privately to Scoggins and Kimo, I said, "Nothing about the farm. Nothing about how to find us. I mean it."

"You know these guys?" Kimo said.

"Of course not."

Annie said, "It's a twenty-minute drive. Where's your vehicle?"

"We walked the last part," Xochitl said.

"Well, then I guess pile in."

We did: Kimo and Scoggins in the bed with two of theirs, Xochitl and I in the back seat, Annie and her husband Harry in front.

"What's the plan?" said Xochitl.

Harry was driving. He said, "The plan is get enough gas so we don't need more for a good long while." His Van Dyke enhanced the Civil War affect. "You have guns? This is a tightly held concern we're stepping into."

I said, "Yes we do. But we aren't soldiers like you."

Xochitl looked at me. "We haven't fought anyone."

"That's all right," said Harry. "Just follow our lead."

"We're not soldiers, either," Annie said. "We found a factory where they cranked these uniforms out by the hundreds. They're good at night, with the side benefit of reminding us not everybody in the South is a redneck."

Harry said, "'Though we are slaves, our God has not forsaken us in our bondage.' I guess that can feel a little hard to reconcile just now, I imagine you feel forsaken just about every day up in…now where did these young people say they're living, Ann?"

"They haven't said."

"The question we ask ourselves," said Harry, "isn't why did God take so many things away from us, but what did He intend to reveal?"

"That's Olivia in back," Annie said, "and that's Edward. Olivia is Harry's niece."

"Are we doing this tonight?" said Xochitl. "Are we going wherever there's gas right now?"

"No time like the present," Harry said.

"I sure am glad to make your acquaintance," Annie said to me, and reached behind the passenger seat to take my hand. "No matter whose plan it is, the world is awfully strange now." We buzzed south on this barren highway while the sun's final phantasmagoria made the west blur and bleed.

"Where do you live?" Xochitl said.

"We're in a little casino next to a newspaper," said Annie. "Which is better than being in a little newspaper next to a casino."

"I know it's fast," Harry said. "But we've been planning and it's time."

"Harry worked in oil and gas. He knows the pipelines."

"There were millions of gallons stored in Oklahoma and Texas and Louisiana, and the pipelines aren't pushing fuel anymore, at least not around here. But millions were still in the system. There's one pipeline that goes through Fort Smith over to Little Rock, and there's one that comes down from

Springfield, Missouri, to a terminal right near here."

"The same town as the first Wal-Mart that was ever built," Annie said.

"Razorback Pipeline, 30,000 barrels a day when it's running. It ends in a tank farm with capacity for almost 200,000 barrels. That's eight million gallons. All these terminals, it's the first place the militias and local governments took. It's already refined and they've been handing it out and using it themselves but there's plenty left, there would have to be. The tank farm where we're headed is a damn garrison. They ship out fuel to who knows where, run by who knows who, and they guard it tight. I worked for TransMontaigne, they built the pipeline and the terminal though they leased it to a big operation in Tulsa. There's real damn soldiers who live at the tank farm. Anyone who tries a simple smash-and-grab without a little finesse…. It won't work."

By this point I was like a dog hearing its name. A big operation in Tulsa? Did that explain why they maybe had power there?

"Do you know what happened?" Annie said. "Nobody seems to know why the electricity went out."

"It was God," said Harry.

Annie said, "Yeah, Harry, well maybe these kind folks know who God was acting through."

Across the median, a car puttered north and Harry waved vaguely, out of general solidarity. Cell towers disappeared into the evening sky.

"There are nine of you?" I said.

Annie's eyes were framed in the headrest and she said, "Right, but too old and too young. I'm afraid we're the best and brightest we've got."

"Perfect-sized brigade," said Harry.

Our tires thudded and now it was black except for our headlights and I may have fallen asleep. I was aware we were exiting, and Annie was saying, "That hotel there, they've got generators on nonstop. That's where the mayor and his staff and their families live." I looked out at an extended-stay suites, its checkerboard of lights surrounded by darkness. They would have guards posted to keep everyone else out, they would trade gas from the reserves they seized for food and medicine, they would be the standard to which the thousands of other people around here aspired: *imagine if we got to live in that building.* Everything was its own ecosystem. From a commercial boulevard that could've been anywhere, Harry turned left and as our headlights swept I could read part of a sign: "Structural Plastic." We parked in a dark empty lot.

Four of them walked four of us into some trees. Someone had a flashlight and they revealed a false fence covered in vines. We stooped inside a burrow and saw shovels gouged into black soil. A tunnel led off into total blackness.

"Here we are," said Annie.

"We go at 4 a.m.," said Harry.

They said the tunnel was almost completed: just a couple final feet of digging and they'd be through to the tank farm property next door. They'd been planning for months. One party would go through the tunnel under cover of darkness and set off firecrackers while another party took advantage of the commotion to bang a tanker truck through the front gate and steal fuel. The tanker was parked a mile away and Harry would drive his people. That was the dangerous part. We just had to be the distraction.

"In the meantime we have food," said Annie.

They set up an LED lantern in the tunnel's mouth and we ate beans and greens and bread. Kimo made shadow puppets.

"Will there be enough time?" Xochitl said. "How much time does it take to fill your tanker? And will all the guards all investigate the firecracker sounds together?"

"It'll work," said Edward, a young firefighter type with a

huge stubbly jaw. "We've been spying on them."

Scoggins and Olivia were flirting in the shadows. I couldn't tell how or if Olivia and Edward were related. This was all very fast, but here we were, waiting and talking for hours.

"I remember a news story," Edward said, "a fuel truck got a flat tire in Pakistan and crashed, and the tank was breached and oil flowed out everywhere. Word spread. Neighbors called each other to say it had happened, to come to the crash and bring bottles and cans. People drove their motorcycles to fill them up, too. Thousands of people! And this was years ago, long before. Unfortunately somebody lit a cigarette and the oil exploded and burned hundreds of them alive. But you see it isn't surprising. What people are forced to do."

I kept waiting for one of them to talk about a missing teen.

Harry drew a map of the tank farm in the dirt. Xochitl took a nap. Kimo stepped outside after promising not to make any light, and I joined him.

"I'm not too nervous," he said. "My grandmother said don't spend time thinking about dying. She said by the time you're old and sick like me, you'll want to."

"We're not old yet," I said.

"Don't worry! I got you and you got me, right?"

"Yes."

"Do you like Xochitl?" he said.

This was a conversation I definitely didn't want to have. I kicked the dirt and looked for the moon; it felt like the past invading: the thousands of other times I'd idly checked the sky.

"I mean do you love her?" said Kimo.

"Not that way," I said. "No."

"Okay. Sometimes you're a one-way street, too."

"…"

"Jon likes her but she doesn't like Jon anymore."

"Scoggins?"

"Now Jon likes Olivia."

I said, "Kimo, I don't know why we're talking about this."

"Well, I'm getting ready to break some heads, boy. Talking is a way I start feeling alive."

"Talk about something else, then."

So he did: a story about a fight he had when he was eleven against a much older kid, how the older kid broke Kimo's arm with a wrench and Kimo went crazy and kicked the older kid until his spleen burst, and a teacher hid him in a computer lab until it was safe to come out. He tried to show me the place his forearm broke, which scarred and later became the site of his first tattoo, but there wasn't enough light.

Edward came out and smoked a cigarette and gave Kimo one, and those orange dots were all we could see.

Hours went by. Harry gave us a watch synchronized to his and drilled us on our roles: on the stroke of four, dig the rest of the way through, come up out of a hill in the tank farm's backmost corner, find a spot hidden from view and begin setting off the firecrackers. Move guerilla style through the back, where the terminal lights would be lowest, set off as many sets of firecrackers as we could, then return to the hole and fill it back in behind us.

"You'll really have enough time to fill a tanker?" said Xochitl.

"We will," Harry said.

Annie gave us hugs and told us be careful. The others waved goodbye. I followed them back into the parking lot and saw a flashlight on Edward holding a crossbow and on Olivia as she took off her blueback clothes and donned some kind of gold blouse that decidedly wasn't camouflage. She heard my footsteps and paused. Harry said, "I almost forgot, here you go, we figured we'd let your girl wear this," and he handed me Olivia's Union uniform. "To be safe."

"It might not fit," Olivia said, and she was gone into their truck, they all were. This time they drove without headlights. I tried to see around this tree thicket but nothing over there was illuminated; I figured that must be part of the terminal security, so as not to provide an easy target at night.

So the four of us sat around that lantern in the dirt, deep inside ourselves. All I heard was our breathing. Xochitl didn't try to wear Olivia's uniform; she tossed it at Scoggins's feet. Probably it was cold in there but I didn't feel it. We hadn't discussed our share of the gas, but I believed Annie would take care of us. Majido's two-month mark was a few days away; I could now see that I hated him, but that didn't stop me from fantasizing about turning up at our assigned meeting spot with a thousand gallons and reveling in his dumbfounded face.

Scoggins said, "I don't think I can do this."

"You will," said Xochitl.

"No, I can't stand up," he said. "I pulled something in my leg."

"…"

"I'm an athlete, I can tell when something's wrong."

"Coward."

"You don't need me," he said. "The more people limping around out there, the more likely we get caught.

"In ten minutes," Xochitl said, "we're all going."

Scoggins gripped his knees, stared at the lantern.

I said, "You haven't been out here. You haven't left the farm since the day you arrived. Admit it."

"…"

"You didn't find the radio in a dumpster. You and Fein haven't been driving around. Those were lies."

"…"

"I just want to hear you say it," I told him. "If you say it, you don't have to come through the tunnel with us."

He looked at Xochitl.

She said, "Also he fucks them all. How many did you

fuck? On the farm he treats them like whores."

Scoggins rubbed together his huge hands and gazed into a middle distance. "It's what they told me to say. Yes. Today's the first time I've been in a car for however long."

"Who told you?" I said.

"Charles."

"Why?"

"…"

"Why?"

"I don't know."

"Where did the radio come from then?"

"We took it. We found it on a pilgrim."

"What pilgrim?" I said. "There haven't been any."

"…"

"…"

Scoggins said, "You shouldn't have stopped what they were doing to me, that first night. I know your hearts were in the right place, but you shouldn't have done it."

The rifle and guns were piled deeper in the tunnel and I imagined putting a barrel in his mouth. But he'd seen me behind the greenhouse. I looked at Kimo, whose eyes were closed in the manner of a fighter before the bell, working himself into a state of recklessness. I breathed and waited for Xochitl to say go.

She did. It was 4 a.m.

The three of us took shovels and guns and firecrackers and matches and we duckwalked far into the tunnel. I was at the front. Kimo also held the lantern. I reached the end and scraped the dirt ahead, trying to be quiet: granules fell at our feet. The tunnel was four feet tall and I realized I hadn't given proper consideration to a cave-in, but that was okay, we'd be out in a moment or two. It was warmer in here, and I figured we only had to dig a foot or so further. I prodded a little harder, and Kimo prepared to extinguish our light as soon as I broke through. The earth was soft and came away easily. I kept expecting fresh air, figuring my blade would puncture a hillock's surface beyond a fence. Giant Kimo wheezed behind me—he was truly crammed in here—and reached out with his own shovel to pull back a few more inches of dirt. I hit a fist-sized rock and pulled it out of the way. Xochitl pushed me from behind, tensing to run out into the tank farm's back field.

I scraped again, with less concern about noise. We were twenty feet in: the burrow and parking lot were far behind us. Annie and Harry were counting on us being out there, were waiting for our distraction. Every minute we delayed was a minute they could be caught. I drove my shovel into the earth wall as far as it would go and kicked it hard, scooped out as much dirt as would come. Kimo had no leverage but he did the same, pulling out a big clod with small roots sticking out. I banged my head on the tunnel ceiling, dug in again, pulled out more soil. How far did we need to go? Could I have misunderstood how much more Harry and Edward said needed to be dug? Could they have miscalculated? Could we be digging in the wrong direction? Kimo pulled my shoulder and I fell back, he wriggled ahead and sat on the floor and kicked his shovel into the wall, cleared another scoop, then another and another. He made a hole that reached several feet deeper into the tunnel wall, too small for a person, and only found more dirt.

Xochitl tapped my shoulder, and I tapped Kimo's. We inched out backwards, and I realized there were noises coming from outside the burrow.

An engine thundered and there were lights. Scoggins was still sitting here massaging his leg. I thought Annie and the others must've returned, I thought something had gone wrong and they were hurrying to tell us the plan was off. I stepped out of the burrow and felt the relief of fresher air.

It wasn't Harry's truck. It was a jeep, and three men in camo uniforms leaped out and I heard weapons clack and one of the men hit my stomach and I fell. They were shouting, pointing guns, Xochitl and Kimo came out squinting and dropped to their knees. We were lined up in their headlights, execution-style. Scoggins also came out, hands up, and I felt satisfaction when they punched him, too.

"Idiots," one of them said. "Fucking morons."

Another man ducked into the burrow and came out laughing savagely.

"Hey, rocket scientists. What, you're invading? Christ, only a half-mile more to go. All you have to dig through is a lumberyard and then go under some train tracks."

I looked at Xochitl. She said, "What do you mean?"

"If you're trying to dig your way into the compound over there, you'll be at it for another month and you'll probably run into some concrete foundations on the way."

"What compound?" Kimo said.

"We don't know what you're talking about," said Xochitl. "We live here now."

They bound our hands behind us with zip-ties. One of them said, "Bullshit. All you've got is guns and shovels. Where's your food? Where's your water?"

"Jackasses trying to tunnel into Fort Knox."

"What's over there?" said Xochitl. "What are you talking about?"

I saw my breath evaporate up out of the headlights. I said, "Who told you we were here? Who said come investigate at four in the morning?"

The soldier who hadn't spoken pointed his muzzle at the pavement. He was missing a front tooth. He said, "They're too stupid to shoot. Put the girl in the car and march the others back to base."

"Yeah," Kimo said. "Who was it who told you?"

The man with the missing tooth said, "There's a waitress who comes by late and brings us coffee, said she saw someone digging around here."

Someone pulled me up. Xochitl shrugged one of them away; I could see her furious face. She knew the only thing I knew: Annie had set us up.

"I want a lawyer," said Scoggins, meaning it humorously.

They put Xochitl in the jeep and lined up the three of us in their headlights and we walked out of the parking lot, turned left, and hiked a two-lane highway with our shadows in front of us like monsters. I couldn't understand this prank. The gold blouse Olivia put on had been a waitress uniform? I grew paranoid: they knew what I'd done to that boy and in retaliation delivered me to a militia.

The world around us had nothing in it, nobody awake and no commerce, so why did it howl? It was still deafening to be out here with all this nothing.

Ten minutes later we took another left. The tank farm's entrance had no fence, no gate: just a truck-width driveway, pitch-black as every other place I'd seen since spring. There was no sense making a break for it. We'd have to take our chances with these military or paramilitary lunkheads, convince them of our harmlessness. In the headlights I saw a few white pickups, a single-story office building, and a drive-up loading rack. My wrists hurt and my hands were numb.

One of the men in the jeep said, "Hold it."

We did. Their weapons clicked again. I looked around and there were no people, I didn't know what I was supposed to be seeing. But maybe they were just going to shoot us after all.

"Did he decide to take a piss while we're gone?"

The jeep's engine switched off, its headlights stayed on.

One of the men said, "Murphy? Murphy, what the fuck, man?"

They were out of the jeep and beside us now, scanning with flashlights that revealed dead grass and utility poles. Presumably somewhere deeper into the property and looming above us were giant tanks filled with gas. These men breathed hard, searching. Kimo bumped against me but I couldn't see his face. Someone's flashlight beam hit Scoggins and lingered, maybe because he was abnormally handsome or maybe because they recognized him. Behind Scoggins I thought I saw a body.

"What's over there?" said someone, his voice tipping into fear. My neck tightened and I shivered.

There was: a body. Away from the driveway and the headlights, on the muddy grass, legs motionless and horizontal. The light scanned elsewhere, then returned...and I saw Olivia in her gold uniform, standing still, her eyes reflecting back at us like a demon's. Styrofoam coffee cups were on the ground around her, as was the body of a guard.

Something whizzed past my face.

A thud, maybe a punch, Kimo dove on top of me and pile-drove me to the pavement, as I was falling the dark released shapes and all I could picture was Olivia standing there like a ghost and this seemed to be purgatory, I hit the asphalt the way Clooney had—face-first—and feet were scraping around us but nobody shouted, it was still quiet, Kimo's weight mashed air out of me and I wanted to make sure Xochitl was all right but everything was above me and my hands were bound and I was under Kimo, it was the confusion of nightmares: the world erupted and made no sense. One of the camouflaged men began to shout but someone hit him.

The shapes.

Had been more people.

Everything was quiet. Nobody moved.

Kimo wriggled off me and got up. I looked at what I presumed was the sky, though it was too dark to tell. Someone dragged me vertical, and clipped the zip-tie from my wrists. It was Harry.

He put a finger to his lips, shone a flashlight at the jeep—Xochitl was fine—then at two of our captors who were on their knees with their hands up, then at Olivia-the-waitress and the unconscious soldier beside her. He whispered, "Chloral hydrate."

I looked around us. There were many shadows: other people in Union uniforms. Two dozen faces. More. Harry said, "Glad you made it."

"You're militia, too," I said.

"What's a militia?" said Harry. "We're people with a common goal."

"…"

"Olivia's been coming here with coffee for weeks. But we couldn't be sure of drugging them all." He waved at the blueback figures around him and they scattered further into the terminal complex. "A lot more men are sleeping in that office up there," Harry said. "Ten more minutes of quiet and we'll be out, and we'll have all the gas we can handle."

I saw a camo-clad body, dead in the headlights. An arrow was stuck in its face.

I said, "Fuck you," and Harry smiled. I said, "Olivia sent these guards to the tunnel. And you didn't know if they'd just shoot us on sight."

"…"

"You needed someone you could sacrifice. While we dug to nowhere."

Harry unfastened Kimo's and Scoggins's wrists, and Annie was here, she helped Xochitl from the jeep. "But you made it," Harry said. "No harm done."

"They left you to die," said one of the guards, from his knees. "You're just gonna take that?"

Annie placed a gun against his head. "Inside voices," she said.

"You'll get some of the gas, too," said Harry. "Come with me."

Kimo, Scoggins and I strode with him up a hill behind the loading rack, while Xochitl stayed behind. One of the bluebacks met us and whispered something to Harry, and we waited while they strategized. Flashlight blobs were all over the terminal now. Bluebacks were prepping the machinery that would bottom-load fuel into a truck; others were posted outside the office.

To me, Scoggins whispered, "This is so bad."

Someone down the hill shouted: a man's voice, reverberating around this complex, presumably one of the camo-wearing men Harry's group had just captured. I couldn't understand what he was saying, and he was cut short. But it had been loud. I saw the outline of Harry's face, listening, calculating. The other blueback also strained to hear, while he handed Harry a set of keys. We all held our breath. The silence seemed fragile. But it was fine, nobody had been rousted. I heard the blueback whisper, "…650 gallons per minute."

Then a light in the office came on.

"Uh-oh," said Harry.

Gunfire, quasi-distant, like balloons popping—but someone nearby fell. This other blueback covered his flashlight, and Harry had a pistol quite near my face, but he was pointing it elsewhere. More shots, and I smelled cordite.

"We still go!" Harry said. "Keep 'em pinned inside as long as you can! Make sure they don't get near the loading rack! And you," he handed me a flashlight and the keys. "There's a truck parked up there. Get it down to that rack."

"…"

"Now, son. Unless you'd like to stay here shoot some people."

Kimo elbowed me, and we ran: we crested the hill and saw the 3,000-gallon tanker they intended to fill. It was the only one parked up here; the idea had been to put it in neutral and roll it down to the rack without the noise of ignition. Now noise didn't matter. But whoever scouted the tank farm hadn't realized: some security-obsessed proprietor had clamped on a wheel lock.

I went through the keys on this ring, and none fit the big yellow disk of that lock.

The tanker wasn't moving, ignition or no.

There was a fence back here behind a line of trees abutting another property, topped with barbed wire. But even if we climbed the fence and cut the wire, Xochitl was down there in the middle of a firefight.

I said to Kimo, "You look for her, I'll see if one of those guards has the key to that lock."

Scoggins said, "What about me?"

I shone my light on him then switched it off. "I don't care."

Kimo and I rumbled back down the hill. Everybody's flashlights were off. We passed near the spot where we'd last seen Harry, and maybe he was still there: it was too dark to tell. Gunfire was more sporadic, and mostly consisted of bluebacks discouraging the office occupants from exiting. We found the driveway. Someone nearby fired, probably not at us, but metal was whistling through the air and that was insane. It was the reason you drove off the road or sprawled in a ditch or hid on a farm; it was the sum of a dying world's terrors. The jeep's headlights were off now but we stumbled into it. I tripped over something that felt like a body. I heard Kimo stage-whispering Xochitl's name.

I tried to feel through this dead person's pockets, and realized I didn't know whose side he'd been on. I had no choice: I flicked on my flashlight, and saw camouflage. But the pockets were empty. There was another guard, alive, trying to hide in the jeep's wheel well.

He said, "Turn out the fucking light!"

I shone it directly at him: the one with a tooth missing. "Turn it off!"

Someone shot in this direction. I moved further from the jeep, kept the light on him.

"Fuck!" said the guard, and he stood and ran, and I tracked him. Bluebacks began firing at him: a shiny flattop hairdo and camo fatigues. He zigzagged to get away, but the terminal's front lawn was huge, empty and flat. I ran after him bearing light as my armament. There were more shots and I saw him go down.

I found him on the ground, holding his arm. He said, "I surrender, don't shoot."

I turned off the flashlight and jabbed it into his back. I heard a dog or a coyote howl; we were probably close to the road. "There's a lock on the tanker wheel. If you have the key, I won't kill you."

"I have it. I do."

So I marched him through a field crispy with dead grass, and the guns were quiet again. He didn't run. The soldiers in that office had turned out their lights. I wondered if they had night-vision goggles; the bluebacks apparently didn't. We pushed back up the hill and someone grazed against my side. A voice said, "I know a safe place that needs you." It was Xochitl.

"Yeah," I said, "maybe soon to be less safe."

We found Scoggins near the truck.

"We could just get out of here," I said.

"But we need gas," said Kimo.

"Yes," said Xochitl. I clicked the flashlight on Scoggins, who squinted and said nothing.

"You're part of the hack?" said the guard. "Is that what this is?"

Kimo gripped him around the back of his neck.

"Everybody knows it now," the guard said. "Everybody knows this is hackers taking over the grid. But nobody knows who."

Shots resumed; I saw flashes near the office.

"Unlock it," I said.

"Show me your gun first."

Kimo punched his kidney.

"I guess you're gonna have to shoot me."

"Unlock it," I said.

"I don't even have the key. You're gonna have to kill me, right up close. Look me in the eye and do it."

His arm was wounded and hung lifelessly and I remembered Ray pressing a gun barrel against Xochitl's broken hand. What had Elizabeth said? *You are what you can't stop doing.* Kimo punched him again.

But he was tough, much tougher than any of us even pretended to be. He started shouting:

"Up here! Hey! Shoot us! Shoot up here! They're stealing a tanker truck! Hey!"

Kimo slugged him in the back of the head, he fell forward and I lost my grip on him, he squirted away and ran out of the light, still yelling. I saw Xochitl's shape fall, and then there were shots whizzing all around us, and a different voice was hollering: a big wordless sound, Kimo spun around and hip-checked me into the tanker, I lost the flashlight which thumped to the ground and revealed our captive scampering and another form lunging after him, I wheeled around, a bullet hit the tanker close to my head and I dropped and felt a big tire's tread scrape my back, Xochitl was saying something nearby and I couldn't understand her, Kimo was crouched next to me, I could dimly see the guard as he reared to his full height and shouted instructions— "Fire! Fire! Up here! Shoot!"—then someone tackled him—a spine-rattler—and it was the punter: Scoggins laid him out, and they tumbled down the hill and I heard Xochitl saying something but I didn't see her, and I stood and heard those guns, heard more bullets hit the trees behind us, and then a person was coming at me, somehow through some trick of reflected light I could see his figure roaring this way and yes I could hear his footfalls, I braced because he was coming straight at me and there was no time to slink aside, this person had impact and damage in mind, and I heard Xochtil saying a word, and I prepared for the contact that would mash me backwards into the tanker, then from behind me came a hissing and from over my shoulder something orange streaked past my ear and it was an arrow that sunk squarely into the man's chest and he fell and his face landed against the flashlight and it was the guard with the missing tooth and I listened harder and Xochitl was saying my name.

I picked up the flashlight and found her on the other side of the truck.

Kimo was with me, and Edward stepped close with his crossbow. He said, "What's taking so long up here?"

She was face down.

I didn't want to look. I wanted out of there. Just get me alone back out into the dark world and I'd be all right.

She said, *"Dónde estoy?"*

I kneeled and slipped my hand under her hip and rolled her toward me.

She was on her back and I shone the light over her, looking for blood.

She said, *"Híjole."*

Edward leaned over her, tried to help, but she clubbed him away with her cast. A couple more bluebacks surrounded us. The perimeter seemed to be closing.

"Are you hit?" I said. "Are you hurt?"

She propped up on her elbows. I could see a gash where she'd cracked her forehead on something. Kimo patted his hands on her body. She watched him do it. He checked his hands for blood, and finding none he laughed, he tapped a knuckle on the top of my head and left us. Xochitl said, "What hit me?"

I hugged her. My nose was against her neck and something big was in my stomach. I thought I could control it, no problem. Then a heat came into my face and I saw myself at various points in my life, alone and soldiering on because there were no other options, and then I didn't want to control it any longer. I took a moment's break from monitoring the forces within me and one pure fact came into the clear: I discovered I was crying. I shook, I slobbered on Xochitl's neck, she hugged me back. I couldn't stop and it was strange, but I just did it.

The tanker started up. Kimo had found the wheel-lock key in the dead soldier's pockets. We got out of the way. He rolled forward; he didn't turn on the headlights and couldn't see the pathway but it didn't matter: he barreled down the hill drawing gunfire, heading for the loading rack. The bluebacks left us; the action left us. I dripped tears and snot into Xochitl's hair.

"You're a good man," she said.

The scene below was entirely aural—diesel grumble and bullets—until Kimo pressed his brakes and everything lit up red. We could see a dozen bodies on the ground. People scampered around the truck, someone attached a hose, someone else fell.

"Is it smart to shoot at a gas pump?" said Xochitl.

Bluebacks raced around the tanker like a pit crew. Others concentrated fire on the office. It was the kind of madness I'd spent a half-year avoiding. More. Kimo turned off the truck and everything was dark again.

"It could blow up," I said.

"Yes."

"But we're not leaving him alone sitting in the middle of that."

"No." She touched my arm. "Where's Jon?"

We ran down there, and the shots were closer and sounded like bulbs popping. We found the tanker by the loading rack's hum. I felt around for the cabin, the door handle, couldn't find it. I said, "Kimo!" The hose had been pumping for a couple minutes, we were standing there, it was dark, fuel was splashing in the tanker from underneath and it seemed we might get away when someone screamed: "Holy shit!" and "Go! Go! Go!" and the gunfire changed to the rapid thwack of an automatic rifle. Xochtil and I stood on the driver side and the truck shielded us, but we could hear dozens of bullets ripping through the tank and banging off pavement and killing men, hundreds of bullets, a detonation orders of magnitude louder and more terrifying than a few firecrackers.

I had a moment of stupid indignation. The soldiers guarding this place should've let us go. We were taking a tiny fraction of their reserves. Was it worth this much ammunition and bloodshed?

Xochitl and I shouted, "Drive! Drive! Drive! Drive!" but either Kimo couldn't hear or he'd been shot. I didn't know how the fuel loader worked, whether pulling away with a hose still attached would start a leak or a fire, but it didn't matter: just on the tanker's other side was a slaughter. It was hopeless, I couldn't hear any return shots, only the machine gun repeating. We were pinned here, I couldn't see, the bluebacks were dead or in retreat.

For a fraction of a second, by reflex, I felt back for the loneliness I always touched: the sense of my sealed-off bee cell that was always my shame and excuse and comfort, the thing that kept me quiet and uncomplaining because it was the hive into which I'd been born and inside which I'd die. Aloneness. There was no resentment, there was acceptance, because at least I was honest with myself: we're alone, we're alone in life and it's all right, it's the natural order, and the tools that supposedly connected us—television! the Internet! smartphones!—were hilarious, departed lies. As always, I momentarily felt for the comfort of this self-knowledge.

And I found only its absence. Bullets whirred in the air like insects and I didn't know myself.

Who was this messy person, without all his old tranquilizers?

Hopeless, helpless, enmeshed: I thought soon the men in camouflage would come around to this side of the tanker or start shooting our legs from the other side. But there was a new sound, a lower register, audible in gunfire: the tanker's engine restarting.

Kimo!

He did: somehow he got it going.

He stood on the accelerator and the truck moved beneath our backs. Xochitl took my hand and we ran along with it. No light, but a wrenching sound—a pipe snapping free—and the automatic rifle kept firing blindly, I found a truck-step and pulled myself up, dragged Xochitl up with me, we pressed ourselves against the tank and we were off.

The driveway went on forever then the truck turned left and we heard fuel sloshing around. Kimo kept going, I looked back and in the pre-dawn I couldn't tell if anyone was chasing. Xochitl said something in the wind.

It lasted about a half-mile. Then we slowed, and the world was infinitesimally lighter: I could see we were stopping between a car wash and another substation. Our brakes rasped. I jumped off the truck and up to the cabin, pulled open the door and Kimo was lying across the front seats.

There was a lot of blood. It looked black. He said words, nothing I could verify.

Out the shattered front windshield, I saw two sedans pull up.

Bluebacks.

Edward got out of one car, Annie the other.

She said, "You're leaking gas there."

"..."

"It's all right, we'll patch you up. And relax: if you're really working a farm, I promise there were militias that already knew about you."

18

Clooney had New Orleans in mind but never even got us to Shreveport. Something resembling the U.S. Army barricaded the highway north of the city and established that most pedestrian of doomsday phenomena: a sawhorse security checkpoint. A kid with a clipboard turned us away.

We backed up and got down off the highway, where oaks were rusting and a big inflatable gorilla advertising fireworks was still somehow upright. The Tacoma's windows were down and Majido said, "Hear that?"

I did. It was music.

We drove past some franchise restaurants that still showed signs of life—if not food—and the music got louder: steel electric slide, cranked up high.

"Is that live?" said Majido.

Clooney said, "Not unless someone around here resurrected Gregg Allman."

"..."

"Yeah, that's 'Whipping Post.'"

Dozens of people were gathered in the parking lot of a paint-and-collision shop, so many folks that we couldn't even see what they were all looking at. Rawboned dudes in jeans and cowboy boots, women wearing purple college sweatshirts, men in camouflage, families wandering in from both sides: many on tiptoes, straining to see how this miracle was happening. Someone was blasting an old live recording that went on and on, solo after solo, and we parked near a few other cars, and we joined the crowd. As the guitar tapped out coy patterns around the drums, I saw some of the people around us shaking their heads and crying, the religious experience of momentarily regaining a lost thing.

I followed Clooney to the parking lot's boundary and eased ahead to see.

It was a quieter moment in the song. Up front, big men with goatees had their heads bowed and their eyes closed and their faces scrunched. In front of a garage someone had parked twenty more cars, lined them up door-to-door and propped open their hoods. Jumper cables ran from each car's battery, along the grass, to some kind of electrical junction and then a soundboard, and an older guy in a straw hat and flip-flops had hooked up two big speaker stacks from which the guitars now accelerated again.

We listened along with everyone else. The guitar played "London Bridge Is Falling Down" and a little later the singer's voice said, "Lord don't you know I feel like I'm dying."

It ended and the audience went crazy. We did, too. There was still music occasionally—some house we passed through might have a generator and a CD player—but nothing this loud or communal. I hadn't realized I'd missed it.

The man played songs for a long time and the crowd spread out into the street. For a while Majido would call out the titles ("Saturday Night Special!" "The Night They Drove Old Dixie Down!"), and I watched Clooney start assessing people around us. He talked to a kid in a camo hunting jacket but I couldn't hear. The kid showed him the guns he had strapped to his waist and Clooney nodded. Some guys wearing oily baseball caps around us watched this kid with hostility. A couple genuine-looking army men slid forward in the crowd—flak jackets and helmets—and they wanted to enjoy the music, too, and the civilians around them offered a wide berth. Majido sneered at me and my growing-back hairdo, swallowed a pill, and tried to talk to a tall woman in a sundress.

After more songs, Clooney followed the hunting-jacket kid over to an ATV and they got on in tandem formation and drove away.

A man next to me said, "Nothing good has been this loud for a while."

It felt stupid to still be standing there. It's not like we had some pact that said we never let each other out of sight, but usually I was given some hint of a plan. By the time fat Majido had struck out with the ladies in our immediate vicinity, I was no longer charmed by this concert. He said, "You hungry?" and I was. We got in the Tacoma, whose cab felt spacious with two people. I was irritated with Clooney and it was vengeful and good to drive, but then the further we went the more I realized there'd be no way for him to find us again.

"Yeah," said Majido. "Real tragedy to lose that asshole." But he didn't mean it; we'd been together a long time that felt like even longer.

I wanted to say turn back, but there was no telling Majido anything.

We drove the way we'd come, back past the gorilla and under the highway. He skirted south on country lanes, past impoverished houses then west on I-220. But every time a sign pointed toward downtown Shreveport, there was another checkpoint. From afar we saw a small airport with its fleet grounded and tailfins akimbo. Majido seemed to've been here before. He zigged over a river and through a low-rise suburb where cars still obeyed stop signs. He turned the wheel hard, arm-over-arm. We didn't have that much extra gas with us.

He said, "Ah-ha!" We turned right at a car dealership

where the windshields were all smashed. A billboard advertised a casino. We took a ramp up to a bridge and I could see a dark brown river and the tall buildings of Shreveport beyond, but we got halfway across and there were more soldiers and we couldn't pass.

"Please turn around, sir," said one of them.

"Why can't I go downtown? I have a friend who lives over there."

"You don't anymore, sir," said the soldier.

"How do you know who I know? These are public roads. That's public property down there. I want to know what gives you the right."

This burly guy with his sunglasses and his wedding ring actually took a moment to look at the hardware hanging from a strap around his shoulder, and half-smiled.

"What can I do?" Majido said. "What would it take to get into the city?"

"Sir, I'm not authorized to take your questions or engage in speculation with you. I need you to turn around your vehicle and head back that way."

"Do they have electricity in there? Is that what it is? All right. We're going."

We returned west and traded a bottle of amoxicillin for some strawberries.

Majido menaced the autumn sun. I wanted to go back and find Clooney, though I didn't know how. We'd acquired a second rifle in Fort Smith—which is a euphemistic way of saying Majido discovered a dead body while pissing one morning, and the guy had been shot in the face behind a bus station and the rifle was there on the ground, too—and now it was Majido's favorite: he regularly ran a washcloth over its stock and took it apart and cleaned its components, and right now he tapped its barrel against the Tacoma's rear bumper, berry juice on his lips, managing some kind of internal reckoning. Cars went by and children peeked out at him, unblinking.

After a long while he said, "All right. Fuck those guys. We're going in."

"…"

"You can swim, right?"

We left behind the Tacoma, we left everything. We strolled down a riverside walkway behind a shuttered sporting goods store, into a forest and through a field. Then we walked into the water: it was warm and brown and whenever one of us splashed, a cloud of silt gathered around us. It was a thousand feet across and I was swimming in my shoes and Majido was in his dumb boots. But it was all right. Partway across I heard Majido say to himself, "No snakes, no gators. No snakes, no gators."

We came out gasping at the little airport. I saw bayou cypresses and cracked pavement. We dragged ourselves south and found an unguarded trestle bridge and we crossed it and were in downtown Shreveport. Several blocks of skyscrapers were laid out to the west. Riverboat casinos were moored in the brown muck. We pressed our backs against a parking garage.

"Now," Majido said, "what are they protecting down here that's so important?"

Some cars were in this garage, a few passed through the streets, but nobody was out here walking around. This had to be a city of a couple hundred thousand people, but it seemed most of them had been driven out, just as my neighbors and I had been.

Majido tramped ahead and I tagged along. A barbershop was chained up tight, a bank branch was dark, but we saw a few people shuffling into a building with faux Greek columns and we looked up, and a sign said "Hustler Club." Majido cocked his head. He jogged over to the entrance and I followed.

The electric signboard wasn't lit, there was no music or air conditioning, but inside business was brisk. Lantern stations were set up all over the club: a speakeasy vibe. Men reclined on couches and nearly naked women grinded on them. On the central stage, three leather-clad ladies pretended to whip each other with cat o' nine tails. Someone behind a closed door was having sex. A short woman in a sequined teddy greeted us and introduced herself: Annabel. "There's a spot right over here y'all will love," she said, and brought us to a pair of leather chairs near a stripper pole. "Tonight we're serving bourbon, if that's all right."

"That would be mighty fine," said Majido.

She brought two brown drinks. Majido tried to give her mine, but Annabel demurred. The same scene repeated in each break in the darkness: recumbent men straining upward, covering for their awkwardness by feigning awkwardness, pretending to offer control to stone-faced supplicants who pretended they didn't want it.

To Annabel, I said, "Do the lights ever go on? Do you ever have electricity?"

"In here? No, honey."

"How about anywhere in this city?"

She put her foot on the table between Majido and me, touched her own thigh. "New to the Ratchet? You here to save a poor southern girl who needs saving?"

"Absolutely," said Majido.

"So many of these boys come in all dressed up. I like a man who's comfortable." She turned and put her be-thonged rump in Majido's face.

I said, "There's food delivery. It comes into the city where?"

"Oh, good food, for sure," said Annabel. "We can hook you up."

"What do you think happened?" I said. "What do you think made the lights go out?"

She scooted between our chairs and faced me. She bent forward at her hips, so her butt crowded Majido and her boobs pressed against me. Into my ear she said, "Silly. We all died, and we're in heaven. Or maybe the other place."

"…"

"Now," she said, stepping back, "I believe this here's the time when I need to see the skrilla."

Majido looked at me and began unzipping his fly.

"No, shit, not that," said Annabel. "Your money, honey."

"Oh," Majido said, "yeah, this was sort of unscheduled, and we weren't carrying our wallets so maybe—" but Annabel plucked away our glasses and was gone, and two big men rushed from the darkness and rousted us from the club. The sun killed my eyes and Majido sneezed a dozen times.

"Jesus," he said. "Jesus, what were you doing in there?"

"…"

"Is that how you seduce somebody? Christ, man, look at you. Would you stop thinking about what your face looks like for five minutes? Stop worrying what people will think. Jesus. 'Do the lights go on? What made the lights go out?' For once in your fucking life, why don't you be a real man?"

It did take me a long time to realize they treated me badly.

We walked deeper into the city. Five- and ten-story buildings still stood, still had flags whipping around them. A big white structure marked Government Plaza had a few men standing out front, arms folded, casually opining in a post-lunch manner. They wore business suits. We hurried by. A woman wearing a blouse and a skirt moved past us on the sidewalk, first distracted then inspecting us. A library, an empty greeting card store…a diner that seemed open, with people waiting in line behind plate glass. A year ago this scene would've seemed like a Cold War nightmare; now it was tempting for its vague impersonation of what I'd understood "civilization" to mean.

We stepped inside the diner and took a place at the back of the line. There were no tables, nobody eating, no actual evidence of food. The guy in front of us was reading a paperback. A woman slept in a chair. Majido seemed ready to strike up a conversation with somebody, but he sucked his teeth instead. I saw someone's face in the kitchen door's porthole, but nobody came out. Maybe if we waited long enough, somebody's to-go order would be filled. Even with the weirdness and the relative desolation, it was a tiny bit thrilling to be here: months of creeping decline—the holding pattern that came with faith in public institutions, the inner abandoned children in us all, the curdling cooperation, the hunger and inertia, the Springdale woman standing naked in a park offering breast milk to troubled passers-by, the dirty teenage girl we found sleeping in the Tacoma's bed in Texarkana, the pack of very small kids who poured weeping out of a trailer park but when we tried to calm them started kicking and biting us, the suicides-by-hanging we'd started to see more of just the past few days—seemed momentarily reversed in a line for takeout.

The waiting patrons seemed to know each other, or at least to understand and mutually accept what was happening. Finally, an older woman came into the dining room and said, "Nothing today, I'm sorry." And the people grumbled a little, but nothing more. They checked their wind-up wristwatches and looked out the window at the sky and straggled outside. We followed; they dispersed.

Majido and I walked around for a couple hours. Stores were open, a few people were inside, but nobody was doing any business. In a lot marked Artisans Court that advertised an open-air arts fair every Saturday, there were no sleeping people, only a mural of the American flag and the Statue of Liberty and the legend "Second To None." Anywhere else we'd been, this place would've been overrun with folks hoping for handouts. We walked to the building Majido's friend lived in, but the people who answered in his apartment didn't know the friend. A few well-dressed women queued outside a different restaurant. A movie theater and a hipster clothing shop seemed open, but I couldn't tell for what. The few people we saw were white.

I heard a generator's buzz and we followed the sound past an apartment building, via some law offices inside which I saw a person in a full-body animal suit apparently performing calisthenics for onlookers. The generator noise was further east: it came from the parish courthouse, whose lawn was sun-dappled and trimmed and green. We climbed stairs to an engraved archway and inside the door hung an electrolier that worked. The front hall was bright.

Nobody protected the place. We walked right in through a metal detector.

Portraits of old men stared down, and panoramic photographs of Caddo Parish. After months of this, my instinct was to find items to pilfer: the artifacts inside this curio cabinet, or something in a desk. Majido, a former security guard, strutted around the lobby, but we were both careful not to make echoing footsteps. I smelled food: something spicy. It was crazy to be in this place, but every day was crazy.

A kid in uniform was at the end of a long hallway, sitting against a radiator, eating something out of a plastic box. He saw us. Majido wandered over bearing law enforcement's smug entitlement. I stayed closer to the door. Majido's voice became lost in echoes and the kid didn't get up, a victory of posture; the kid wanted to be left alone and here was this jerk. Majido got louder; I still couldn't make out what he was saying as he made big shapes with his arms. And the kid just sighed, and he put down his food, and he sized up Majido and stood…and he was huge. Majido took a step back and the kid in uniform spun him around and pushed him against the lobby wall, and I thought I should run except now it felt like a prison-break movie, how would I get out of Shreveport? Would they just let me walk out?

"Hey!" said Majido. "Jesus! Hey!"

I said, "What are you eating over there?"

"Huh?" said the kid.

I moved closer. He was six-foot-six and had his knee

against Majido's back.

"I said what's that you're eating?"

He looked at his plastic box with the fork sticking out, back over on the radiator. "Neckbones. I think pork."

"Sounds good."

He almost smiled. "It's terrible. Probably not pork. Might be cat."

Majido managed to squeeze enough air out of his lungs: "What'd I say?"

"You didn't say anything, fool. One look and I know you don't belong here."

"Ahh! C'mon, lemme go."

I said, "I guess it's not very good here."

The kid removed his knee from Majido and stepped away. His bald scalp and muscles shone in the electric light. He said, "Yeah, whatever."

"..."

"Why you even wandering in here? Bothering people when they eat?"

"Well, I'm an agent of chaos," said Majido.

"If it's not very good here," said the kid, "then take a walk."

"Seems like your job should be run us out of town," I said. "If there's so many people guarding the city, how can you let us get away once we're in?"

The uniformed kid resumed his place by the radiator, picked up his fork again. "Dude, if you want to hang around these parts and catch yourself a big dose of crazy, you can feel free."

"..."

"Okay fine," he said, "I just arrested you. You got the right to remain whatever. That make you happy, being under arrest? Go down there, right around the corner there. Go through that door, talk to the man." He scooped out another neckbone and bit down. The pause before he chewed broke my heart a little.

We followed his instructions. There wasn't anything else to do. Majido crumpled his nose at me, jeered like a child.

The door around the corner led into a large courtroom: a cavernous, glass-ceilinged place with several rows of pews for onlookers, leather magistrate chairs and a wide semicircular table—all empty—leading up to the judge's bench and a wood balcony high above. One man was in here, on the bench, white head down and writing. He heard us come in.

We were small, approaching Oz from below. Who wouldn't hear echoes from a thousand tribunal railroad jobs? And this is the reason for institutions: the heavens may fall, but people will ever fear faceless things in pretty rooms. The man finished writing and focused on us, and we were close enough to him that I could see some social switch flip. He stood quickly, self-effacement in his posture, an acknowledgment of his own mild rudeness.

"Hey! Hi there. Welcome." He stepped down from the bench and came around to our side. "Mikey Dallenbach. How are you guys doing?" He had silver hair but seemed young: a pale handsome guy in a white dress shirt with the sleeves rolled up and the collar undone, an architect staying late at the office. He shook our hands and said, "Have a seat, if you'd like," and we did. We sat at the big lawyers' table and he stood with his hip against it. The lights in here weren't on, but the glass ceiling made it bright. "How can I help you?" said Mikey.

"I wouldn't say no to some food," Majido said.

"Of course, of course. Absolutely, we'll get you something. What would you like?"

Majido wasn't dumb. He waited for the other shoe to drop, but Mikey just smiled at him. So he said, "Uh, rice?"

"Just rice."

"Yeah. Yes. Sure, I don't want to…impose."

Mikey spread his fingers and wrinkled his brow comically.

I said, "Do you know what's happening? Why the power

is out and when it's coming back?"

He assessed us. His teeth were clean, his stubble only a day old. "Oh, you don't live in Shreveport. You're visitors."

"…"

"I'm sorry, I mistook you for constituents. Welcome to our city. What's that they say? 'A City On The Grow.'"

"Thanks," Majido said.

"Yeah, the electricity," said Mikey. "That's the big one. Unfortunately I don't think anyone around here knows what happened. We've had emissaries from the federal government going parish to parish, but the story changes. They always seem vaguely optimistic, but it strikes me bureaucrats are born that way." He interrupted himself and asked me, "Do you really want anything? We'll get some sandwiches for you guys. Do you like crayfish?"

"Okay, thanks," I said.

"Of course. You're guests. Well, you'll find our people are doing okay. Life-goes-on, sort of thing. We lived millions of years without it, people did all right. I guess there's an adjustment period. But what people want out of life hasn't changed. Enough food, shelter from the storm, a way to be productive, a way to connect with other people. Love and be loved. I guess that's what life is when you trim away the fat, cut out the unnecessary wires."

Majido said, "I got a buddy here, born and raised. Somebody else is living in his apartment."

"That's strange," said Mikey. "We'll help you find him for sure. We'll give Clark his name. I'm sorry about that…it must've been a shock."

"The city's guarded," Majido said. "You're keeping people out."

"…"

"There are soldiers across the river, and we came here south on the highway. You've got army roadblocks set up to keep people from coming in."

Mikey cocked his head like a parrot.

"And where are all the people who live here?" said Majido. "It's a ghost town. You kicked them all out?"

"We definitely did not," Mikey said. "I'm not sure what you're even…. It's not like I run the city or anything. I'm a judge, and I hope I'm a good representative of the parish, but I can tell you with all due seriousness and intent everybody is welcome in the city of Shreveport. The more the merrier."

"…"

"Guys, this is pretty strange. *You're* here."

"We swam," said Majido. "They wouldn't let us come over the bridge so we swam in. Look at us."

"You look fine to me. I don't know what to say, we'll…let's go out right now, the three of us, and you can show me what you're talking about. I'm happy to do it. I'm frustrated you've had a bad time in our city but I have to believe it's a misunderstanding."

I looked up at the balcony, then behind us, the way we'd come in. I figured Mikey was stalling with nonsense, and someone was about to burst in and detain us.

Mikey said, "Wait, are you guys pulling my leg?"

"…"

"All right. I'm sorry your friend doesn't live in the same apartment, and obviously you can't call him or text him. That's frustrating, but nobody's been kicked out. Everybody's allowed in. Life's a little slower now, we're all figuring this out." His expression grew wizened. "Is this because we've got generators in the courthouse?"

I looked at the portraits on the walls: white men in robes, from ancient oils to full-color photographs, powdered wigs to fussy comb-overs. I said, "They make you sit for one of those things?"

Mikey blinked, saw where I was pointing. "Oh, yeah. It's tradition, right? But we ran out of wall space. I'm hanging in the back hall. I get to pass my own goofy mug back and forth on the way to chambers."

"I know what I saw," Majido said. "We had to drive all

around the city, you've got it choked off."

"Guys," he said, "tell you what. Let me get someone to bring you some food. That's the first order of hospitality, all right? And when you're done eating, we'll walk around the city and you'll show me what you're talking about, and in the meantime we'll work on seeing who knows your friend. I'll personally send Clark over to your friend's apartment—what used to be your friend's apartment—and we'll get to the bottom of it. Cool? Sound okay?"

"..."

"You'll see with your own eyes. Everything's calm, everything's normal. As normal as it can be." He pushed away from the table, nodded at us dryly, and strode out the courtroom door.

Majido stood and his chair rolled away. "He's not getting us food."

"..."

"He's crazy or lying."

"..."

Majido looked up as the sun appeared from between clouds and made shadow-grids across our faces. "Maybe both."

We waited. When Mikey didn't come back right away with army men, it was possible to believe he was fetching food. But then it took *too* long, we sat there twenty minutes, half-an-hour, and it seemed he wasn't coming back at all. Majido walked up to the judge's bench and examined the papers Mikey had left behind. I followed and saw: an official-looking legal brief with a "FILED" stamp across the top, on which Mikey had been stenciling an accomplished and elaborate silhouette of a person falling from the sky, arms and legs outstretched, with one hand gripping the handle of a supermarket shopping cart, which was also falling and whose contents were spraying out into the wind. We looked at each other, and there was nothing to do but laugh a little.

"So it's all bullshit," said Majido.

He walked down the back stairs into the hallway behind the bench. I went, too: and it was true, the judges' portraits really did carry on down the hall. It was quiet and dark, but I could see that Mikey's photograph actually was up there. He was serious and his robes looked sateen.

The door to his chambers was locked. He hadn't come back this way. Where had he gone? Had he run? There was a fire exit: Majido pushed it open and no alarm sounded. The sun made him sneeze again, he fumbled for his sunglasses and the fishing hat, we were outside in a small courtyard and the uniformed kid—the big bailiff who'd been eating neckbones—was out here smoking a cigarette. The sight of us made him grimace.

"What the fuck is going on in this place?" Majido said.

"Yeah," said the kid, blowing smoke.

"You're Clark?"

"I am."

"Judge Mikey told us you'll figure out what happened to my friend."

"Well," said Clark, "I'm not gonna do that."

Majido sneezed ten times and we watched him. He said, "Are there crayfish? He was going out to get us some crayfish."

"…"

"They forced the people who lived in this city out of their homes," Majido said. "Why'd you stay?"

"Because they let me," said Clark.

"So there *is* food."

"Sometimes you got to choose," Clark said. "Give up the daughters, give up the guests, that kind of thing. Neither option is very good but you got to choose. How do you boys like it right now out there in the big world?"

"It has its moments," said Majido. "Today we saw a concert."

"People are crazy and there ain't no crayfish." He said it to me, looking directly down into my dumb expression. His uniform was a size too small and strained against his enormous biceps. In his mind, he was living proof of his own story. But I thought: strong or weak, it didn't matter, the things we told ourselves on a long drive or sitting in an abandoned courthouse lobby were nothing, what we pretended we believed about the next day didn't matter, it all broke down before the truth of those you met and what they were prepared to do for you, or to you.

Then again, those you met were probably lying, too.

"At least things ain't violent in here," said Clark. "Maybe sometimes a little tense, is all."

Majido said, "Where does the food come into Shreveport?"

Clark pulverized his cigarette against the courthouse. "Probably time for you boys to get out, yeah?"

"How do you make the army guys stay?" said Majido.

". . ."

"The army guys set up all around this place. The ones your boss pretends he doesn't know anything about."

"Well," the kid said. "I guess they must think they're guarding a place that's still standing." He swaggered away, through the courtyard and back inside.

Majido looked at me and okay, yes, I felt unnerved. But hadn't I been making peace with a lonesome dusty death my whole life? Hadn't my uncompromising choices kept me untethered, which was probably why I was still alive? I gave Majido a withering look back and it really did hurt him, my hard shell.

We walked around this walled-off downtown some more, and saw a brigade of troopers guarding an old brick building on Elvis Presley Avenue. Maybe it was a makeshift food repository but we couldn't get close. Majido chose a tall apartment building on Cotton St. and we climbed through a broken door and up a dozen stories onto the roof. But what was there to see? A dead spaghetti interchange and a couple abandoned highways. A greenbelt west and north of the city.

Some suburbs south. And every downtown access point roadblocked by lazy toy soldiers. The horizon was flat. The river rusted east.

We got out. We strolled down Texas St., walked right out on the center stripe up the bridge's back hump, and approached the soldiers who'd turned us away a few hours ago from behind. They were surprised to see anyone leaving. They didn't recognize us, and didn't stir much. We walked back to the Tacoma and I saw a rabbit in some bushes, looking frightened and forlorn.

Majido drove us back north around the city and into the sunset, past the inflatable gorilla. When I saw that the concert crowd had dispersed: that was the first moment I felt panic over potentially losing Clooney. We got out and the DJ in the straw hat was hanging with friends, drinking wine from the bottle. He wore a sweatshirt that said "Crazy Cat Lady." We asked if he knew where Clooney was and described him.

"Pull up a lawn chair, guys," he said. It was getting chilly but they were bare-legs-crossed and reminiscing about the songs they'd just played: old cosmic cowboys too cool to worry about end times. Majido sat and accepted a long swig. One of the other dudes said, "If he got mixed up with those Visigoth kids, I bet I know where he is." Majido tossed me the keys.

He said, "I'll be right here, reaping what I sow."

By myself, I drove the Tacoma down a highway into darkness. I didn't drive much then. I left the dome light on so I could see scribbled-down directions. The art to not crashing in such total blackness was not to stare at the white line; the white line made you lose balance and veer off into the void.

I passed nothing for a good while, then I saw a sign and stopped where a hay bale had a snowman painted on its side. This was a Christmas tree farm and a zoo, abandoned, and an old plastic sign strung up between trees invited families to make a wish with Santa Claus. I turned left, kept going, saw the fuel gauge quivering below the one-eighth mark, watched my headlights take and give back each mile I crossed. I hadn't realized it would be so rural, and the further I went the less likely it seemed I'd run across Clooney. But I wanted to know what he was doing and who he was with.

The directions said take one more right and then keep going and look for three cow skulls on pikes. But now it was farmland and there was no moon; I clicked on the high-beams and leaned forward squinting. And I pressed down my foot, mad with impatience.

The way he'd detached from us, just getting on an ATV with a stranger and vanishing, the charming matter-of-fact shrug he'd given me, the little eye-roll. After so many weeks…such a nothing little gesture couldn't be the end.

When was the last time I was alone in a car?

I found the skulls and slowed. They demanded privacy: a harbinger. I still couldn't see any light other than my own. I crept forward, inspecting. Clooney was a needle in a stack of needles. He was a screen that invited projection, or he was a bug zapper whose laugh I liked. I rolled, just a few miles per hour. When I wasn't paying attention the road had turned to dirt and it seemed like a moonscape out there. A fence followed on my right. The posts materialized and vanished. But up ahead, something leaned against one of the posts, clearer every inch of my approach: an oversized post that became a shape that became a gate-guardian sculpture that became a human body. I stopped. A motionless human body, upright, clothed and propped and sagging. My high-beams were too bright, the body was washed-out and colorless. I felt for the Tacoma's headlight switch but didn't want to click, didn't want to know, not really. I idled a long time, trying to come up with a way out of it.

Then I clicked and the light was less direct and I could see it was a camouflage uniform. I rolled forward. It was a uniform like the ones we'd been seeing all day: a woodland disruptive pattern, computer generated. It was empty. The boots were attached to empty pants, the coat was draped across a wood post and barbed wire, the helmet balanced on top with goggles strapped in place. It looked like a scarecrow, and I guess so did I.

Something hit the driver side door, I felt it in my left side, and I heard it: a thump and the sound of smearing against glass, I jumped so hard I smacked my forehead on the Tacoma's ceiling, my foot accelerated the truck by instinct, I pulled away, and couldn't see anything, couldn't see what had hit me, but I heard someone shouting, "Wait! Wait!"

My head swiveled, I tried to see behind me, something was banging against the truck but I yanked around my neck, felt adrift, couldn't see. I rolled down the window and looked out and a red man was out there naked. He was barefoot and naked, and he was red because my brake lights bathed him. He was young and short and squat, brawny and neckless and buzzcutted, and crying. He came around the passenger side and slapped the window. Behind him, now I could see a few points of electric light: a ranch house. I unlocked the door, he opened it, clanged it against his knee while hurrying, yelped in pain, hopped into the cabin.

"Drive!" he said. "Just drive!"

I didn't. I took the keys and got out.

"They were gonna kill me!" he said. I found a Mexican blanket in the Tacoma's bed and passed it through the window. He covered himself and curled up shivering. I asked how many people were around here, I asked if he'd seen someone fitting Clooney's description. He might've been 18, maybe younger. He buried his face in the blanket and wouldn't speak more.

I told myself Clooney wasn't out there. He was probably already back at the concert venue, drinking wine and waiting for me. To the soldier in the front seat I said, "Do they call themselves Visigoths?" but he didn't answer. There was nothing else to do.

I brought a flashlight and walked up the ranch house driveway. It was a squat structure, tiny and dark and nowhere.

This wasn't the act of a brave person. I didn't feel brave. I just wanted my leader back.

I heard voices. Shouting. Maybe laughing. Were there other soldiers tied up around here, being tortured? I reached the house, put my ear to the front door. I continued around the side, shining my light into land that went on forever. There was something in me that said don't worry. Don't worry, because I wasn't important enough to be at the center of something big.

I turned the corner into a back yard and saw a campfire.

They didn't seem to be soldiers. There were seven or eight of them in big wooden chairs, toasting marshmallows on sticks. Lives were happening everywhere. I turned off my light and had the advantage. Unseen, I stalked the fire's perimeter, listening, hoping for some clue. It absolutely could've been the end of the road for me. It absolutely could've been a group of cannibals. All I wanted was to ascertain Clooney wasn't among them, that he wasn't tied up somewhere, and I'd leave without making contact.

I heard his voice. He was one of the silhouettes; he was among them.

I emerged into the firelight and heard guns click but bee-lined straight to him, where he sat in a chair. He saw me coming and got up and said, "Hey!" and he saw my expression and said, "Aww," and hugged me. And I hugged him back, I was a little taller, I felt him press and the relief melted me. Nothing had to change.

They handed me a bag of marshmallows and I sat and ate. The Visigoths viewed themselves as a resistance. One of them said, "Everybody outside the checkpoints looks inside and says it's not fair, what makes them so special? I'll say this for the people inside the city: they're giving us something to unify around. Something to strive for." They were plotting an invasion of Shreveport.

I didn't tell them they could just swim in.

Clooney said, "These boys were also just telling me

about what Tulsa's like now."

"Someone already did that invasion," said one of them. "Wish I'd been there."

"We can do the same for Shreveport," another said. "Gotta steal enough oil and gas reserves for seed capital, right? You get known for being a good place, you start attracting other people who've got fuel who want to live there."

"So what they were telling me," said Clooney. "If a person was to go up to Tulsa with a significant amount of gas, that person would be granted admission. And there's food and power and people living lives."

"I heard the streetlights are on," said one of the Visigoths around the campfire.

"I heard there's doctors and central heat," another said.

"But we're gonna be the founding fathers of New Shreveport."

"Except we're not calling it that."

"Just time to get the flat-earther fucks out of there. Accept the world as it really is."

"I was goddamn born and raised."

They wanted guards and gates, too. They just wanted to be on the inside. Guards and gates were damn enticing. I didn't ask about the naked man. I didn't say anything.

That night they got drunk on cans of Dixie and Clooney pretended to get drunk, too, but I could see him pouring out beer while nobody else was watching. I ate the whole bag of marshmallows because nobody stopped me. A couple of the Visigoths were arguing politics and a few others had fallen asleep in their chairs. The fire weakened. I felt something on my shoulder, and it was Clooney's hand. I looked at it. It was warm and it stayed a long while, and the combination of the fire's remaining heat and the cool autumn at our backs made me happy.

I listened to them talk, and felt drowsy, sated, safe. I wondered if now Clooney and I were Visigoths, too.

The hand on my shoulder wiggled for attention. He mouthed the words *follow me*. We got up and my heart's tempo went wild, we left the firelight and I turned on my flashlight but he covered it with his hand and I turned it off. I trailed the sound of his footfalls until we were around the ranch house's other side. He took the flashlight from my hand and shone it on a steel object resting on the brown grass. A fifty-gallon tank.

He whispered, "It's full of gas."

"…"

"Who are *these* guys?" he said. "Screw these guys. I want central heat."

And we did: we dead-lifted that tank and wobbled out onto the front lawn, and I thought there was no way he could've known I'd be here with the truck, what could his plans have been? He was the greatest improviser and I loved him.

And I flushed with relief that nobody had to get hurt. We slammed the tank down into the Tacoma's bed and hurried to get in, the naked man was in there sleeping and I shoved him between us, and Clooney grabbed the keys and we peeled out laughing like crazy people.

19

Kimo was critical. We stretched him beneath blankets, across the seats of a smaller tanker Annie gave us. The bluebacks didn't have real doctors, either. They said they were giving us four hundred gallons but there was no way to verify. Scoggins, Harry and many other bluebacks were dead or missing. I drove with Kimo's feet in my lap. Xochitl crouched on the passenger-side floor and pressed her hand on his waxen cheek.

We neared the ghost of I-49, the road that would take us past those golf courses with dead people in the trees, the road where Clooney was shot in the face, the fastest way back to the farmhouse…yet I knew if I just stayed on Route 102 we'd reach Tulsa in maybe three hours. From down there, Xochitl couldn't see where we drove. Kimo was unconscious.

Surely we had enough gas to get in. Just keep going west, see if it was true.

Because if it was true: they would have doctors and plasma and central heat. We could be surer of saving Kimo. Couldn't I turn around and drive right back to the farm, tell Elizabeth about my buried gas?

I paused at the entrance ramp.

I almost posed the question to Xochitl. I almost turned her distress for Kimo into permission.

But I followed the new morning onto the interstate. It might not be true about Tulsa, and also we had to get back and clean house.

It was only a day later. I don't know what I expected. I was surprised by snow on the ground. I was surprised by overgrown weeds in the hills. After Exit 10 the signs for Lodging and Food and Gas were clean and buoyant and sure of themselves.

Yes, the snow was still bad this far north and we pummeled down the ramp. But off the highway there were tracks: someone had been through here with an actual, real plow. I scanned the white tiers receding across the plain, checked the rearview, felt naked. *Someone around here had enough resources and time to plow the damn street!* And with all this gas, what a prize we'd make now! And isn't that always the way? The more you've got, the less communal you feel, and the more set upon from all sides.

Loaded down as the truck was, we did well in the drifts that remained. And the plow-tracks continued further east, further toward our home. My companions didn't know, and I didn't say anything. When I looked down at Xochitl, I kept a calm mask.

Twenty miles from the farmhouse…fifteen…ten…who had plowed? When had they done it? If we'd come this way yesterday, would they have stopped us? It felt like waking up and realizing you live next to a superpower.

Finally, just as the lifeless farms began, the plow-tracks ended and we met a three-foot snow barrier. I gunned it and battered in, finding it more melted than yesterday. Also we were taller and heavier and our wheels did spin asymmetrically and it felt crazy, but there were no other options. Nobody inside these tiny ranch houses stuck their heads outside at our commotion. We passed under phone and electric wires and they felt poignant to me; it was so easy to forget that things might never change back. We had one more turn to take and then we'd run into our own plow-marks from yesterday. I floored it, and swerved.

Xochitl was checking Kimo's pulse. I could feel his feet shivering.

Our momentum stalled. I backed up, revved it hard again, rocketed forward and heard our gas slosh. I kept thinking I saw the turn. This was so amateurish. People out here were organized.

But I decided we would make it. I just decided. I backed way up and smashed ahead, skidded, again and again. And there it was: a stop sign and a left turn, and evidence of yesterday's trip south via makeshift cowcatcher.

"Home soon," I told them.

We arrived, down the quarter-mile driveway and I couldn't help myself: I honked the tanker's horn. The white farmhouse looked smaller than in my memory and dirty in the snow, and nobody raced out to greet us and I thought there was a chance the farm had been raided. I climbed out from beneath Kimo's feet and jumped down and realized I was so tired I could barely stand. I didn't see any unfamiliar vehicles or any damage or dead bodies. I called for help, also anticipating praise.

They came out—Ben and Maribel and Morales and Paola and several others—and they seemed less chipper than yesterday. They patted my back and helped Xochitl out and admired the tanker, but it was a subdued welcome. I asked Maribel if anything was wrong and she said nothing other than Kimo being hurt, and I wondered if actually they were always like this, and maybe my mind had exaggerated the intensity of their fellowship. Maybe, after the gun battle, I was the one who'd changed.

They carried Kimo into the house. I looked at Ben and he said, "I'm not a doctor."

"I know," I said.

"You look almost as bad."

"I have to talk with Elizabeth."

"Does that thing have fuel in it?" said Ben.

"Supposed to be four hundred gallons."

He grinned and scratched his arm, and I didn't want him to say anything else. It was perfect.

I glanced down the hill, into the valley beyond the first shack: a single undifferentiated shape white with virginal snow. I hadn't really recognized its beauty before we left. The blue sky was warm and something flashed in my vision, maybe the false information of a capillary popping in my brain, or exhaustion. There was no life down there, not yet, but under that snow and ground the components of next year's survival were percolating.

I went inside. Ben had long since indexed the blood types of every resident who knew theirs. Several women with O-negative were lining up for Kimo. They put his giant frame in the central room, behind the stone fireplace, and hung bed sheets around him. Xochitl and I had bartered for an extensive first-aid kit that had needles and rubber tubing they could use for a transfusion. But nobody here could excavate bullets.

Maribel pushed me down the hall and said, "You need to rest. Whatever it is can wait."

"…"

"Let me get the generator running. Let the kitchen cook a hot meal."

"Don't let Charles out of anybody's sight," I said. "He's been lying the whole time."

She was everywhere, blocking me, herding me into her cubicle. She spun past me and danced and now was legitimately chipper. She said, "You sleep. Who doesn't lie a little?"

I fell on her mattress and she rubbed my shoulders and I lost time. I dreamed that I awoke inside that same cubicle, got up, walked back to the central room and found it populated with children. There was Young Maribel in a silly dress

wearing opera gloves and Young Fein sneering when he
thought nobody was watching and Young Kimo was
unconscious and bleeding, and Young Ben cooked in the
kitchen directing a team of other seven-year-olds, and Young
Charles was berating some other children, and Young
Elizabeth in her veil was sitting at a table, watching all the
others, writing it all down in a book. I sat across from her.
She lifted her veil. She had the face of a normal little girl. Her
eyes were purple. She said, "Do you think he did this because
we're women?"

I woke and it was partly dark out and the adult Maribel
had burrowed into my armpit, and she was snoring like a fat
king. Something metallic was gouging my stomach: hunger. It
wasn't the evening I'd returned. It was the next day's dawn.

I sat with Kimo inside his tiny tabernacle while many
others slept on the floor near the fireplace. He was gray and
unconscious and they'd wrapped gauze around his midsection
but it seeped crimson. I couldn't make his jackstraw tattoos
cohere into something I understood. Yes, yes, gentle giant:
except what role had he played in whatever Charles was really
doing?

I ate pancakes and then in the back bedroom I presented
my theories to Elizabeth:

"There's no way in the world every other human in the
area has mysteriously overlooked this place for seven months.
We just saw two pretty big armies basically fight an actual war
thirty miles away. Someone plowed the highway all the way
east from Anderson and then when they got close to us they
just stopped. And Charles has *not* been sending out people to
scout the area. Scoggins told us directly that he hadn't been
off the farm since he got here, that it was a big lie, he wasn't
driving around at all. He said they got that radio from
pilgrims."

"..."

"I know: what pilgrims? But put that aside. I've seen
Charles and Fein and Scoggins in the back barn, I've seen

them dragging supplies around. If someone's really been driving anywhere other than Xochitl and me, it's been very close by, to drop off food. Charles has been in touch with a militia, he's been dealing with them. It has to be. One night I heard a truck, I saw Charles and Fein walking back from the main road. Of course all he's worried about is defending this place. It's already under attack!"

"…"

"And building a wall around the farm, y'know, it means he probably has dreams of eventually fighting them off, which based on the firepower that's out there that we've just seen…is not ever going to happen."

She had a steaming cup of tea on her desk, and she seemed to be looking at it. She said, "I don't know what—"

"You know we've seen them," I said. "Marching around. Xochitl and I saw one standing out on the road just out there at the end of our driveway. Who's in charge of the food inventory?"

"Ultimately Charles is," she said.

She didn't move. I was choking with anger. We were silent.

And I thought: *oh no, what if she already knows, and what if she authorized it?*

I wanted to see her face. I had the arrogant belief, after all this, that I'd be able to read the truth.

It all made sense, except it made *more* sense if Elizabeth knew. She wasn't dumb. Wouldn't she ask about provision totals, wouldn't she notice missing amounts? Probably? Maybe? I didn't know how much free rein Charles had. Maybe she was too lofty and academic to notice. But exposing that kind of lie…what would it do to this place? Would people care they were paying a tariff—protection money—without knowing it? Why had she kept it a secret? What would she do to protect these facts?

I said, so calmly, "Did you already know all this, Elizabeth?"

She folded together her fingers and hunched over the desk, sort of a functionary's jurisdictional droop. She said, "Would it be terrible if I did?"

"…"

"If Charles making a deal like that was what it took to protect us?"

"Are you really asking?"

"I am."

"If you did this without telling anyone," I said. "That would be pretty terrible, yeah."

"…"

"Because what if whoever it is changes their mind, and meanwhile the rest of us have no idea they're even out there, eying us?"

She looked around the room. I wanted to tear off that veil. Right then it seemed the height of abstract impotence, guarding one's face like that: *I don't like being judged by my appearance so rather than try and change anything for the better I'll shut down the entire transaction.* All the veiled among us made secrets, or appeared to. I thought about my dream, Young Elizabeth with purple eyes, and I thought for sure the real Elizabeth was about to show me her true expression: horror or shame.

But she said, "Wait, then where did the radio come from?"

"You tell me," I said.

"I don't know that. He handed it to me the day I handed it to you. He had someone driving around checking up on you, that's what he said."

"…"

"…"

I said, "Fein and Scoggins didn't find it in a dumpster. I'm a hundred percent sure."

"Then it came from a soldier?" said Elizabeth. But of course not, why would a group of men who could blackmail us for food want us to be in touch with the outside world via radio? One of the first things Xochitl told me was that no soldiers had been to the farm, but Kimo found that cut barbed wire…these things I'd been told and the things I'd seen—quaintly, in the past I would've called them facts— alternately reassured and hoodwinked. I looked down at my own hands. Without realizing it, I'd snagged a novelty nameplate from the desk that featured a silhouette of a person on a tractor and a legend that read "This Is How I Roll," and I was turning it over in my hands, squeezing and flexing it with my fists…and my brain transmogrified it into that pry-bar. The one Fein had given me, the one I swung futilely at Charles's back.

The radio.

Trembling in that tunnel, Scoggins had said: *You shouldn't have stopped what they were doing to me, that first night. I know your hearts were in the right place, but you shouldn't have done it.*

Oh no.

I said, "Charles was looking for a way out."

I got up, I left Elizabeth's room, I walked out the side door. The air was warmer than freezing, the snow along the walkway that led to the livestock pens had iced over and gotten lumpy and dirty. I retrieved an ax from the back woodpile. Elizabeth was behind me, following. I detoured behind the generator's enclosure and heard it happily chugging. Somebody or something had chipped away pink paint from the enclosure's rear clapboard, and left shavings in the snow like a spray of blood. I passed Annie's tanker and clomped through drifts and Elizabeth kept pace, saying nothing, and nobody saw us: down a shoveled path, beyond some trees, and then along a utility road that led deep into the property. This was the way to the cinderblock barracks where they held me those many weeks before.

Elizabeth's voice bobbed as she said, "What do you think is happening?"

There were no vehicles parked outside the barracks. There were tracks in the snow, but they were like cement. Nobody had pulled up here in days.

I tried the barracks door and it was locked. I knocked and didn't hear a response. I swung the ax against the doorknob and it sparked. I looked around us, to see if anyone was watching. I swung again and a splinter of metal pinwheeled out and hit Elizabeth in her veil.

She stepped back. "It's all right," she said. "I'm all right."

I figured that the cowboy with the leather holster and the forearm flower tattoo would surely lunge out of the woods and stop this, because the people who control things and invent things have the eternal advantage over those of us who don't. But I swung again and felt spirits blow past me and against my neck, but it was actually the colder air from inside the barracks, rushing toward equilibrium.

The door was open. It was dark in the barracks. Nobody scurried into the sunlight. Elizabeth rushed past me and she said, "No no no no no no no."

It didn't really smell like anything.

But there were bodies: a bearded man sitting up on the cot under which I'd once cowered, a blonde woman on Fein's old cot with her arms around a child, two boys huddled in a corner. I didn't know their faces. None of them stirred. The water jug was gone. The table and the magazines were still here.

Elizabeth touched them all. I stayed in the doorframe and the wind outside blew snow down from the trees. The barracks had no heat. These poor pilgrims had died from exposure.

Elizabeth said, "Where is he?"

He was out by Ben's greenhouse with Fein, removing snow from the pilings for his presumptive wall. Elizabeth brought forty of us down out of the house to confront him. He handed over the holster and he said, "I'll bet that one killed the punter," and pointed at me.

We all looked back at him and made our judgmental mouths tiny.

20

I felt guilt.

I did, and maybe I shouldn't have, but Charles didn't interrogate pilgrims for admission anymore. He grew harsher because of me, and the fuss I'd made. After I'd interrupted Scoggins's inquisition, Charles had decided no more pilgrims: he couldn't trust anyone enough to let them stay or let them go.

He took their possessions. That frozen family had been carrying the radio.

Fein knew. Presumably Scoggins had known, too. Did it haunt them? They said so. They were tearful. Charles said what he'd done was a worse torment than being forced to leave the army rangers, to which I probably still didn't believe he'd ever belonged. I didn't know them as men, couldn't know whether it was pure sociopathy. I remembered Ray in the forest with a gun grinding into Xochitl's hand. Charles and Fein and Scoggins and Ray and Majido…if there was electricity tomorrow, they wouldn't be kings or jailbirds: they'd be real estate agents and auto mechanics and middle-school teachers. In the abstract this notion wasn't shocking: the evil that lurks, etc. But to be presented with it in the flesh, to know what had been done in our names.

Charles said the deaths were my fault. Without my wan protests, he'd never have been driven so far. In response I asked him what had happened to my former bunkmates Conrad and Bob, and anyone else who'd fallen ill over the past seven months. He didn't answer.

It was a bruising few days for the farm. Elizabeth convened a forum and admitted that Charles had skimmed food and that she'd suspected he was trading it. She promised she hadn't known the specifics: that he'd been dealing with a pair of brothers who controlled fighters near the Missouri/Oklahoma border. Charles gave them food and in exchange, for now, they left us alone. Elizabeth also swore she knew nothing about what happened in those barracks.

It was an easy vote: they removed her from the council. After the ballots were counted, people scattered tearful and despondent, without nominating anyone new.

By giving us the radio rather than smashing it against a rock, Charles had hoped we could find more people and more weapons. He'd hoped we'd find a way out; he wanted to get us out from under a thumb we knew nothing about.

The worst part was how reasonable it all was. That was the true horror.

Maribel came into the kitchen. Ben was scrubbing something at the sink that might not have needed to be scrubbed. She began talking to one of us, both us, as though the conversation had already begun: "...and I don't understand how you can do all that and not tell anyone. People take things over now? You let people freeze to death? You let them die?" She was pulling preserves out of cabinets, dusting the tops, acting like it was a challenge. "Children. Little kids."

I realized she wasn't wearing her veil. It legitimately shocked me. Well, she sometimes got hot or frustrated and lifted it—probably everyone had seen her face—but had she ever walked around not even wearing that cowl? It was personal religion revealed as mere stubbornness. She said, "I hope we kill him," and flashed a look at me. She didn't know whether to resume her position as keeper of the generator.

"Now children are a luxury of the bourgeois," said Ben.

I said, "Is that a quote I'm supposed to know? Who said that?"

He turned with wet hands. "I said it."

I inspected a fine series of scratches in the kitchen's flower wallpaper at my eye level. They seemed fresh. I tried to imagine them being made accidentally.

"If it's factions and warfare," said Ben, "we're not going to win. There are too many hungry people." He looked at me. "And I suppose it's right. Who are we to deserve this bounty when everyone else waits for help that never comes?"

I said, "But who is anyone? Who's the kid who inherits a billion dollars? Who's the college or church with its tax-free lucre? Who are the descendants of the men who burned down Black Wall Street? Who's the man born strong enough to hurt weaker people?"

"Okay," he said, "fair. Who is anyone?"

It was so easy for me to be righteous. It was so easy to forget I'd been stealing from the collective, too.

Ben said, "Power will always be a thing whether we want it to be or not."

"But we don't have enough food," Maribel said. "There's too many people."

"Yes."

I said, "It's fine to be charitable in theory, but when everything is being parceled out, sometimes you have to sacrifice your ideals to make sure—"

Then there was a shattering explosion. It forced adrenaline into my eyeballs and my breath rushed away and I tried to understand what had happened, trained by the new world to be ready for anything, and I saw an organic mess spattered on a cabinet and sliding down it. Glass rattled to the floor. Ben lurched away.

Maribel had thrown a jar of preserves across the room and it had burst against the cabinet. She said, *"Where are the people who are supposed to save us!"*

I looked at her, couldn't breathe.

"How do people not even know what happened! How could nobody come to even explain it! How is nobody even being punished! Where the fuck are the people who are supposed to save us!"

People swung into the kitchen. They wore masks of concern. They gave her space, as one would give a rabid dog, but it was over, she was done. She began to crumple and cry. They put their arms around her and she cried more: maybe beneath everything else, she wanted to know that being Elizabeth's sister hadn't gone from being a great blessing to a terrible curse.

They told her: it will be okay. They told her: we aren't alone. They told her: help will come eventually. I took a turn and offered her tiny shoulder a squeeze.

And Maribel was a person who could be talked out of a mood. Soon enough she was laughing sadly, red-faced and reassured, they took her away to the main room and I stayed behind with Ben.

"I should go talk to her," I said, standing next to him with our butts against the countertop. He didn't respond, but he was thinking. About what? About tomorrow's menu, Kimo's health, Charles's treachery, Elizabeth's complicity, a math problem? He was tired. He slept deep in the burrows of some other bedroom at the back of the house, but others said his half-cubicle was usually empty. I said, "But with me and Maribel, it's not…ah, amorous, y'know?"

"I knew something was going on," he said. "I knew there was food missing. And I heard those fools talking a few times."

"Oh."

"Yeah."

"But you didn't really know. You didn't know what they were doing."

"A lot of willful myopia in the world," said Ben. "I didn't have to put the whole thing together, I just had to ask one question."

"…"

"And now what? Personally I'd like to give every last scrap of food away. No more hoarding, no more grasshopper stocking up for winter. No more choosing who lives and dies because they live here or don't. How are we any better than the people who know what happened to the electricity, off somewhere in the populated parts of the world squirreling away information? You all would be fine. You're young and strong, you'd figure something out."

"You're young enough," I said. "You're strong. Everyone relies on you."

"I just know a few tricks."

"…"

"I break it down logically. At some point it doesn't matter if there's a God allowing this to happen. It doesn't matter because it *seems* like there is. All this nothing happening. All this abandonment." His voice cracked. "Maybe there are places where everything is bright and warm and everything works, but here the callous lack of an answer definitely feels like God."

I did it:

I found myself doing it:

I kissed him.

On the mouth, pretty hard, and I wanted to take it back but not really.

What's the feeling? When you feel like an avalanche of flowers inside you has been held back forever and just once you let it go, and you're filled with color and indignation, you're almost crying but almost laughing, you're weak and strong and you're allowing yourself this one time, allowing yourself disaster, the unfairness of everything is obvious but you just do it anyway. I wasn't the same. I couldn't stay lonely like that anymore.

He was surprised but didn't recoil, but he didn't kiss back.

I finally said, "I'm sorry."

"No," said Ben. "It's okay. Nobody has done that to me in a long while."

I withdrew, stood alongside him again, we both looked at the locked walk-in freezer. I thought about who might still have a copy of the key. I said, "When you talk you sound like a robot."

"You're not the first person to say that." He made a little whirring mechanical noise with his mouth. "So now I guess I can tell you my secret," and he looked at me funny, no eyelids and head strangely cocked, and I felt wound tighter than ever, wondering what else could go wrong, and he stuck out an elbow and turned his shoulders, whirred more, bent at the waist, tilted his chin vertically then horizontally…and I realized he was popping and locking. He was doing The Robot. And he was good at it. I laughed and my eyes were wet.

They asked Ben to take one of the council spots, and he said no. They sure didn't ask me.

At night, Maribel told me that months before, she'd noticed a little boy behind the side vegetable plots and he wouldn't speak to her and wouldn't come near, and every day for a week she left cornbread wrapped in paper near the tree line and it disappeared, and she hadn't told anybody. She never saw him with an adult, and he stopped coming back, and she told herself he was fine, and now she worried the rest of his family had also been detained in that barracks.

"I'm not very motherly," she said, from the spot beneath my armpit.

"Have you talked with Elizabeth?" I said, and she pretended to be asleep.

I was listening to people talk more. I heard cheery words in loud voices and despairing words in soft ones. Everyone had recriminations: for themselves, for Elizabeth. I sat behind the hanging bed sheets, watching Kimo's chest rise and fall, and I heard them second-guess, heard them say they always suspected the farm was too good to be true, heard them worry about what came next. The generator chugged on. We had water and hot food and even sometimes lights. I lost track of the days. It might've been New Year's.

Should we have tried the radio again? Should we have found a place in the larger world? We were leery.

Was a drop-off due soon? Would a militia be paying us a visit? How did it work? The barracks in the woods was empty; they presumably had Charles and Fein locked away somewhere on the far reaches of the property. I guessed someone was extracting information about what came next. Someone said, "How are we supposed to feel? They're picking a bad time to get even quieter about what's going on," and someone else said, "I thought we were supposed to be making decisions together so this never happens again," and someone else said, "This is exactly how it always happens, you can't stop people from keeping secrets," and, "We'd do better if we left the farm," and, "We'd do better if we ran the farm," and, "Elizabeth should be in jail with them."

One cold day, a week later, as rainwater rattled the gutters, I left Ben holding court in the kitchen about some timeworn technique for cleaning beets and I stood outside and watched puddles splash and snow melt, this tidy view of forever that seemed like a calm place about to be turned to ash in a disaster movie. In that moment it was clear to me that we'd been living between epochs: what seemed like a self-sustaining secession was an eye-blink of independence before the spider ensnared us again, the systems that would create whatever came next. And viewed in this light, wasn't it possible that *we* were the bad guys? Wasn't it possible that we terrified locals who were still hanging on and starving through winter? That tales of Elizabeth's farm—where food was hoarded and pilgrims were tortured—had become a reason parents told their children to come in before dark? Maybe the coming era of these border brothers wouldn't be so bad.

Xochitl came outside, too. In the clammy air our breaths steamed out. We hadn't been on a run since Arkansas. She said, "Do you think he'll ever wake up?"

"…"

She was short, I was tall. The black cast on her hand was filthy. Ben said she could probably take it off, the bones were probably as healed as they'd get.

"I don't care why anymore," she said. "I don't even think about it anymore."

"Why what?"

"Why there's no electricity. Somebody did something, somebody didn't do something."

"Ah."

"I used to bug you about it," she said.

"Yes."

"A big bomb went off. Bad people took over the government. Aliens invaded." She snorted. "I'm an alien. I invaded."

"…"

"I realized you were right the whole time. It doesn't matter. The big things don't matter. It's only the little things."

This was my philosophy? I didn't think so, but who knew.

"I was just listening to the rain before," she said, "and every so often it sounded like somebody clicking on a computer. Over and over, I couldn't stop hearing that little part, click-click. My head keeps wanting to hear things, but what's the point when those things are gone."

"…"

"But maybe it can be okay," she said.

I said, "Xochitl."

"…"

"At the oil terminal, when I thought you died…" but she shook her head.

"Don't." She made dimples without smiling. "Oof. What happened to the dangerous man?"

But I had convinced myself that the dangerous man was never me. I convinced myself they'd been persistently, eternally wrong.

She seemed about to say something else when two women, veiled and unveiled, came cackling into the side yard, returning from the outhouse. Xochitl clammed up.

Yes, we would be outraged and fearful across a negotiating table, and those snowplowing border brothers would see it—having only experienced Charles's swagger—and understand there was another truth.

The women stopped to chat with us. Indeed, people seemed less afraid of me, now that there were more obvious devils.

After a while, Xochitl excused herself and stepped back inside and I listened to these women talk for a few moments more—Susan and...Kim?—then I excused myself and followed the left turn Xochitl had made toward the kitchen, and I pushed the door but something was holding it closed. I shoved harder and felt the door bend, and Ben's voice said, "Please give us a minute."

I said, "It's me."

"Just one minute," he said, and I thought I heard vomiting.

Elizabeth stepped into the dining room, behind me, and said, "I need you." She wore a too-big sweatshirt that said "University Of Hard Knox." I looked at the kitchen door, bit my lip, followed Elizabeth deep into the house. They hadn't taken away her room yet.

She didn't sit behind the desk. She paced.

She said, "Did I ever tell you the real story of how Maribel's hands got like that?"

"..."

"The real story is: nobody knows. It wasn't some high school girl trying to fling acid on her, because there would've been witnesses. There was no lawsuit, no college tuition paid for. She came home crying one day and her hands were wrecked. She wouldn't tell our mom and dad what happened. We took her to the hospital and they called the police. She wouldn't say anything. Chemical burns like that could be bleach or ammonia, drain cleaner or oven cleaner, leaky batteries, lye, sulfuric acid…but did she do it to herself? Did someone else do it? The police were convinced nobody in the family did it to her, so they gave up. And she wouldn't talk about it. What do you do? Oh well, life went on, and Maribel had disfigured hands.

"But some time later, she started telling stories. The one about the jealous girl who threw acid on her. The one about the boyfriend whose crack pipe blew up near her hands. The one about a little boy in the woods who fell into a campfire who she saved by patting his clothes out. My parents didn't want to talk about it, they didn't care that Maribel was pathologically lying and losing track of those lies. I thought it was deeply messed up. You don't want to say what really happened, okay. But, what? You're trying to make yourself seem more interesting? I know for a fact she told you one thing about her hands, but if we asked other people around here, for sure she told them a different story."

Her veil swayed as she paced. I saw the underside of her chin, and maybe a hint of lower lip.

"Why am I saying all this? Because I want to know your reaction. What happens when you know someone's lying, and maybe doing it out of self-preservation, but maybe just doing it because they can't stop doing it?"

"…"

"All right," she said. "Because I want your help."

"You want me to be Charles."

"No. No more of that. I'm not on the council anymore, I don't have any authority anyway. But no more of that. Sonya came to me this morning."

"…"

"We found a woman wandering up the driveway this morning."

"…"

"And she says she's Jon Scoggins's long-lost wife."

Scoggins's wife?

The one he was separated from in their tony Dallas suburb? The one who'd abandoned their house by the time he hitchhiked back from his gas-related kidnapping? The one he left a note for with instructions to head north and look for him in Oklahoma City or Tulsa? It seemed impossible, we were more than a hundred miles away from those places, we were nowhere, what clues could she have used to track him to this farm?

Elizabeth said, "I can see you doing the math. You've put up with Maribel. Will you talk to this woman?"

"She used Scoggins's name?" I said. "She said his name before anyone else said it?"

"I've talked to her. Others have talked to her. She definitely knows him. Definitely."

Had Scoggins left breadcrumbs for his wife as he traveled east?

"And you were with him," said Elizabeth. "You spent those last couple days with him."

Could she merely be a crazed pro football fan?

"My point bringing up Maribel is just to say: sometimes the story matters, and I guess sometimes the story doesn't matter. The wife is down in that same cabin where we had the radio. I don't have much clout around here anymore. But will you go down and see what you think?"

But what was the point? There'd be no turning someone away a week after our grisly discovery. The wife would stay. The wife was in.

I sloshed down there. I knocked and entered. Someone had moved the radio and its daisy chain of batteries, and they'd deconstructed Ben's worktable and set up one of the cots and several chairs.

Sonya the retired English professor was here, seated facing the door, and another woman was sitting with her back turned. Sonya held up a preemptory finger without looking at me, continued speaking. "I hate to say it, but my ex-husband and I used to refer to your hometown as 'Cancer City' instead of 'Kansas City,' everyone there smoked!"

"Oh," the woman said, "it's much better now. It's been ten years maybe…you can't smoke inside most places anymore."

"Well, it was a great pleasure to meet you, Tiffany. I'm so glad to have you with us, I want you to know you're welcome, and you just let any of us know if you're getting hungry or thirsty. We'll take care of you."

"Thank you, ma'am."

"You look very well, you're a lovely girl. I'm sure you're hoping to see…. Jon really is off the farm right now and we're not sure when he's due back, but I think it's a good suggestion: let's have you sit a while with one of the people here who knows him best."

"That would be amazing," the wife said.

We were going with missing-in-action. I wasn't the man for this. Sonya smiled glassily at me, got up, pretended to dust off her seat with an invisible handkerchief. The rain came harder in the Midwestern way, becoming a sheet of noise that smelled like ozone. I felt the echo of a thrill that rain provoked in younger days: that nobody could blame me for staying in and attending to my various insignificant projects.

"Here he is now," said Sonya. "I'll leave you to it."

We stepped past each other; Sonya took a deep breath and jogged into the downpour. I wondered what I'd say, how much I would lie. *Your husband was a coward and probably a murderer.* I clacked my knuckles on the cot—the exact spot where I slept those first weeks and nursed my grievances— and then tumbled into the chair. I said, "It's nice to meet you, my name—"

And I looked at her, and I knew her.

She was grinning at me, an ellipses in her eyes. Waiting for me to catch up.

It was:

"Olivia?"

The woman from the back of Harry and Annie's pickup, the one who impersonated a waitress to fool those guards, the one whose chicanery began the invasion of the oil terminal down in Arkansas. She was wearing a puffy winter coat and she unzipped it and revealed the collar of a blueback Union uniform.

"Surprise," she said.

I felt punctured and didn't exactly yet know why.

"Oh, you quiet types," said Olivia. "I never would've believed it, you're about the last person. A sneaky snake, you are. Coming down to help us, acting all innocent."

I was racing, trying to figure it: how could she have found the farm? Was there a tracker on the tanker they gave us? But for a tracker didn't you need a satellite or the Internet?

She said, "Okay, fair play: we lied, too. But there are lies and there are *lies*."

What did I know?

"I didn't come in armed," she said. "We knew I'd be searched."

Olivia shows up, talks her way in by claiming to be....

"You thought you'd get away with it forever," she said.

How did she know Scoggins's wife was maybe out there looking for him?

She said, "There was always going to be a price."

The boy's face. The rock in my hand.

"You have Jon," I said.

"Had," said Olivia. "I'm sorry to say your friend didn't make it. He was shot up pretty bad, but we did get him out of there. And before he died, he told us a lot."

"..."

"About this place. And about you personally, dear heart,

and the bad bad thing you did."

I was the reason he hadn't wound up like that frozen family. I was the reason he'd been with us in Arkansas. "Jon doesn't know the bad thing I did."

She said, "Oh, you're wrong. He spilled your secret."

I shivered. The only question was how, and I knew with a bottomless feeling in my stomach, the entire lesson of the past year: it didn't matter how.

"We never get the gas without your big guy being a hero," she said. "So we would've left you alone. But then Jon told us what you did…. And that, we can't forgive." She tilted her chin down; her eyes held disaster.

There were new sounds outside the shack, pops much louder than rain.

"Yes, they were watching," she said. "As soon as they saw you step in here, that was the signal."

I looked at the door.

She said, "Because before it started, we wanted you personally to know why."

I ran out.

Behind me I heard her say, "He was thirteen!"

Bluebacks were in the fields.

They jostled through snow, firing guns into the rain. People up the hill scrambled, a door slammed, I saw a body on the slope. I ran up in that direction, toward the house, and someone fired at me from long distance, the bullet sighed in the snow. A person was face down; arterial blood discharged into the white. I ran around the side of the farmhouse, where the blank vegetable plots receded in mist, and I saw Ben, wounded in his hip, scuttling on hands-and-knees. More pops, glass shattered, people on both sides were shouting. Somebody fired on the bluebacks from inside the house, using weapons I'd never seen.

I crouched over Ben and helped him up. He said it wasn't bad, but it looked terrible.

They hadn't surrounded us. From this vantage I could

see them slushing up toward the house, taking cover behind a short stone wall and fence posts and a lifeless rose thicket, an advance worthy of Gettysburg. I could also see a way behind us, through the empty vegetable plots: into the steam that rose from snow, through a break in the trees. That way was west: toward Tulsa.

"Can you run?" I said, and Ben nodded doubtfully. I told him to wait there. He tugged my shirt, daubed me with his blood, and he shook my hand, hard. I said, "Cut it out, I'll be right back."

The bluebacks were focused on the front of the house, whence someone was shooting at them, and I crashed through the side entrance and nearly had my throat slit by Maribel, who charged me with a penknife. I said, "We gotta go!"

The windows were shattering. Bullets were coming through walls. People were bleeding and dead. Maribel followed me, still unveiled, holding my hand. The main room was warm. Women were crouched by the windows, firing out into the rain, and it was deafening.

Someone shouted, "More ammo in the kitchen!" and I saw Xochitl run there, head down, holding a rifle.

I followed, I swung into the kitchen: and that's where everybody was huddled, men holding their wives, people praying, veiled women covering each other's heads, Paola, Morales, the kitchen attendants, the farmhands, the singers, the seamstresses, all stunned and operating under the assumption that Charles—not I—had done this to them.

Over gunfire, I said, "Let's go! Get out of here! Everybody out!" and they looked at me, and they looked around, and they stayed on the cement floor, and I said, "We can make it! We can make it!" and I turned to head back out the kitchen door and we all watched as a woman standing in the dining room—it was Breanne—took a bullet in her face, and her blood and bone spattered across the wall.

Xochitl was beside me. She touched Ben's blood on my

shirt.

Maribel was over in the main room, crouched behind the fireplace with a few other people, fastened below Kimo's dying figure. That way: back that way, down the hall, out through the door I'd just destroyed coming in…liberation. And between here and there? These women: untrained and desperate, veiled and not, lifting their heads into the line of fire to squeeze off more rounds, to protect us for however many more minutes before the inevitable came crashing in. My fault, my fault, the nightmare from which I'd never really woken.

My legs were tensed; I was probably ready to make a run for it. That I wanted the others to come try with me wasn't much of an excuse. I knew how Scoggins had heard what I'd done to that bluebacked boy. Xochitl held my hand and I didn't care: I wasn't letting go.

We heard a voice trying to be heard between the terrible bursts.

It was saying, "Stop! Stop! Stop!"

I looked out the kitchen window. Elizabeth had walked onto the front porch in her stupid sweatshirt and her stupid veil and was waving her arms. I heard Maribel shout, "Lizzy! Don't!"

Our women stopped firing. They might've been out of bullets. But the bluebacks were still shooting, Elizabeth was still standing, she ducked her head but walked further out onto the porch still waving her arms. Now I could only see her from behind. She was foolish as a referee. I expected to see her fall.

Then I did let go of Xochtil's unbroken hand, bolted up and out of the kitchen, brainless, palms raised like a victim in a train robbery. I felt wet on my face, is how I knew I was outside. Someone down there shot again. I could see them emerging: their stupid uniforms, their empty faces. I scurried toward Elizabeth and I stood in front of her. Then she grabbed my shirt and stood in front of me. Then we stood side by side, and the bluebacks seemed convinced nobody would shoot at them and they approached: nobody I recognized from the week before.

I decided I could explain what happened. The boy had killed the man I loved.

Surely they'd believe me.

ABOUT THE AUTHOR

Christopher Harris is the author of four novels, *Slotback Rhapsody*, *The Big Clear*, *War On Sound* and *Tulsa*. He lives in Amherst, MA, and Los Angeles, CA, USA.

Made in the USA
Middletown, DE
17 September 2018